# TREAD SOFTLY

## JJ MARSH

D1115164

TRISKELE BOOKS

Cover design: JD Smith

Published by Prewett Publishing.
All enquiries to admin@beatrice-stubbs.com

First printing, 2013

ISBN 978-3-9523970-7-7

For Florian, with love, respect and admiration

# Chapter One

The bells struck seven. Tiago was late. Taking a last swig of *Estrella Galicia* for luck, he gathered keys, mobile, jacket, the CD and the flowers. Were roses too much? Maybe if they were red, signalling an obvious agenda. But yellow should be innocent enough. No, leave them, it's embarrassing. No, take them, it's a lovely gesture. Yellow rosebuds could signify the start of something.

Gazing into the fragrant whorls was only making him later, definitely a negative message on a first date. He ran out the door, leaping the stairs three at a time. On the second landing, Doña Llorente, complete with shopping, dogs and inhaler, blocked his path. He greeted her with a wave, the spaniels with a pat, and on impulse, thrust the flowers into her hand.

With a gallant bow, he slipped past before she got her breath back. He hit the street and recognised a smart decision. Ana wouldn't want flowers. Independent music with quirky artwork, perhaps, but no old-fashioned gestures. The right choice. Saved from cliché and into Doña Llorente's good books.

His instinct to reach for a cigarette was countered by a desire for fresh breath. At least for the greeting kisses. His smile spread as he recalled the email. Not only word for word, but every single character.

Meet me @ *El Papagaio* on Sunday, 19.00.
Let's NOT talk about work. Ax.

One extra letter. An X. Its effect was disproportionate, but still. Ana Luisa Herrero had sent him a kiss. It had taken him an hour and a half to compose a reply, and another fifteen minutes debating the pros and cons of adding a kiss.

OK. Looking forward to it. Tx

He sped up, almost breaking into a run.

The uplight illuminated a cartoonish parrot, painted in primary colours, as he approached the door. A solitary smoker stood outside, leaning against an empty table. He didn't return Tiago's *Buenas tardes*.

The restaurant was unusually empty. But Tiago only ever came in here on week nights after work, so had no idea about the bar's weekend trade. Two men sitting at a corner table looked up and nodded. The only other person was a barman Tiago didn't recognise. Strange not to see Enrique. Perhaps he didn't work weekends.

But most importantly, Ana was later than him. Relieved, he sat facing the door. He would order two beers. Or should he wait? No, he needed a drink. And maybe some olives, mainly to give him something to do with his hands. He sent her a rapid text message.

The barman approached, unsmiling.

"Two beers and a ..."

"She's in the back." He jerked his head towards the rear of the room.

Tiago glanced in the same direction and frowned.

The barman shrugged. "She said you should go in the back. She's waiting."

Tiago scrambled from his seat, confused. In all the time he'd been coming here, he'd never been 'in the back'. He didn't even know there was another room. Was it the same sort of 'back room' as the one in *Gatos*? Everyone knew what went on in that kind of place. He got up and followed the barman's louche stroll. He knew he was being watched.

The lack of clientele, the new barman, the silence ... something felt wrong. He stopped. The front door opened and the smoker returned, locking the door behind him. Tiago's pulse pounded as the barman pressed a hand to his shoulder, guiding him firmly through the door. When he resisted, he was shoved forwards, falling across the jamb onto all fours. Fear shot through his veins like acid as he tried to make out where he was.

A door opened ahead of him, blue light and cold air spilling into the dark corridor. The fridge room. His scalp contracted as he saw the chair inside, with attachments. Every nerve urged him to run, but he had no idea which way. He pushed himself to his feet and turned to face the men behind him.

"What's going on? What do you want?"

Without answering, they moved forwards. He attempted to duck past, tripped over rubbish bags and landed on the floor.

They dragged him to his feet and into the fridge. He twisted and bucked like a fish on a line, but the smoker and barman wrestled him into the chair. His arms were cuffed behind him, his legs spread and secured at knees and ankles with leather straps. Shallow breaths made small panicky clouds in the cold air as he tried to keep from shaking. He heard the suction of the closing door. He scanned the four unfamiliar faces, searching for an explanation. The two older men from the corner table were relaxed and unhurried. One had a missing forefinger, the other's face sagged on one side. A pair of tough old tomcats. The smoker and the barman, both built like bulls, wore identical tense expressions. Muscle, no doubt. But who the hell would send four heavies after him? And where did Ana fit in?

His voice was unsteady. "Look, I don't know what the problem is, but we can work something out, I'm sure. Please, can we talk? What have I done?"

No one moved.

The greyer of the tomcats spoke. His voice was hoarse and

creaky, as if it didn't get out much.

"No, Tiago. No more talking. That is part of your problem. You were warned. Twice. There is no third chance." He motioned to the smoker, who handed something to the barman. A pair of garden shears. They both donned plastic gloves.

Tiago shook his head, unable to speak, blinking to clear his vision. He had no idea what warnings he was talking about. No one had tried to dissuade him from pursuing Ana. His colleagues even encouraged him. Were these men some Portuguese relatives come to defend her honour? He hadn't even kissed her yet.

"You see, Tiago, it's like gambling. Only join the game if you can afford to take the losses."

Two figures approached, but through his flooded eyes, he could no longer differentiate between individuals. As he rocked and yanked against his restraints, he squeezed his lids shut and screamed, a desperate howl bouncing off white-tiled walls and indifferent ears. When his lungs could produce nothing more than hyperventilating gasps, the hoarse and rasping voice came to its conclusion.

"When a man sticks something where he shouldn't, he must be prepared to lose it."

# Chapter Two

The smell of flesh was giddying. *Chorizo*, sausage, *cecina* and air-dried hams hung overhead; *pintxos* arrayed on the bar looked like individual works of art, spiked anchovies, layered peppers, tortilla slices and salted cod vying for attention; and the glass of *Txakoli*, wearing a light coat of condensation, reflected the sunshine streaming through the windows.

Beatrice sighed with anticipation. It was very hard to make a decision. She gazed at the shoppers on Calle de Edouardo Dato and caught her reflection in the glass door. Good God, she looked almost happy! An involuntary smile; things must be improving. She showed the barman her snacks, although the quantity stretched the definition of the word, and settled into a leather banquette to enjoy her lunch.

Content to observe the patrons and eavesdrop on the intriguing sounds of Basque, she chose not to pick up her novel, her guidebook or her map. The bar seemed a popular location for workmen, who stayed mere minutes, washing down their *tapas* with beer or cups of wine. She enjoyed the respectful nods she received from each new wave of diners and began to feel quite at home.

Meal over, she lined up her toothpicks so the barman could count them and charge her accordingly. It reminded her of *Go Sushi!* in Hoxton, another 'healthy' place which cruelly tempted diners into over-indulgence. Thoughts of home swelled a dull yearning. Not homesickness. Not nostalgia. Just an ache for the familiar. How absurd. She'd only been in Spain a week.

She ordered another glass of rosé, picked up her phone and dialled the Classics and Ancient History Department of Exeter University. Hang the expense, she needed to hear his voice.

"Professor Bailey, good afternoon?"

"Hello Matthew, it's me."

"Beatrice? Are you all right?"

"Absolutely. Only phoning to make you jealous. I've just finished the most wonderful lunch in a Spanish bar. They have these *tapas* things, but bigger. I've never seen such imaginative use of anchovies."

His relief was audible. "You are a truly heartless woman. I'm sitting here, grading first-year essays, grinding my teeth and weeping. These people use apostrophes as decoration, scattering them across their texts like glitter. And for my lunch, I had tinned ravioli."

Beatrice gave a belly laugh and checked to see if she was disturbing other diners. But all heads were turned in the opposite direction. A young brunette walked through the gaggle of blue-clad workers, ignoring their undisguised ogling and semi-audible comments. She spotted Beatrice and, with a friendly smile, seated herself at the bar.

Beatrice returned her attention to Matthew. "Now I know you're lying. You would never eat tinned ravioli."

"Ordinarily not. However, I was babysitting Luke this morning and he baulked at what his mother had provided for his lunch. Seemed a shame to waste it. But now I understand the poor little chap's reservations. Hideous slop. He made short work of my carrot soup instead. You see, my grandson already shows excellent taste. How are you enjoying ... where are you now? Santander?"

"Vitoria-Gasteiz today. And tomorrow. Glorious. I've barely even scratched the surface, so I think I'll hang on for a couple of days. Rest my feet."

The brunette, quite unmistakeably, was listening. Not only that, but watching Beatrice in the mirror. Her long hair, like a chocolate waterfall, cascaded down a suede shirt. The textures lent a softness to her unapproachable air.

"Oh dear. You need to go easy on the feet, at your age. Have you seen the Artium yet?"

"It's not my feet, it's my shoes. Blisters. And anyway, I'm all arted out after the Guggenheim. The Artium's on the agenda for tomorrow. Tonight I'm meeting a connection of Tanya's, the exchange student, pen-friend, whatever she is. She stayed with us one summer, remember?"

"Of course. Andrea Something?

"Ana Something. Lord knows if I'll recognise her. Last time I saw her, she was all elbows and knees with a mouth full of metal. She's taking me for *parillada de mariscos*."

He exhaled. "How I wish I could join you. My particular weakness is fresh seafood. But envy, I remind myself, is a deadly sin. Now, it's mid-afternoon and your calling me via mobile is ruinously expensive. Enjoy your siesta and I'll speak to you tomorrow. Are you keeping out of trouble, Old Thing?"

"Believe me, I am the picture of innocence. Everything is fine, Matthew, and I'm enjoying a rest from it all. Love to the girls and we'll talk tomorrow."

"Very well. Hurry back, in your own time."

She smiled and ended the call. Before she even replaced the handset in her bag, the dark-haired girl had approached, standing opposite. Her expression was expectant.

"Beatrice Stubbs." The accent disconcerted Beatrice, evoking more of an Irish Colleen than a Spanish Carmen. Her face, open and intelligent, bore signs of tension in the upper lip and brow.

"Correct. And you are ...?"

"Ana Something." She smiled.

"Good Lord." Beatrice assessed the soft skin, straight white teeth and elegant proportions. The laughter in the girl's eyes gave the only clue to the gauche exchange student she had met nine years earlier.

"Or Ana Luisa Herrero, if you want the whole story." She held out her hand. Beatrice shook it, still lost for words.

Ana slid into the seat opposite, rested her elbows on the table and looked into Beatrice's eyes. "Guess how I found you?"

"I've no idea. Sniffer dog?"

The girl laughed, drawing attention from the whole bar. "I'm a journalist. Getting information out of people is my speciality. It's good to see you again. Must be, what, ten years? But I remember you very well. Mainly because you didn't patronise us and enjoyed good food. And because you were a police detective with the London Met. Apart from an air hostess, I couldn't think of a cooler job."

Beatrice recovered her voice. "Well, I thought I remembered *you*, but I would never have recognised that girl ..."

"... all elbows and knees with a mouth full of metal? Ah, don't worry. Serves me right. I shouldn't have been earwigging."

"Earwigs never hear good of themselves. No, what I wanted to say is that you have blossomed into a genuine beauty, Ana. And you wear it well."

"Cheers. Anyway, I went to your hotel. A stranger in Vitoria is going to ask for *tapas* recommendations, right? I spoke to the receptionist and tracked you down."

"Congratulations. But while I applaud your skill, I can't help asking myself why you would bother? We have an appointment this evening, and I feel sure I gave you my mobile number in case of difficulties. Why did you need to track me here?"

The girl's face darkened, her focus turned inward and her whole body seemed to sag.

"Beatrice, I'm after your help. And I needed to explain to you in person. A colleague and I have been working on a particular story. We think we've found something suspicious. The problem is that he's disappeared."

"Your colleague?"

Ana nodded, her jaw clenched. "We all had a drink together

after work on Friday. But this morning, he didn't turn up for work and missed the weekly update. I had to busk it on his behalf. I've called him and been round to his apartment, but there's no reply."

"Well, it's only just after lunchtime. Maybe he took the morning off."

"He'd have let me know. He's not the type to drop a colleague in it."

Beatrice considered. A young man, a journalist. Rarely the sort to inform colleagues when chasing a story, or anything else. Missing for under twenty-four hours. No police force in the world would even blink. Young people could be so very naïve.

She adopted a conciliatory expression but before she could reply, Ana continued.

"Yes, I know. I've already been to the station and the local guys won't touch it. But I know something is wrong. I got a text message from him on Sunday evening." She slid her phone from her breast pocket and focused on finding the message.

She turned the screen towards Beatrice.

"HA! Estoy aquí - EP. SM, OK? Tx

Beatrice rubbed her eyes. Surely she should be dozing in her hotel room rather than listening to a flighty female who'd had a dust-up with a boyfriend speaking in code.

Ana explained. "HA means *Hola* Ana. *Estoy aquí* means I'm here and EP probably stands for our favourite bar, *El Papagaio*. SM, OK? Is *San Miguel* OK for you?"

"Ana. He expected you for a date, you didn't turn up and he's probably sulking. Men tend to do that."

"But listen. There was no date. I spent the weekend in the mountains. We hadn't made any arrangements for Sunday night. And now, he's completely vanished. No one will take this seriously but I feel something's very wrong. Please, humour me. The first twenty-four hours are crucial, I know that from my experience on the crime desk. Time's slipping away. I need to think like a cop. And I have one right in front of me. Would you at least give me some pointers? Where would *you* start?"

The girl wasn't mad, just desperate. Beatrice recognised the conviction in the deep brown eyes. She dropped her voice below the labourers' banter and the sounds of Shakira from the speakers.

"What's your friend's name?"

"Tiago Vínculo. Hence the Tx at the end of the message. Which is also weird."

"Why?"

"Tiago never puts kisses on his messages."

"Maybe it was a slip of the thumb," Beatrice suggested.

Ana linked her hands together and rested her chin on her knuckles.

"The thing is, I get a lot of attention, from men, because of the way I look. My mum was Portuguese and my dad's Irish. Guess they gave me good genes. I grew up in Ireland and encountered more than my fair share of charmers who turned out to be chancers. So I've learnt to be suspicious of male friends, you know, alert for any hidden intentions. For that reason, I never make empty gestures, like adding kisses to my signature, telling people I love them, or anything which could be misinterpreted. My mantra is, only do it if you mean it. My friends all know that and I expect the same from them. So why would Tiago, one of my best friends, suddenly choose to send me a kiss?"

Beatrice recognised the habitual tug of curiosity. Pieces of a puzzle and the old urge to find out the meaning behind the fragments. Ideas began bubbling. Why not? She could offer Ana some advice. After all, what harm could it do?

"Right. Let's see what we can do. But first things first, I need to buy some comfy shoes."

# Chapter Three

"Papí! Papí!"

Arturo de Aguirre straightened from his inspection of the young vines. He lifted his head towards the sound of his son's voice, shielding his eyes against the low October sun. Basajaun was waving from the garden terrace at the top of the vineyard. As Aguirre waved back, he saw his wife join the boy, her mobile to her ear. His phone rang, so he moved a few paces away from his waiting workers to take her call.

"Marisol? Is everything all right?"

"*Yes. Basajaun's waving goodbye. We're going into Vitoria to meet Inez for lunch, maybe do some shopping. I've left you some food in the fridge.*"

"You're taking him shopping? I thought he was home from school because he was sick."

"*He had a temperature, that's all. But he's bored, hanging around the house, so I'll take him with me to see his sister.*"

Aguirre considered his response. "You can take him to lunch today. Tomorrow, he goes to school. His education is vital, Marisol."

"*So is his health. See you later.*" She rang off.

Aguirre watched the pair of them walk towards the Jaguar XK, Basajaun skipping and hopping and jumping about with his usual excess of energy. It was not good enough. Aguirre would wait until the weekend, letting her think he had forgotten, before making an announcement. Any future decisions regarding Basajaun's attendance at school would be taken by him alone. The trouble with Marisol? She was used to bringing up girls. She'd done a good job, mostly. Paz and Inez already married and several possibilities lined up for Luz when she finished her studies. But his son's destiny lay in the business. His education must be taken seriously. Time he assumed paternal control.

Aguirre turned back to the two workers, who waited for his approval.

"OK. I'm happy with the quality here. But this section needs frost protection while the vines are so young. That must be finished first." He checked his watch. "Go and have some lunch. I'll be back by two to supervise the process."

*Left you some food in the fridge.* Who did she think she was talking to? He would go out for lunch and use the opportunity to pay a visit. Striding back to the house, Aguirre debated whether to call first. He decided not. Surprise generally worked in his favour.

His timing was perfect. Most of the staff at Alava Exports were already in the canteen, enabling him to enter the building unnoticed. The security guard and receptionist barely blinked at such a familiar face, simply smiled and wished him a good afternoon. The little secretary who defended her boss's privacy like a yappy chihuahua was absent. No one to warn Angel Rosado of his approaching nemesis. Excellent.

His son-in-law remained in his office, on the phone. His habit of standing and staring out the window while talking made it even easier to surprise him. Aguirre opened the door almost noiselessly. Almost. But Angel turned and recognised his visitor. His expression of alarm gave everything away.

"I have to go, someone's just walked in. Thanks for your advice and I'll call you back later."

Angel extended a hand and forced an implausible smile. He was a dreadful actor. And Aguirre had seen a few. Some of the most painful evenings of his life had taken place during Marisol's amateur theatre period.

"Angel. How are you?" He didn't wait for a reply. "Our wives have decided to lunch together, so I thought you might be lonely. I've come to take you out. We'll go somewhere nice and have a chat."

Angel looked down, his long lashes hiding his eyes. "That's a kind gesture, but today I planned to eat in the canteen. Show my face to the workers, you know?"

Aguirre nodded his approval. "An excellent idea. Good to break bread with the staff once in a while. You can do that tomorrow. Come. You'll need a jacket, the wind is sharp."


Everything about Angel irritated Aguirre. His fastidious way of dressing, his constantly miserable expression, the grateful smile he gave to the waiter who handed him the menu, not to mention his spineless capitulation to everything his wife demanded. True, Inez was a forceful opponent. Aguirre himself recalled stand-up screaming confrontations even when she was a child. But he always got the upper hand and she respected him for that. Angel let her win. That was a mistake and he would never regain her respect. Weak. No wonder everyone despised him, including his wife.

"We'll have the *Menú del día. Revuelto de setas, txipirones,* and the house white." Scrambled egg with mushrooms, followed by squid in its own ink. Aguirre handed the menu back without looking, waiting for Angel to protest. His son-in-law always had a bad reaction to mushrooms and disliked the way the black ink stained his teeth. But Angel shrugged his acquiescence and asked for some water. His every movement invited bullying. He only had himself to blame.

"By the way, you haven't yet congratulated me," said Aguirre, flicking out his napkin.

Angel's wince showed he understood, but he faked an innocent enquiry. "With so many successes to admire, where do I start?"

So slimy, so false. It was hard to believe the man was a Spaniard.

Aguirre ignored the sycophancy. "I'm to be a grandfather, for the second time. Paz is due the end of April. As you can imagine, Marisol is deliriously happy."

"Congratulations. That was quick. Surely Ramón isn't one yet?"

"No. His first birthday, as you well know, is this Thursday. Don't forget the party starts at twelve, with lunch at two. So Paz and Guido's children will only be eighteen months apart, which I believe is a very good thing."

"I'm surprised to hear you say that, when there's such a huge gap between the girls and Basajaun."

"Not surprising at all. I was determined to have a son. That took a little longer."

A silence swelled, punctured by the waiter's arrival with a carafe of house white and a bottle of water.

Aguirre sent back the wine and ordered a bottle of his own produce, *Castelo de Aguirre Blanco*. Not the best on the menu, but he was making a point. A point Angel, despite his limited intelligence, would recognise.

"As for my grandchildren," he continued, "wouldn't it be wonderful if they had cousins of a similar age?"

Angel didn't reply, looking around the room, as if the answer lay with one of their fellow diners.

Aguirre dropped his voice and adopted an expression of concern, such as might be worn by a prurient chat show host. "I mean, there's no problem, is there? You know Marisol and I would do anything we could to help."

The boy shook his head. "I don't think anything is wrong. It just hasn't happened yet."

Aguirre kept his eyes on him, waiting for something more.

Angel changed the subject. "I've been meaning to ask you something. I still don't know whether you resolved the problem with the paperwork. I haven't heard anything more from Saez, but other people have been asking questions."

The waiter placed a basket of bread and two dishes of scrambled egg in front of them. Aguirre gave him a curt nod of dismissal and tore into a roll.

"The paperwork issue is no more. A typical example of a minion getting carried away beyond his brief. The company have assured me it won't happen again. And in turn, you will promise me that next time you have an external audit, you talk to the organ-grinder. Not the monkey."

"Of course, I promise. Although I had no idea he was a trainee. What about that journalist? He told me a missing person's report was filed on Saez." Angel's eyes scanned Aguirre's face.

"Nonsense. The company relocated him, at my request."

"Relocated? Do you know where?"

"I don't recall. Somewhere out in the sticks, they said. I expect he left a young woman behind, who can't believe she's been dropped. Far more romantic, not to mention kinder on the ego, to invent a disappearance. Anyway, where he went is immaterial. He's gone and that journalist is unlikely to return. So if anyone else asks, send them directly to me. Eat your lunch, Angel, it's why we're here. Perhaps that is part of your problem. You're not eating right."

Angel blinked at his plate and dabbed at the oily, eggy mess with some bread. His voice was weak, pathetic.

"As I said, I'm not aware of a problem. I think it's simply a question of time."

"Maybe." Aguirre poured the wine, studying the colour before raising his glass to his nose. He inhaled deeply and allowed the light fruits, the clean flowers and hints of green to fill his nostrils. He opened his eyes and held his glass toward Angel.

"*Topa*! And here's to future successes. For both of us."

"*Topa*. To success," Angel responded with minimal enthusiasm, but held his glass steady for the chinking.

Aguirre sipped at his wine, pleased with the light effervescence and lively body. This could hold its own against Portuguese *vinho verde* any day. He trained his eyes on Angel.

"A question of time. Yes, it's possible you're right. So let's give it until Christmas and then we'll look at the problem again."

Angel stared into his wine, the downward pull of his mouth reflecting the rim of the glass. Aguirre lifted a forkful of mushroom and smiled. He was rather looking forward to the rest of lunch.

# Chapter Four

Beatrice stood in the doorway of the Residencia, handbag over her arm, cardigan slung over her summer dress and sore feet slipped into brand new flip-flops. Ana, wearing jeans, held out a helmet.

"It's a moped."

Ana shook her head. "That's like saying an Aston Martin is a car. This is a Vespa. A design classic and lifestyle statement. And the only way to travel in the city. Shall we go?"

"I didn't realise this would be our mode of transport. I'm not exactly dressed for motorbike riding. Do you think I should change?"

"Not at all. I've ridden this in a skirt before. So long as you can get your leg over, it's just a question of tucking yourself in. Come on, let's get going. When I lean, you follow, OK?"

With a deep breath, Beatrice wedged the helmet over her head, swung her leg over and ensured she was decent. The bike's engine whizzed up like a lawnmower and she grasped Ana's waist as they sped forward into the traffic. It was exhilarating, dodging in and out of lanes, creeping between queues of cars to be the first at the lights. The limitations of four wheels did not apply to the little bike. The wide leather seat was comfortable and despite her exposure, Beatrice felt surprisingly safe. In fact, she enjoyed the sense of being right in the middle of things. If only Matthew could see her. Actually, probably best he couldn't.

Ana bumped up onto the pavement in front of an apartment building, switched off the engine and pulled down the stand with her heel.

"This is Tiago's place. He lives at the top."

"You're allowed to park it on the pavement?" Beatrice heaved off her helmet, choosing not to worry about what had happened to her hair.

"You can park a Vespa anywhere. Let's go."

Ana rang Tiago's bell first and they both waited with a strange sense of anticipation. No reply. She didn't try a second time. Instead, she pressed her finger on the bell directly beneath. When a male voice answered, Ana spoke in Spanish. Beatrice listened, clueless, but impressed at how many syllables per minute the girl could manage. The buzzer sounded and Ana pushed open the door. She stopped and looked into Beatrice's eyes.

"You're a British writer, OK? Your book is about European journalism and you're following me around to learn how it works. I'll translate and you can tell me what questions I should ask."

Beatrice responded with an obedient nod.

Ana looked back again. "And if they believe that, they'll believe anything. You've got police stamped all over you. Well, nothing we can do about that now."

Gregorio Torres opened his apartment door wearing a black T-shirt, stonewashed jeans and a bad-tempered scowl. He appeared to be late twenties, tall and well-built. His dark colouring and deep eyes could have been attractive, but a heavy jaw tilted him into Desperate Dan territory. As he surveyed Ana, the scowl lifted, only to return when he spotted Beatrice. He shot several questions at Ana and a few dirty looks at Beatrice, before leaning against the door frame, arms folded.

Ana took out her notebook and began asking questions. Without turning, she relayed the information to Beatrice.

"He saw Tiago on Saturday – talked about football – seemed

normal – wasn't here on Sunday so didn't see or hear him at all."

"Where was he if not here?" asked Beatrice and waited while Ana translated. He raised his eyebrows at her, but answered the question.

"In his family's village. It was the day of the *txoko*. It's a Basque custom where all the men get together and cook a meal for everyone," Ana said.

"What a lovely idea!" exclaimed Beatrice.

Gregorio looked at her in surprise and a slow smile softened his expression. He nodded.

"Yes," he said, in English. "It is."

Ana glanced at Beatrice before firing off several more questions in Spanish. He answered with more openness but as Beatrice could see from Ana's expression, no useful information was forthcoming. Finally, Ana shook his hand and said her goodbyes. Gregorio politely extended his hand to Beatrice. She shook it and made an effort. "*Muchas gracias.*"

"You're welcome," he replied.


On the way down the stairs, Ana seemed despondent.

"So Gregorio didn't come home on Sunday and went straight to work from his village. He has no idea if Tiago was here on Sunday night or not. No one else is likely to know. Tiago's is the only flat on the top floor."

"The penthouse?" asked Beatrice.

"More like the attic," Ana replied. "We may as well try a couple more, you never know," she added, pressing the bell on the next landing. As they waited, Ana looked sideways at Beatrice.

"Guess what Gregorio does for a living?" she whispered.

Beatrice thought. "From first impressions, I'd have him down as a truck mechanic. No, maybe a cattle brander. Well, something rough and tough, anyway. The lead singer in the Spanish equivalent of Status Quo?"

"Tut, tut. For a detective, your powers of observation are

shocking. Did you not see his hands?"

Someone moved behind the door and the sounds of locks rattled.

Beatrice turned to Ana. "No, I didn't. He kept them folded under his armpits. Why?"

Ana's smile lifted her cheeks into russet apples. "He's a manicurist."

"Really?"

"Yep. Hard as nails." The door opened. "*Buenas dias*, Doña Llorente!"

Dismounting the Vespa outside *El Papagaio*, Beatrice handed her helmet to Ana and tried once again to brush the dog hair from her dress. Tiago's neighbours had been little use, and the interviews, mostly conducted at front doors, had proved surprisingly tiring. Beatrice's frustration at being excluded from the conversation and having to wait for Ana to translate tested her patience. On top of which, the asthmatic woman with the dogs had the most grating voice Beatrice could ever remember hearing. Worse still, it was obvious that she rarely had a captive audience, so she'd made the most of it.

"So, apart from the fact that woman can talk faster than I ever thought possible, I understood very little of what Doña Llorente was saying. But I gather she saw him on Sunday."

"Yes, and you were right to suggest the step-by-step approach. I could literally see her remembering. She gave me a lot of details. He was dressed to kill, as she put it, he was in a hurry, tearing out the door, but stopped to give her a present, those flowers. She had no doubts about the time, either. Just after seven o'clock."

"And he sent you a text at what time exactly?"

Ana didn't need to check. "Nineteen minutes past. As you saw, the bar is a ten-minute walk from his place."

Beatrice thought about it. A bunch of yellow roses. She doubted Tiago had bought them for his asthmatic neighbour.

Did he change his mind?

Ana locked the bike and turned to face the restaurant. "Here we go."

The interior was lively; groups of people chatting at tables, a crowd at the bar and half a dozen men standing watching football on a small television set high in the corner. Two young women threaded their way through the patrons, carrying trays of beer, carafes of wine and some intriguing-looking snacks.

Ana made straight for the bar, where a jowly man in his sixties was pouring a beer. She beckoned Beatrice to join her.

"*Hola*, Enrique! Can I introduce you to a friend of mine? This is Beatrice and she's a journalist for a travel magazine. I told her to talk to you." She turned to Beatrice. "No one knows Basque cuisine like Enrique."

Enrique beamed and wiped his hands on a cloth. "*Hola*, Ana. And hello, Ana's friend, Beatrice. Take a seat and I'll join you in a minute." He waved at an empty table towards the front of the room, away from the sighs and groans below the TV set.

At least ninety percent of the men in the bar watched Ana walk to their table. Some even tore their eyes away from the football. She ignored them and sat with her back to the window. She hoicked one foot up to rest on the opposite knee and dropped her voice.

"Enrique's a good guy. And when it comes to the food and drink of the region, he'll talk the ears off you."

"Sounds like we might get along. Although I do wish you'd warn me as to my undercover roles a bit earlier. Acting's never been my strong point."

"But asking questions and eating will give you no bother. Here he comes."

Enrique joined them with a tray bearing glasses, two carafes of wine; one white, one red, and a selection of tiny canapés.

Beatrice smiled. "Ana tells me you are an expert on local dishes."

"Not an expert. *The* expert. I know the best restaurants in San Sebastian, the best wines from the Rioja and the best recipes from Bilbao to Vitoria. What do you want to know?"

Ana's expression was pleasantly enquiring and innocent, a match for Enrique's. Beatrice was on her own. Enrique opened his hands, offering his knowledge to her on a plate.

"Well, for a start, can you tell me what these are?" she said, pointing to the little snacks on the tray.

"Good question. Let me introduce you to some of our local delicacies. Salt cod croquettes with nuts. You will love them. Tell me you are not vegetarian."

Even if Beatrice had been a committed vegan, the hostile expression on Enrique's face would have forced her to lie. As it was, she shook her head.

"No, I will eat anything."

Enrique's approval spread across his face. "Good. British and Americans with their fussy intolerances ..." He waved a hand in front of his face, rolled his eyes and then pointed at a terracotta dish. "This is beautiful. Prawn and bacon topped with a homemade vinaigrette. And *Txalupa*; mushrooms and cream, covered with cheese in a pastry boat. And the speciality of the house, our secret tuna mix topped with anchovy and chives. Try, please. These are for you."

"How very kind!" Beatrice's delight was genuine. Lunch seemed a long time ago. She selected the messy-looking boat, which would force Ana to take over the conversation.

Enrique poured white wine and watched Beatrice eat, nodding his satisfaction. "Ana, try something. You never eat my *pintxos* and it hurts my feelings."

Ana picked up a croquette. "Nothing personal. It's just, when we come in here, it's usually after work. I don't want to spoil my appetite for dinner."

"It doesn't seem to bother the others. Jaime, Tiago, Maria-José; they always have something. Think of it as an appetiser."

Beatrice watched Ana in her peripheral vision. The girl's

manner was totally relaxed as if she hadn't even heard the name. She bit into a croquette.

"Bloody hell, these *are* good. See, you've broken the dam now. In six months' time, I'll be the same size as Maria-José."

Enrique laughed, showing long, yellowing teeth. "She has an appetite, most certainly. Beatrice, try a croquette. Save the tuna till last. You will never eat anything as perfect anywhere in Vitoria."

Beatrice obliged.

Ana wiped her fingers and took a sip of wine. "Did Maria-José come in at the weekend, Enrique? I have a feeling I agreed to meet them, but totally forgot."

Enrique's face seemed unchanged. "No. I haven't seen her since last Friday. When you all came in together. They're good, aren't they? The nuts add something special to this croquette."

Beatrice agreed. "They are sublime. I could live on this food forever." This was her kind of interrogation. Her job was eating and appreciating fine food while Ana did the tricky stuff.

"What about Tiago? Was he here?"

Enrique poured more wine and frowned. "Tiago? No. In fact the place was very quiet all day on Saturday. Everyone deserted me."

Ana smiled. "And Sunday?"

A look of puzzlement crossed Enrique's face. "Ana, we're closed on Sundays. That shows how often you come in at weekends if you don't know that. I spent Sunday with my parents-in-law. To be honest, I'd rather open the bar than drive over there, but my wife insists."

Now Ana looked puzzled. Beatrice finished her croquette, caught Ana's eye and made a tiny twisting motion with her hand.

"Does anyone else have the keys to this place?"

"*El Papagaio*? Of course not. Why would anyone have the keys?"

Ana looked to Beatrice. The girl clearly needed guidance.

Beatrice decided to trust him. "Enrique, the truth is that I'm not a travel writer. I'm a police detective from London. Ana asked me to help her find Tiago. He's gone missing and the last place we think he was ... well, Ana can explain."

Ana pulled out her phone and explained her analysis of Tiago's last message.

Enrique shook his head and rolled his eyes once more. "You women. Too many soap operas. Always searching for the dramatic. EP is not *El Papagaio*. The bar was closed on Sunday so no one was here. But EP could be *El Periódico de Alava*. It's much more likely he went to the newspaper office and asked you to join him there. And he's probably chasing some lead or other right now, while you're panicking over nothing."

To Beatrice, that made perfect sense. She hadn't even questioned Ana's interpretation of the text and accepted it at face value.

Ana set her jaw. "And *San Miguel*?"

"SM could mean many different things. Who knows what goes on behind closed doors?" Enrique nudged Beatrice and she joined in his laughter.

Ana looked from one to the other as Enrique handed Beatrice the tuna fish.

"Even if you are nothing more than a police detective, I can see you are a woman who appreciates good food. Eat. This will be a moment of revelation."

He was right about that.


The crescendo of excitement built by the football fans was soon deflated by the groans of a near miss. Beatrice, like everyone else, glanced at the screen to watch the replayed moment. The scrambling figures, high colour and garbled commentary made as much sense to her as a computer game, so she picked up the tuna and opened her mouth. That was when she saw it. A camera. She stopped, eyes fixed on the small device high in the corner of the room, with a tiny red light announcing its presence. Replay.

"Enrique ..."

He followed her eyes. "That doesn't work. I must call the engineers. It's crazy, spending all that money on a security system which doesn't even function. I should ask for my money back. Now, tell me, is that the most delicious thing you ever put in your mouth?"

# Chapter Five

Rita's hair spilt over her pillow, a matt-black tangle and as light-absorbent as Guinness. Her lips released a puff of air on each exhale and her shoulders rose and fell with her deep-sleep breathing. From the other bed, Luz watched for several moments, finally turning her head to see the luminous blue digits of the alarm clock. 01.43. Time to move.

She lifted the duvet clear of her legs and waited. Rita never woke, not even in the early hours of Sunday mornings, when clubbers returned from the city. But Luz took no chances. Especially this time. She pushed herself up on her elbows and slid her feet to the floor, stopped and listened.

"Puh ... puh ..."

The rucksack was ready, hurriedly packed while Rita had been running through her Bryan Adams repertoire in the shower, and stuffed casually under the communal desk. Luz scooped up her trainers and her keys, listened for a couple of seconds, and then slipped into the corridor. The lock clicked softly behind her. She paused, scanning the corridor for movement and padded towards the bathroom to dress.

Only two windows of the residence building were lit as Luz zipped up her black fleecy jacket. Her red pea coat would have been warmer, but too recognisable in the unlikely event anyone was looking. Instead, she pulled out a long fluorescent strip to loop over her shoulder and around her waist, unlocked her bike and checked the lights. Safety first. She was her mother's daughter. *But if she knew what I was doing right now ...* She snorted a dry laugh at the thought. With one more glance around, she swung herself into the saddle and headed towards Reyes Católicos, her breath visible and her heart already racing.

Cold tightened her cheeks as she pedalled along the colonnade and through the campus paths. A familiar sense of exhilaration and guilt filled her. There was no doubt. Taking Rita and Pilar to his restaurant tonight had been a stupid, unnecessary risk. They'd spotted the attraction immediately.

Pilar had peeped over the top of her menu. "Luz, I swear that waiter's tongue is hanging out. Why don't you give him your number?"

"I noticed that too! He can't keep his eyes off you. At first I thought it was great service, but now I suspect he has another reason for being so attentive. Pilar's right. Just leave your number and see what happens. It's time you had some fun."

"Rita! Keep your voice down. He's just after a decent tip. These guys are struggling to survive on the minimum wage and he's probably got a wife and three kids to support."

"Don't think so. No wedding ring. Beautiful eyes. Is it possible to get an eyelash transplant? If so, I want his."

"You can have his eyelashes, but I want his bum. Which bit do you want, Luz?"

Luz had joined in the shrieks of laughter, blushing and refusing to look in his direction. The tension was obvious and she couldn't hope to get away with being that close again.

Traffic was sparse as she sped past the hospital, moving from patches of street light to tree shadows in a comforting rhythm. She shook her head. The freshman Luz of a year ago would have seen rapists and psychopaths in every opaque corner. Now, she'd even befriended the night. She turned into Calle Valentin Jalón, sweating and exhilarated. This battle between body and mind brought back memories of being a child. Her mother, always insisting on decorum, correct behaviour and toeing the line, while her father encouraged wildness, breaking the rules and grabbing as much fun as possible. How things had changed as soon as she'd hit puberty. Game over. Still, the imprints remained. Luz's sensible head, in her mother's voice, told her she had already taken a huge risk tonight and she must be an idiot to get on her bike and take a second. Her body ignored the dampening maternal tones of her conscience and encouraged her to hurry, filling her with expectation and the cravings of an addict. That voice didn't belong to her father, though. That was all her own work.

The apartment block was in darkness so she was careful to make no noise as she locked her bike to the fire escape. She checked her watch. If the bus was on time, she had about three minutes to prepare. Creeping up the iron steps, breathing through her mouth, she shivered with excitement and fear. This was insane. So many things could go wrong. If someone saw her, if the door was locked, if he'd been delayed, if he'd brought someone home ... she stopped, her confidence faltering for the first time. In the cold stillness of the night, three steps from the top, she argued with herself, the rational against the passionate.

He wouldn't mess about with anyone else. He loved her. She didn't doubt him. Even the girls had seen it in his eyes this evening.

But he wouldn't expect to see her tonight. As far as he was concerned, she'd gone home with her friends and he wouldn't see her till tomorrow afternoon. He was free and he was a man. Men only ever thought with their ... she shook her head. That was a stupid cliché designed to make women paranoid. Didn't she trust him? After he'd made absurd amounts of effort to see her while keeping their relationship secret.

Perhaps the secrecy was for his own benefit. If he had someone else, the two lives could easily be kept apart. Until

Luz turned up at his apartment, coming face-to-face with some Turkish beauty with honey-blonde hair. Her face flushed hot with embarrassment and humiliation.

Why did she put herself through these imaginary scenarios? Even if Tunçay arrived home now, alone, surprised and delighted, all the joy had gone from the moment. She felt jealous, betrayed and mistrustful, which was as far from the intended romantic mood as she could get. She'd spoilt it. All by herself.

She turned around and silently descended the fire escape, eyes fixed on the metal steps ahead. On reaching the last, she felt in her jeans pocket for the key to unlock the bike. A movement caught her eye.

"Luz?"

Adrenalin flooded her system and she dropped the key. Tunçay stepped away from the wall, a faint light glinting off his glasses.

"What are you doing here?" he whispered. "You gave me a terrible fright. I came round the back with scraps for the cat and thought we had burglars!"

His expression was impossible to read but Luz could hear the smile in his voice.

"I was just taking out my mobile to call the police when you turned around and came back down. Not a burglar at all, but my beautiful, mysterious lover creeping around my house in the middle of the night!"

Luz dropped her head but laughed with him. "It was supposed to be a surprise."

He pulled her into his arms and kissed the top of her head. "More of a shock, I'd say. What was the plan?"

She looked up at him and he smoothed back the hair from her temples with gentle fingers.

"I was going to use the fire door. You said it's never locked. Then I was going to get into your room, undress and warm the bed for you."

"So why didn't you?"

"I ... changed my mind. I thought it might not be such a good idea after all."

His eyes searched her face. "It's a brilliant idea. Brilliant but completely crazy. Riding around the city at two in the morning is dangerous. And how did you plan to unlock my apartment without a key? Not that I care what the neighbours think, but someone might have seen you and called the police. And most of all, Crazy Lady, my number one worry is how on earth we're going to get any sleep tonight."

All the elation and desire which had propelled her out of bed returned, and Luz kissed him, drawing his tongue into her mouth, pressing her body hard against his, feeling the heat spread in her groin. He broke the kiss with a small moan.

"Upstairs. Now. Let's stick to your plan, but how about you use the conventional stairs and take my key. Leave the door open. I'll feed the cat, which will give you two minutes. Then I'll 'come home' and get the best surprise of my life. You may as well keep that key, by the way. Just in case you get the urge to surprise me again."

Luz gave him the thumbs-up and ran round to the front door, grinning all over her face.

# Chapter Six

"Shit."

Ana entered the little hotel room, dumped her handbag onto the desk and sat on the end of the bed, hands dangling between her knees.

"Shit, shit, shit."

Beatrice opened the tiny window in a feeble attempt to overcome the smell of damp. "Shit indeed. And with classic misjudgement, I revealed my profession."

"Don't beat yourself up. I thought it was a good move. Until he started lying."

"Several things occur to me. First, Enrique's trying to hide something, but not particularly well. And unfortunately, thanks to my incompetence, he knows we're trying to find it. Under normal circumstances, I'd demand the weekend footage recorded on that camera, but I have no jurisdiction here. We must talk to the police."

Ana shrugged. "I've tried that already and they dismissed me as a sensationalist. Although I suppose Stubbs of the Met might carry more weight. OK, we'll give it a go. What were the other things?"

"Alibis. Both Gregorio and Enrique gave us a detailed account of their whereabouts on Sunday, including several witnesses. Possibly both are telling the truth, but such efficient accounts might suggest preparation. And something feels odd about those flowers."

"Doña Llorente's flowers?"

Beatrice pulled out the little kettle from the cupboard, along with the tiny tubes of coffee, slim selection of teas and milk substitutes. "Can I offer you a drink?"

"Have you no mini-bar?"

"Unfortunately not. I could order room service?"

"No, I'm grand. The flowers?"

"Tiago was rushing out the door, dressed well, late for an appointment, probably scheduled for seven o'clock, with a bouquet of roses. He had no idea his neighbour would be arriving home at that moment, but decided to give her the flowers he was carrying. If he believed he was on his way to meet you, for some kind of romantic liaison, he may have bought flowers but bottled out at the last minute. And Doña Llorente benefitted from his indecision."

Ana's eyebrows rose. "Jesus."

"What is it?"

"Tiago's nickname is '*Depende*' meaning 'it depends'. He's famous, so much so it's a running joke, for being the most indecisive person on the news-gathering team."

Beatrice sat down beside Ana. "Right, we need to go through every possible scenario until we work out the most likely sequence of events which fits with the elements we know. Then we test our theories, one by one."

"Brilliant. Thing is, do we have to do it here? This place is depressing."

Looking around the room, Beatrice acknowledged the drawbacks. The minuscule amount of light, the pervasive whiff of mould and the ancient furnishings combined to create a grim echo of 1960s bedsits.

Ana elbowed her. "Look, say no if you want, but I have a spare room, a big balcony and a well-equipped kitchen. You realise that staying at mine would put you at risk of questions and queries at any hour of the day or night. But it's got windows and it doesn't stink."

Beatrice considered for all of fifteen seconds. "I'll take you up on that. Thank you, you're very kind. It's only for a couple of days, as I need to press on with my itinerary. But you can rely on my full support until I depart. Do you happen to have broadband?"

Balancing a suitcase on the moped was out of the question, so with some relief, Beatrice took a taxi to Calle Cuchillería. She paid the driver and walked down the busy pedestrian street, dragging her baggage behind her. The tall, cluttered buildings either side and the spread of cafe tables outside every other bar gave the street a narrow, almost mediaeval appearance. Washing and flags dangled overhead, rippling in the wind. The walls between the shops and bars bore murals, peeling fliers, graffiti and the occasional stone relief. Music pounded out of several doorways and Beatrice looked up at the balconies and open windows, wondering how the residents got any sleep. Crowded, colourful and just the kind of place a tourist would label 'a discovery'.

Ana opened the door with a smile. "Come in. What the hell have you got in that case? It's almost as big as you. We won't both get in the lift with that. You go ahead, fourth floor. I'll come up the stairs."

She pointed to the open lift doors behind her and raced off up the stone stairwell. She was right, the space inside was tight, barely enough room for three people. Beatrice manhandled her suitcase into position, squeezed in beside it and pressed the button for the fourth floor. With a ponderous pause, the doors closed and so began the slowest lift journey Beatrice had ever experienced. On arrival, the doors eventually opened to reveal Ana waiting.

"So, let's get this inside and then we'd better shift. I've called the local police and they've given us an appointment in twenty minutes. God, this thing weighs more than my Vespa!" She heaved the bag onto the landing, pulled out the handle and wheeled it into the apartment.

"Don't exaggerate. And I'm on an extended holiday, so I brought everything I might need."

"Including your golf clubs?"

The living room was filled with brightness: a yellow sofa, lively Kahlo colours on the walls and a washed-out turquoise table, covered with magazines. The only scent in the air was fabric conditioner from the clothes drying on the balcony.

"You're in there, and the bathroom's next door." Ana indicated a door on the right, which opened onto a small, cosy room. The bed was covered with a quilt in jewel patches of ruby, gold and jade.

"It's a beautiful apartment. The décor is a delight. So cheerful. You live here alone?"

"Yeah. I bought it as an investment, planning to get a lodger, but I discovered I prefer living alone. So I'm always skint, but at least I have my privacy. Now, come on, dump your bag and let's go. You can pay tribute to my soft furnishings when we get back. First, we have to talk to the police."


The architecture of the police station was a peculiar blend of austere and pompous, giving an unwelcoming impression. Prepared for hostility, Beatrice considered her approach as she and Ana waited in the bland foyer. In the past, the knowledge that she worked for London's Metropolitan Police had raised hackles. On more than one occasion, representatives of local forces, especially those holding the same rank as herself, felt patronised and belittled by her; as if she thought them incompetent. Once or twice, they might have been right. Therefore, in Spain and not in an official capacity, she would need to be extremely diplomatic. At least she was wearing flip-flops. It would be impossible to pull rank in flip-flops.

"Good afternoon." The man standing in the doorway had only one eyebrow. Where the other should have been was shiny scar tissue, reaching up to his hairline. Probably clean-shaven this morning, his chin now showed a distinct shadow. Black hair flopped over his forehead, partially hiding the scar. His dark eyes flicked from one to the other without smiling.

Ana rose. "Detective, thanks for seeing us. As I mentioned, Beatrice Stubbs is a detective inspector with the Met in London. Beatrice, this is Detective Milandro."

He held out his hand. "You are on holiday, Detective Stubbs?"

Beatrice's first challenge. Her title was Detective Inspector, and Ana had introduced her as such. But to correct him at this stage would be counter-productive and unnecessary. She wasn't at work. She shook his hand.

"That's right. Exploring the north coast of Spain. Ana is an old friend and she asked me for help, so I offered my advice. That's why we're here – to hand over what we know to the professionals."

He cast a neutral look in Ana's direction. "Come through. I can give you half an hour."

He took them through a security door and escorted them along a corridor. An obscenely fat man came out of an office and stared at them as they passed. He grunted in response to Ana's greeting and said something to Milandro, who motioned for them to enter an interview room on the right. He spoke quietly to the slug-like man in the corridor, leaving the door open.

Beatrice dropped her voice. "What are they saying?"

"I've no clue. They're talking in Basque."

Milandro joined them and closed the door.

"Who was he?" asked Ana.

Milandro seemed amused by her blunt query. "He is my superior officer, Detective Inspector Salgado. He likes to know what is going on."

Ana gave a contemptuous look at the mirrored window, as if Salgado were on the other side. "And what did you tell him?"

"That I don't know what's going on. I hope you can enlighten me."

His expression remained attentive and he asked several smart questions regarding their assumptions. Beatrice's respect for the man grew, particularly as he seemed one of the few men who didn't appear awed by Ana's appearance.

He looked up from his notepad and directly at Ana. "So you think he was expecting to meet you? For some kind of date?"

Ana shrugged. "It looks that way. The flowers, the neighbour's description of him as 'dressed to kill', and most importantly, the text message."

Milandro made some more notes and Beatrice scrutinised the man for clues. Lean and muscular, he looked like a runner. His face, no older than forty, bore signs of stress and more scar tissue was visible on both hands. It must have been burns, perhaps an explosion. He raised his head to meet Beatrice's stare, waited till she looked away and returned his attention to Ana.

"Why would he think you had a date? You say you made no plans to meet him on Sunday and there was no more intimacy than friendship. How did he get the wrong idea?"

Ana shook her head. "I don't know. When he sent that message, I was on my way back from Sierra de la Demanda. The bus was full of soldiers and incredibly noisy. So I didn't hear it and only noticed there was a message when I got home. By then it was after midnight so I didn't answer. But when I read it again the next morning, I thought it was weird. I meant to ask him what he was playing at when I got to work. But as I told you, he didn't show up."

"Is it possible the message was meant for someone else, another 'A'? And he sent it to the wrong person?"

"I suppose. But I know him pretty well, and his circle of friends. I can't think of anyone who begins with 'A' apart from me."

"Men are good at keeping secrets." Milandro looked at Beatrice. "If the young man assumed there was a date, he must have had a good reason. Ana says she made no arrangement, so how else might Tiago have got the wrong idea?"

Beatrice thought about it. "Could someone have sent him a message on your behalf? Someone who knew you'd be out of town?"

Ana frowned. "No one knew I was going to Sierra de la Demanda because I only decided myself on Saturday morning. As for someone using my email, they'd have to know my password. I change it every week. And my phone is always with me. So I can't see how."

Beatrice checked Milandro. He looked back but gave no reaction. His silence seemed to be permission to continue. So she did.

"How would you ask someone for a date?" she thought aloud. "Face-to-face, over the phone, by email, by text, by sticking a note in his pocket? The first two are out, as he knows you and your voice so well."

Milandro agreed. "And I assume he knows your handwriting, as you work closely together at the paper?"

"Yeah," Ana nodded, "he takes the piss out of my writing. I learnt italics at school and still write like something out of the nineteenth century. He'd know if it was me or not."

Milandro made a respectful open-hand gesture to Beatrice, indicating she could continue. She began to like this man. A genuinely decent sort.

"So email or text are our only options. He couldn't have received either while you were in the bar on Friday otherwise he would have reacted. He must have received it on Saturday or Sunday, while you were in the mountains. Have you checked the sent folder from both your phone and email?"

Ana picked up her phone and began scrolling back through her messages.

"How long is your vacation, Detective Stubbs?" asked Milandro.

"Till Christmas. It's more of a sabbatical than a holiday.

Trying to decide if retirement would suit me."

"Judging by current events, I would suggest not." Milandro pointedly looked at Ana and back to Beatrice with one raised eyebrow.

Ana put her phone back on the table. "Nothing was sent from my personal email. I'll check my work one when I get into the office. And like I said, my phone is with me always."

"So what next? You would be able to ask for the CCTV recordings. Are you going to interview the bar owner of *El Papagaio*?" Beatrice asked Milandro.

"Possibly. Ladies, please let me know if you find any more information. I have to leave you now as I must make some calls. Thank you for your assistance in this matter. Detective Stubbs, could you tell me the name of your hotel or give a mobile number? In case I need to contact you."

"You can contact her at my place," said Ana. "Calle Cuchillería, I think you have my details."

Milandro's single brow rose again.

Beatrice withdrew a card, clearly stating her identity as Detective Inspector Stubbs of the Met. "My mobile is bottom right."

Milandro read it and slipped it into his shirt pocket. "Thanks. Have a pleasant evening and thank you for sharing your information. Goodbye."

Ana seemed as buoyant as Beatrice on leaving the police station, but had to return to the newspaper offices to update her editor on the story. She dropped Beatrice off at Calle Cuchillería and sped off, hair flying from under her helmet.

After a brief visit to the supermarket, Beatrice returned to Ana's building, recited several verses of 'The Rime of the Ancient Mariner' as the lift inched upwards and won the battle of wills with the lock on Ana's apartment door. She made herself some tea and sat on the balcony with her laptop, intending to check her emails, but found herself constantly distracted by the activity from the street below. She realised, once again, that she was smiling. This break, only a week old, was proving excellent for her health. A plethora of art, fine food and awe-inspiring scenery accompanied by good wine, a ride on a moped and a little adventure was all it took to recharge her batteries. Just look at her now.

The sound of her mobile ringing brought her back to the moment.

"Hello, Beatrice Stubbs speaking?"

"Stubbs, my team are dealing with a series of major incidents involving trafficked weapons. The media are nipping my ankles over cover-ups from the 1970s, the terrorist threat has been raised to amber and the government wants expenditure cuts but improved levels of service, if you please. On top of which, I am one detective down. Because said detective is taking a well-earned sabbatical in order to rest and recuperate before getting back to work. So can you explain why, at the end of another hellish day of defensive strokes and damage control, I received a call from the Spanish police asking me to keep my people out of their jurisdiction?"

"Sir, it's not really ..."

"The question was rhetorical. Good God, woman, even when you are not at work, you cause me headaches. What the hell are you playing at? If you want to do bloody detective work, get back here. But leave the Spanish police alone, stop telling other people how to do their jobs and keep your nose out of what doesn't concern you. If I have to make another call such as this, there will be no need to discuss your future at the Metropolitan Police in the New Year. Do I make myself transparently clear?"

"Yes, sir. I wasn't trying to tell anyone ..."

Hamilton cut her off with a pantomime sigh. "You are in Spain, DI Stubbs. Go native. Eat calamari, have a siesta, drink some sangria. Run with some bulls, if you're that bloody bored. But for once in your life, stop interfering. That is an order. Good evening to you."

# Chapter Seven

Ripples responded to the breeze, fluttering across the surface of the water with a sound like distant applause. Jeremy stretched and yawned. He damn well deserved a round of applause for getting up at seven in the morning. Marcus would have dragged them out of their tents even earlier, had it been light enough. As it was, he must have been up a good half hour ahead of them to get the fire going and prepare breakfast. Amazing sort, really. Just the type to keep both morale and discipline on track. Five creased and sour faces had brightened up after sausage, beans and bacon, mopped up with yesterday's bread. Protein and carbs, essential for today's forty-seven kilometre route.

Lots of groans and grunts from the chaps as they took to their bikes, not to mention a fair bit of ribbing. His own backside was tender on the saddle and his calves seemed to be screaming as he massaged in sun lotion, feeling an absolute twerp as he could see his breath in the autumn air. Whose damn fool idea was this anyway?

"Lactic acid, that's all it is," called Marcus, adjusting his helmet. "Best thing is to get the muscles moving. Nice easy one to start us off and we'll tackle the hills after lunch."

Jeremy sighed and double-checked his panniers. He wouldn't make the mistake of sloppy packing and holding up the others a second time. They made sure they left their camping spot in pristine condition, dumped the rubbish in the municipal bin and headed out of town in single file.

The inlet curved away to a perfect U, allowing for a flat, gentle ride and an opportunity to take in the views. Despite the morning chill, one could see a fine day was in the offing. Cloudless sky, mist rising from the forests beyond and the sun heralded its imminent arrival with an intense white-gold glow from the other side of the reservoir. He enjoyed the rhythm of pumping legs, team spirit and collective sense of tackling a challenge. Nevertheless, his physical discomforts were not quite forgotten. It appeared he was not the only one.

"*Sometimes, I feel*
*Like my arse is on fire*
*Sometimes, I feel*
*Like my arse is on fire*"

Laughter spread even as far as Marcus when Laurence's hearty baritone resonated along the line. Five voices joined in, creating a half-decent harmony.

"*Sometimes, I feel*
*Like my arse is on fire*
*A long, long way*
*From my home*"

The pace began to quicken as they made their way towards the dam and Jeremy felt a very simple, pure kind of pleasure. He knew he would remember this, in his dotage, as one of the happiest days of his life.

"Marcus? What say we have a photo op when we get to the dam?" Simon shouted. He'd become awfully fond of sharing their activities on Facebook, which necessitated regular stops, especially when their route passed anything tourist-worthy.

Marcus did not respond, but as they passed the massive edifice, made a crisp, military gesture to indicate left. Most of the chaps stayed on their bikes as Simon fiddled about with his gadget. Marcus removed his wraparound sunglasses.

"I told you yesterday, Harris, that you are entitled to no more than four of these stops per day. That's one down, three to go.

Choose wisely."

"Wilco. Best get a group shot now then. Come along, ladies, into position."

Laurence rolled his eyes but swung his bike to face Simon. The group lined up with surprising efficiency, Jeremy taking the spot furthest from the road. He attempted a kind of nonchalant smile, as if photographs were a silly affectation he could take or leave.

"One sec ..." Simon called, messing about with the camera.

Jeremy joined in the sighs, leant on his handlebars and studied the scale of the brickwork from top to bottom. His eyes registered a shape in the water, something oddly natural and yet not. Looked like a marble bust; shoulders, back and upper arms, but no visible head or lower body. Jeremy squinted and he tried to account for the *trompe d'oeil* with a logical explanation.

"OK, sorry about that. Say Camembert, everyone. Jeremy! Where the hell are you off to?"

"Hold that." Jeremy swung his leg off the bike and handed it to Laurence. He scrabbled down the slope, annoyed by the uselessness of his cycle shoes on this terrain, focusing on his progress, not his target. He reached the fence and climbed over without a second's hesitation. Now he kept his eyes on the shape. He could already see it wasn't marble, or a bust. The indigo lines were veins and the cold blue he had mistaken for stone was pale, dead flesh. A body, face down. Legs dangled into deeper water, obscured by plants and black hair floated gently around the head. He reached the edge of the water and saw a hand bobbing along with the ripples. Fingers which must have held pencils, scratched heads, typed letters and caressed cheeks, now silently decomposing in cold, dark water. Jeremy's stomach contracted.

"Jez?" Marcus jumped down from the fence. "Something wrong?"

The usual clipped tones were softer and the friendly diminutive didn't go unnoticed. Relief in familiarity unlocked Jeremy's jaw.

"I'll say. Dead body. We should call the authorities. Simon's best with the lingo. Would you mind giving him a shout?"

The sun crept over the hills in the east, adding a cheerful light to the macabre scene. Yells ricocheted up and down the slope and some of the others came down for a closer look.

"What a horrible way to go."

"Do you suppose he was fishing and fell in?"

"I doubt it, Laurence. Unless he was fly-fishing in the buff."

"Poor bugger."

Jeremy ignored it all. There was something wrong with the legs. Bodies float horizontally, unless something was dragging the ankles down. Jeremy scanned the scene and spotted a dangling branch a few yards ahead. It took seconds to break it off and return to the corpse.

Marcus frowned. "Look here, I wouldn't touch it if I were you."

"I'm not going to touch it. I just want to know what's weighing it down."

"Best leave that sort of thing to the police, I'd say. For all we know, this could be a crime scene. Jez?"

Crouching on the bank, Jeremy lowered the branch into the water and made a slow sweep beneath the body. He met resistance, as expected, under the legs. So he tried to draw the branch, and the body, closer. But something gave way, the branch broke the surface and Jeremy fell backwards. However, the momentum he had instigated continued, to the dumbstruck horror of the men on the bank. Legs freed, the body sank, rolled and resurfaced, horizontal and face up.

"Jesus Christ!"

Jeremy's eyes registered the image for only a second before he turned to heave up his breakfast. But no matter how tightly he closed his lids, he would never be able to erase the image of what he'd just seen. A siren approached.

# Chapter Eight

At the *Feira do Vino,* all roads lead to Castelo de Aguirre. An exhibition stand to suit his status, at last. The centrepiece, sitting at the junction of five aisles, clearly announced his importance to the world. After attending the biggest trade fair in the country for ten consecutive years, finally, he was king. He'd allowed his daughters to select the décor, on condition he had final veto. The girls proved useful in such roles. He'd suggested red and yellow; dynamic and forceful colours, an attention-grabbing logo and beautiful young girls serving the wine. His daughters turned up their noses in perfect synchrony, comparing his design ideas to the marketing of McDonald's. Now, returning after a long lunch, he acknowledged his intelligence in allowing them a free hand.

Dark green baize flooring muffled the sounds of footfalls, establishing gravitas. The much-debated backdrop, an artist's rendering of vineyards, hinted at taste, discretion and subtlety. Three wide steps invited one in, the carved stone bar, gilded tables and chairs with blood-red cushions offered a sense of luxury, and the final touch – welcoming smiles from Paz and Inez. Neither of his daughters could be described as young or beautiful, but their knowledge of the product was second only to his own. Behind the bar, two of his most respected tasters, whose ancient faces resembled the gargoyles on the granite, poured samples and advised visitors. The cumulative effect needed no shrieking logo. Quite simply, here was the real thing. Old World wine, Old World style.

The ebb and flow of guests remained constant during the day, easily managed by the four representatives of the estate, leaving Aguirre to mingle and network. Occasionally he spent an hour or so on the stand. As well as giving the punters an opportunity to meet the man himself, it meant one of the others could take a break, refill the brochure racks, open more bottles, clean glasses and rearrange the furniture. His appearance always guaranteed a swell of interest, not least from the international wine journalists, who appeared with tedious regularity to trot out the same unimaginative questions.

Paz escorted a pair of buyers down the steps, shaking hands and smiling, before turning her attention to her father. Her hair, swept into a French pleat, was a complex arrangement of blonde highlights sprayed into submission.

"Good lunch?" she asked.

"Outstanding." Aguirre lowered himself into a gilded chair, feeling sleepy and satisfied. "In the eyes of the *Denominacion de Origen*, I can do no wrong. Everything going well here?"

Paz checked the stand, her eyes sharp. "Yes. That woman over there is a British importer. Inez's English is better than mine, so she dealt with her. I took the Valencians. They placed a decent order for next year's Crianza. The couple at the bar are time-wasters, in my opinion. I'll relieve Salbatore in a minute and get rid of them."

Aguirre smiled, confident his daughter's hard-sell charm would chase off the most persistent freeloader. Paz began wiping tables, reorganising displays and restoring the stand to its usual immaculate condition. All the time he watched her, she watched everything else. Nothing escaped her attention; her father, her sister, the employees, the punters. She reminded him of a hawk, scanning her terrain, ready to swoop. They were good girls. Real assets. At least two of his daughters took after him. Luz, unfortunately, had inherited her mother's stubborn streak. An Aguirre girl at university; it was absurd, indulgent and a waste of time. Yet Marisol seemed to be as proud of Luz reading law as she was of her first grandson. Occasionally he regretted marrying such a short-sighted woman.

His phone rang. Aguirre answered, irritation already in place. As he listened to the hoarse tones relaying the latest, his frown deepened and his jaw muscles tensed. His impatience grew until he could take it no longer.

"*Basta!* Enough! Take him a case of wine. Tell him to forget it. He knows nothing and there's nothing to know. The situation has been resolved and a pair of scavenging dogs looking for scraps is no cause for concern. I'll make sure he's not bothered again. All he needs to do is keep quiet and talk to no one. Be friendly, but let him know we expect him to keep his head. In fact, say exactly those words; we hope he can keep his head. That should shut him up."

Aguirre ended the call and scowled. Paz checked his expression and obviously misinterpreted it. She stalked across to the bar, dismissed both bar staff and stretched back her lips in an alarming smile. The bird of prey was on the hunt.

"Señor Aguirre?"

Before he'd even turned his head, Aguirre knew it was a journalist. This one was typical. Too-long hair and dressed in a cheap suit, he had the eager optimism of someone new to the job. The only point of any interest was the camera crew.

Aguirre stood with a charming smile. "Yes, I'm Arturo de Aguirre. How can I help?"

Lights arranged, furry sound boom in position, cameras and faces pointing in his direction drew more attention from passers-by than usual. A shiny sheen of sweat appeared on the journalist's brow as he checked his equipment. The boy needed to relax; after all, he was dealing with a professional. Aguirre signalled to Paz for one of the cheaper bottles, and with a circular gesture, requested glasses for the whole party. Not only articulate, accessible and an excellent interviewee, but generous.

An all-round good guy.

"So, Señor Aguirre, we're all set. Oh, good idea!" the journalist exclaimed as Paz set the wine on the table between them. "We should have an example of the famous product in shot."

"Please make sure *all* our guests are served, my dear," said Aguirre, nodding at the crew. He returned the appreciative smiles. His mobile vibrated silently against his ribcage, but he ignored it.

Wine served, the young man addressed Aguirre. "I'd like to begin by asking you about the product, its history and finally ask your views on how you explain its amazing popularity. Is that OK?"

"You're the boss," responded Aguirre, despite all the evidence to the contrary.

The few curious onlookers had built to a small crowd, all stretching and leaning to get a better view of one of Spain's best-known icons. The camera operator counted down and, with a quick wipe of his face, the greenhorn began.

"One of the greatest Spanish success stories of the past few years has been the rise of white Rioja. Once the poor cousin to Spain's flagship red, one vineyard has championed the white Viura grape and boosted demand, both domestic and foreign, for this fresh, citrusy wine. Castelo de Aguirre is the brand which has come to represent the renaissance of the region's white wine.

"Today, we're lucky to interview the viniculturist himself, the man behind the brand, Arturo de Aguirre. Thank you for talking to us, Señor Aguirre."

Aguirre dropped his voice to a more authoritative register. "Happy to oblige. Every opportunity to spread the word is welcome."

"Can you begin by telling us about white Rioja? What makes it so special?"

Aguirre angled himself towards his interviewer, projecting his voice past the microphone towards the knot of observers.

"Everything. From nose to palate to finish, this is an exceptional wine which can stand comparison with any Australian Chardonnay or Californian Sauvignon Blanc. Not only can it compete with the wines of the New World, but it takes on French Chablis, Portuguese vinho verde and Italian Pinot Grigio."

The journalist took a breath for his next question but Aguirre anticipated him.

"You're going to ask me why? Good question. Tastes change. For the past two decades, we have seen a trend to the fruit-focused, crowd-pleasing, oaky whites. Easy to drink, higher in alcoholic content and even the driest has a sweetness on the palate. Wines such as our neighbours' Verdejo or Albariño also favour this tropical fruit robustness. Add to this accessible taste the power of New World marketing, and you understand why the traditional white has fallen out of favour."

Inexperienced he may have been, but the boy recognised his cue. "But white Rioja is now one of the most popular wines in Europe, grabbing a huge slice of market share from other white wines. Where did this sudden interest in traditional whites spring from?"

Aguirre gave an understanding nod. "Another good question. To find the answer, we must look backwards. Rioja, in contemporary public perception, stands for fine red wine. It was not always so. In the nineteenth century, the region was famous for its white wine. Have you ever asked yourself why red wine is described in Spanish as *viño tinto*? Tinted wine? Not as in other countries: *rouge*, *rosso*, red or *negre*? Because the majority of the region's output was white and as a result, subject to higher tax. So the wily viniculturists added a 'tint' of red to their best-selling whites, avoiding tax and spreading the name of Rioja all over the globe."

A murmur rustled through the onlookers. Not only was he an entertaining speaker, but he taught them something as well. He kept his eyes on the journalist.

"Fascinating. So why has the general public, not only at

home, but abroad, embraced white Rioja again?"

"If I knew the answer to that, I would retire, right now." The laughter came, as expected, and this time Aguirre bestowed a gracious smile on his audience.

"All I can do is guess. After twenty years of the mass-produced uniformity of sunny, fruity and disposable wines, the traditional, time-honoured methods have once more been recognised for delivering depth. Open a bulk-produced Chardonnay and a white Rioja and compare. At first taste, the Chardonnay comes out fighting. Consistent to the last drop, it tells you of the maker and his methods. A reliable if unexciting wine. The Rioja, with a more savoury, green-apple note to begin, develops an earthy, mouth-coating taste, revealing its mineral sources, and deferring finally to a buttery lemon finish. A journey from first taste to last, it tells you of the soil, the climate, the land. That is not simply a wine. That is an adventure."

His rhetoric, his gestures, his passionate evocation of the sensory experience brought forth a round of applause. He spotted Inez and Paz exchanging a look of familiar admiration. Yes, they'd seen it all before. But like a fine Gran Reserva, every year he just got better.

The journalist, quite delighted with his coup, shook Aguirre's hand more times than was necessary, before finally following his crew to the exit. Or perhaps he was just drunk. Paz had ensured their guests were well-lubricated, just as soon as the interview was over, and the atmosphere was celebratory.

Aguirre slipped into the back room, amongst the wine boxes and publicity material to make a call. It went to voicemail. He smiled. So much the better.

"Tomas, it's Arturo. Arturo Aguirre. I hear the fire we put out is still smouldering. A collaborative effort is now required. For all our sakes, we must extinguish this once and for all. I know I can count on you. Keep me informed. Goodbye."

He glared at the cases of his famous product, seeing nothing.

This whole business was becoming an irritant. Just like an infection in the vines, it had to be treated at source, otherwise it would spread like a virus, damaging crops, vintages and reputations. Something like this had to be ripped out at the roots. It was time to call in some favours.

# Chapter Nine

The front door slammed and Beatrice jerked awake. The clock read 08.13. Ana must have left for work. Beatrice threw back the duvet and stared at the carpet. She'd guessed Ana wouldn't accept this easily. The girl's lack of respect for authority had come to the fore last night, making it harder to convince her that Beatrice had no choice but to back off. A reluctant truce was reached, after arguing back and forth till gone midnight. Beatrice's hands were tied but her mind was not. She would stay in the background, advising Ana on techniques and lines of enquiry until the end of the week. Then the girl would be on her own.

To her credit, Ana didn't sulk, instead giving Beatrice the story Tiago was pursuing; a vanishing junior accountant. Sounded rather dull, but Tiago's disappearance aroused more suspicion. With everyone, it seemed, but the police. Beatrice shook herself. She would devote no more hours to fuming at that sly, two-faced, duplicitous Milandro. She stomped into the bathroom. Rotten little rat; *I have calls to make.* He wasted no time. Nasty, untrustworthy snake. To think she'd respected him, when all the while he was waiting to drop her in it. She turned the water to full blast as if to wash away her thoughts.

How frustrating journalism must be. To have almost as many facts and opinions as the police, but without the authority of the law to investigate.

Once dried, dressed and her blisters plastered, Beatrice

sought the kitchen.

A note was stuck to the fridge: *Help yourself to whatever you fancy. I recommend the rashers. Coffee machine on stove. Back at lunchtime unless any developments. Ana.*

Whilst tucking into bacon, eggs and mushrooms, Beatrice made a mind-map of all she knew in pen, adding assumptions in pencil, placing Tiago Vínculo at the centre. She retrieved her tourist guide from her handbag, identifying Tiago's apartment block and its proximity to *El Papagaio*. The accountancy firm with the absent accountant sat in the central bank and finance sector. All within spitting distance. She trawled the firm's photographs, their address, and attempted to read some of the *El Periódico* archive logged by Tiago. But her poor grasp of even basic Spanish made this a fruitless exercise.

Yes, the Internet opened many doors, but there was no substitute for the real thing. Beatrice wanted to be out there, talking to the people, pressing the editor, checking Tiago's communications. Impossible. Hamilton would explode in a cloud of indignation and serge suiting if he heard the merest hint of her involvement. And Matthew would most certainly take a dim view of her detour into detecting while she was supposed to be taking a complete break.

Matthew. He had no idea where she was and intended to call the hotel today. She washed up and went in search of her mobile, releasing her hair to do its worst. The sun cast huge rhomboids of light across Ana's living room, so Beatrice settled into the sofa, tucked up her legs like a cat on a cushion and prepared to put a positive spin on her extended stay in Vitoria.

She was still thinking of the most suitable terminology when running footsteps approached the door. Beatrice got to her feet as a key rattled back and forth. Ana burst in, breathing heavily, but pale as porridge.

"Just heard – a body's been found – at the bottom of a dam – near the Ullíbarri-Gamboa Reservoir – huge fuss at the paper – water for half the province comes from there – police won't confirm identity – we have to go – come on – your boss can just swivel."

She thrust an aggressive middle finger in the direction of the telephone.

Beatrice obeyed and put on her flip-flops; her sense of foreboding and concern growing. But as they hurried down the stairs, she couldn't help practising that gesture and whispering the word 'swivel' with a secretive smile.

The morgue, situated in the same grounds as Santiago Apostol Hospital, had its own car park surrounded by trees, effectively screening it from those who would rather not be reminded of their own mortality. Ana parked the moped as far from the entrance of the low, sober-looking building as it was possible to go. Beatrice dismounted and saw why. A police car sat squarely in front of the main doors.

It would be foolhardy to cross paths with Milandro the day after he'd reported her to Hamilton. Ana obviously had the same thought and indicated the walkway along the side of the building. As they approached, Beatrice could see that the building did in fact have two storeys, but one was below ground. On this side, a deep trench ran alongside the wall. Large frosted-glass windows allowed natural light to penetrate but prevented any ghoulish curiosity. A handrail ensured no one could fall in and a set of metal steps descended to a fire escape door. Stainless steel ashtrays indicated the smokers' corner.

Ana's phone trilled an upbeat melody. She answered, leaning on the rail, muttering a few words in Spanish, but mostly listening. Autumn leaves and litter had blown into the trench and caught in spiders' webs, giving the place an abandoned quality. Beatrice moved a little further along, concerned about being seen from the car park.

Ana ended her call. "That was Jaime, the editor at the paper. He's been talking to the cyclists who found the body. Male, young, no ID, no personal belongings and the face was unrecognisable, they say. Could be anyone."

Beatrice rested her hand on Ana's arm. "So there's every possibility it was some poor hiker who took a tumble."

The girl shook her head. "I have a bad feeling about this. We'll wait for the police to leave and then find out for ourselves who it is and how he died."

"Will the coroner give out that kind of information?"

"No." Ana's attention was caught by movement in the car park. The police vehicle pulled away, followed by an unmarked car, with Milandro clearly visible in the driver's seat. Fortunately, he faced front. Beatrice released her breath and looked at Ana to continue.

"Now what?"

"Now this. Can I borrow your phone? I'm going to call Karel, the coroner's assistant, who will tell us what we want to know."

Beatrice handed her mobile over, wondering why Ana didn't use her own.

"Is Carol a friend of yours?"

"More of a stalker who owes me a favour. Hence the need for your phone." She scrolled through her own phone and punched the number into Beatrice's keypad.

Beatrice stared at her. "Why does she owe you a favour?"

Ana frowned at her for a second before her face cleared. "Not Carol, Karel. He's a six-foot four Dutch doctor. And he owes me because I didn't apply for a restraining order." She pressed the call button and her expression hardened.

"Karel? This is Ana Herrero. I want to talk to you. Outside, by the smoking area. Yes, now would be good. Tell them you need the bathroom."

Two minutes later, the door crunched open and a tall man in a white coat emerged. He stooped to avoid banging his head on the door frame and Beatrice noticed the gesture was well practised. As well as his impressive height, Karel had the broad shoulders of a swimmer, thick fair hair and strong features. His expression was wary, searching Ana's face before acknowledging

Beatrice with a bow of his head.

"Hello, Ana. I was surprised to hear from you."

"I'll bet. But it's not actually you I'm interested in. I need some information."

Karel gave a sad smile in Beatrice's direction. "Unrequited love, you see. If she'd only give me a chance ..."

Ana interrupted. "She can't understand you. That's my bodyguard and she doesn't speak any English."

Beatrice kept her face stony, searching for a gesture which might indicate both incomprehension and physical power. She settled for folding her arms.

"Where is she from, because I speak several ...?"

"Karel, who is it? The body they found near the reservoir."

Karel dropped his eyes. "Ana, I can't ..."

"I need to know who it is and how he died." Her voice contained no hint of a polite request, just clear determination.

"We can't even give the police cause of death with any certainty yet."

"So you know who it is and you think you know how he died. Come on, Karel. Is it Tiago Vínculo?"

"Yes." His mouth dragged down in sympathy. "I'm sorry, Ana. I know he was a close friend."

Ana swallowed once but her voice remained steady. "Thank you. How? I already know it wasn't an accident."

Karel opened his palms. "*We* don't even know that yet. His bruising is consistent with a fall. If he slipped from the top, bumping into stones and rock, it could have been the impact of any one of those that killed him. We can't make any definitive assessments till after the examination." He rubbed his eye, as if tired.

Beatrice should have known Ana would spot a liar's tic.

Stepping forward so he had no choice but to look at her, Ana stood directly in front of Karel. "What else? You know more than just bruises. Tell me, Karel. I think you owe me that."

He scrunched up his face in discomfort. "You're a journalist.

Giving you any information could get me in a lot of trouble."

"This isn't for the paper, it's for me. What is it?"

He shoved his hands deep into the pockets of his white coat and glanced again at Beatrice. Ana moved into his line of sight.

"Karel ..."

"She really doesn't understand English? I mean, I'll tell you, but I don't know that woman and she makes me nervous."

"She hasn't got a clue. I promise. Look, your toilet break is starting to get suspiciously long, so do us both a favour and tell me what else you've found."

Karel's eyes flicked to the fire door. "You cannot, under any circumstances, use this in a story. OK? The body had another injury, which can't be explained by the fall."

"What?"

"Someone cut off his nose."

"Jesus, Mary and Joseph ..."

Thankfully, Karel's attempt to comfort Ana in an embrace meant that he didn't see Beatrice clap a horrified hand to her mouth. By the time Ana had pushed him away and he looked back, Beatrice had regained her composure. Arms folded, chin high and eyes suspicious – she looked every inch a foreign security officer. But inside the implications hit her like a series of electric shocks.

# Chapter Ten

Bells rang across the courtyard, breaking into Luz's contented doze and announcing four o'clock. Her stomach swooped with a thrill when she realised where she was. And who with. Her risk-taking was getting worse. Bringing him back to the campus, back to her room, she must have lost her mind. Perhaps that was why she couldn't stop smiling. She nuzzled against Tunçay's chest and closed her eyes. She refused to watch the clock digits count away her remaining moments of happiness. He slept on, no doubt exhausted by late shifts, early mornings and limited sleep in between. Selfishness and lust, greed and need, was she taking more than she gave? Her guilt surfaced and she pulled away to look at his face.

Without his glasses, he looked younger, more naïve, and his face had relaxed completely. She smiled. His chest rose and fell, dark hair converging to an arrow which pointed beneath the duvet. Luz wanted to follow that arrow with her fingertips to see where it might lead, but she had no time. Always the same story – there was never enough time.

She kissed his cheek. "Wake up. It's past four."

He didn't open his eyes but breathed deeply, stretching out his arm and pulling her onto his chest.

She laughed and kissed him again. "Come on. We've got to get out of here. Rita will be back in less than twenty minutes."

"No. I can't move. I'm not going anywhere."

She laughed again, but a quiver of panic limited her smile. She shoved him, a dead weight. The clock flicked to 16.10. Her panic morphed into anger. She wanted to shout at him, threaten him, even hurt him. Anything to make him move. He opened his eyes.

"Is that the best you can do?" he asked, his smile sleepy.

She pounced, tickling his ribs, stomach, armpit, back, neck, wherever presented itself as he writhed and pleaded under her attack. Finally he rolled off the bed, gasping.

"That'll teach you. Come on, we have to get dressed." She jumped off the bed and picked up her underwear. He caught her ankle.

"You won't even give me an opportunity for revenge? Come on, I'm not going to see you again for five whole days." He slid his hand up the inside of her leg.

"No! Tunçay, please don't do this. We have to get dressed and get out." She dragged on her knickers and hooked herself into her bra. "I knew it was a bad idea to come here. I can't relax and you can't take it seriously. We mustn't get caught!"

All humour dropped from his face and he got to his feet. Luz looked away from his semi-erect penis and handed him his clothes. He sat on the bed to dress, his expression tired and sullen. Neither spoke until a trill emanated from Luz's phone. She read the message and sighed with relief.

"Rita's going for a sauna with Pilar and Mariana. She won't be back for another hour, at least. Wait, I have to reply, she wants me to join them."

She keyed in a swift excuse and glanced up to see Tunçay's face unchanged. He looked as if he'd had enough. She threw the phone onto the table, sat beside him and looped her arm around his neck.

"I'm sorry for hassling you. I just get so terrified of being caught that I tend to ..."

"Caught with a Turk? Am I really that embarrassing?"

She sat back, shocked. "No! No, Tunçay, it's not you. I told you that. My parents are incredibly strict. They have plans for me, and don't want anything, or anyone, to get in the way."

He stood up and pulled his cigarettes from his jacket.

"You can't smoke here. She'll smell it. Look, let's go outside."

He lit the cigarette, opened the window and blew the smoke into the cold air. "We can't go outside. You might be seen with me. People would talk and then your family would find out and then ... then what, Luz? Would it be the end of the world?"

Luz couldn't meet his eyes. She gazed at her fingernails and thought about his question. The end of the world? No. Only the end of hers. Her father would remove her from the university overnight, her mother would take her through the express checkout in the husband supermarket and her working womb would be the only interest she would hold. Her headlong rush towards independence, a hard-fought victory of five years' education would disappear as if it had never existed except in her own imagination.

Tunçay squeezed the butt under the tap, took a tissue and wrapped it carefully, before dropping it in the bin. She smiled, letting him know she appreciated the gesture, even though she'd have to dig it out and dispose of it more thoroughly after he'd gone. He sat down beside her and took her hand.

"I know this isn't easy for you. OK, your family is traditional. You could never introduce me to your parents. You, an heiress, and me, a Turkish waiter. The shame! I understand that. If you want the truth, I would also be ashamed to take you home to my family. I'm sorry if that hurts you, but I think we can be honest now. I'm Muslim and to have a serious relationship with anyone outside my faith would cause ..." He shook his head. "I don't know what it would cause and I'd never try to find out. No matter that you are the daughter of a highly successful businessman, you are still a Catholic."

The way he said it: Catholic, as if it was dirty. Luz's eyes stung but she blinked away the tears, breathing fiercely through her nose. She sat beside him on the bed, holding his hand and wondering if this was the end of her first relationship.

"Listen to me, Luz. I feel very strongly for you and I'm happy we met. I don't know if we can plan too far ahead. Our being together would hurt a lot of other people we love. But for me, that's the future. What I want to know is – do we have a present?"

It hardly ever stopped at a kiss. Luz found herself tugging at his jeans almost immediately. And after such a dance alongside the abyss, she needed that physical affirmation of his need. His love. Quick, urgent and intense, they were dressed and saying farewells within twenty minutes. Luz opened all the windows, sprayed deodorant and took the bin to the waste disposal chute in the corridor. She stopped at the vending machine for two *espressi* – one to drink and one to soak up any odours in the room. She made her bed, spread out her books to reinforce the lie that she'd been studying and sat in the armchair staring at the ceiling.

Her eyes were in the sky but her head was in the sand. Yes, she'd won the battle to go to university, to study law. Her parents were even convinced it might be of benefit to them and their business. It had never been stated explicitly, but they'd given her five years. A long leash, but still a leash. Four years to go and then what?

# Chapter Eleven

At the *El Periódico* offices, Beatrice sat in the meeting room, fidgeting. Ana had only gone downstairs to collect their guest, but unease stretched every second. Since the meeting with love-struck Karel, Beatrice was reluctant to let the girl out of her sight. Especially as the information about Tiago's body had galvanised Ana into frenetic activity; the threat implicit in his mutilation serving as catalyst rather than check. But she insisted the news they'd received at the mortuary remained their secret. Beatrice somehow doubted she was protecting her source and more keeping her cards close to her chest.

The activity log at the paper's server showed Ana's computer had been accessed on Saturday morning, while Ana herself was on a bus passing Logroño. Tiago's computer at the newspaper contained few leads, as he preferred to use his own laptop. Official tape barred entry to his apartment so the only trace of the original story remained in Ana's memory. Fortunately, a memory of superior quality.

"The guy's name was Miguel Saez and he worked for GFS, Gasteiz Financial Services. The company does audits, performs due diligence and generally checks the books for small to medium-sized companies. He went missing about three weeks ago, maybe more, and the police seemed to think he'd done a runner. I don't think they closed the case but they definitely weren't chucking resources at it either. So his girlfriend contacted the paper to try and publicise the issue. Not exactly a hot story, so our editor assigned it to Tiago. He resented being given such a dud, at first, but then he got the wind under his tail and you couldn't hold him back. Tiago's theory was this: Saez had accidentally found some sensitive information and was paid to disappear. Saez's girlfriend – what was her name? Whatever. She confirmed their relationship was volatile, he had few ties here and no family. Tiago believed he'd just taken the cash and gone. The girlfriend insists he would never do that, but how well does anyone really know a partner? Word of warning, though. I suggest we tackle that subject very carefully when we meet her. She's pretty scary. What the hell was her name?"

"Margarita Xarra."

A curly-haired woman entered the room and stomped up to Beatrice, her bag slung across her chest and one hand thrust forward. Short and square, she wore tight jeans and a glittery blue sweatshirt which bore the words 'Too Hot To Handle'. Beatrice estimated her to be early forties, aggressive and best given a wide berth. Ana followed her into the office and stood just inside the door, giving Beatrice a wide-eyed look of mock alarm.

Beatrice jumped to her feet, shook hands and attempted a greeting in Spanish. After that, conversation would be down to Ana.

"*Buenas dias, Señora Xarra. Muchas graçias ...*"

"I can speak English. You're the London detective?" Her tone was sceptical and her eyes were hard as she took in Beatrice's flip-flops.

"Yes. I am a detective, but I'm on holiday at the moment. My name is Beatrice Stubbs."

She dug deeply in her bag. "I don't care if you're on holiday or not. If you are a detective, you can help find Miguel. I brought everything I have. Why don't you sit down?" It wasn't a suggestion.

She yanked out a folder stuffed with papers and plonked herself opposite Ana and Beatrice. As the woman rifled through the papers, Beatrice voiced her concern.

"Miss Xarra, if you have some evidence relating to Miguel's disappearance, you really should give it to the police."

Margarita's head snapped up to face Beatrice. "I'm not stupid. The police have seen all this stuff. I tried to explain but the truth is I don't really understand it either. I'm not an accountant, but I'm not stupid. I know Miguel hasn't just left me, and I know whatever happened to him is connected to this." She stabbed a forefinger at the papers in front of her.

"I've been through this with the police, several times. I've been through it with your colleague and answered every one of his questions. And now I have to do it all over again with you."

The woman's pugilistic attitude rankled with Beatrice. They were hardly duty-bound to find her missing boyfriend. All they could do was offer assistance. And here was this female acting as if she were under sufferance.

Margarita evidently sensed the change in atmosphere, or registered the aggression in her tone. "But if it helps Miguel, I'll do it again and again until someone finds out what happened," she added, looking from one to the other, her expression no less confrontational.

Beatrice conceded. "I appreciate this is difficult, especially the repetition. Could you start at the beginning and tell us as much as you can about Miguel?"

"Miguel. We've been together for two years, almost. He's Galician. Not physically attractive at first glance but he has a good heart. He's a junior accountant with GFS. Because he was new to the company, they only allowed him to assist on most jobs, doing the boring bits. I can't give you any detail because we don't talk about his work. Boring like you wouldn't believe. Sends me to sleep. But a while back, around two and a half months ago, he got an opportunity to take over a job. He wouldn't shut up about it."

She pushed a brochure towards them. "You'll have to make photocopies; I'm not giving you the originals. The job was at Alava Exports, which handles some of the regional wine trade. Miguel was so excited and determined to prove himself, he worked extra hours at the weekend, checking and double-checking. It really pissed me off. We argued a lot around then."

Ana cleared her throat. "Very often, when a couple's relationship has been through a rough patch, the police take the easy option and presume he ran off. What did you say to convince them otherwise?"

Ana's subtle probing failed. Margarita's eyes flashed and her voice rose.

"How can I prove something *didn't* happen? Tell me! What can I say to a lazy son-of-a-bitch police officer who just wants to close the file? I *know* Miguel would never do that. He's a noble, honourable man and he loved me. We planned to get engaged at Christmas, so why would he run away? He told me he was under my spell."

Beatrice dropped her voice to a gentle reassuring pitch. "That's very romantic. He sounds like a charming man. Margarita, the first journalist you spoke to believed Miguel was paid to disappear. Think carefully. Could he, under any circumstances, have accepted that kind of offer?"

Margarita shook her head, slowly, but with absolute conviction, a faint smile on her face. "No. For money? No. His parents died some time back and as the only son, everything came to him. He works because he loves it, not because he needs the money."

Alarm bells rang in Beatrice's mind. A young man, no family, madly in love with an older woman, vanishes completely. "Do you know if Miguel had made a will?"

The question seemed unexpected. Margarita blinked, her face smoothed into a thoughtful calm. For the first time, Beatrice could see the natural beauty previously masked by defensive hostility.

Margarita pursed her lips. "I don't know, but I doubt it. We've never talked about it. We talked about a pre-nuptial agreement, though. That was my idea. He didn't want to discuss divorce before we'd even got married. But I want to sign a piece of paper saying everything he has before he marries me, he gets to keep. I'm not interested in his money."

So that answered that.


Forty minutes later, they said their goodbyes and Beatrice watched Margarita follow Ana out of the room. The short woman even managed to convey aggression in her walk: head down, shoulders back, like a prop forward. The pile of photocopies on the table sapped Beatrice's energy. All the painstaking legwork would be down to her and Ana; no detective sergeants to assist, no forensic expertise to call upon, and the strong possibility that any relevant papers were long gone. Or in Spanish.

"You must be Beatrice Stubbs."

The man resting his hands on the table wore an open-necked denim shirt, demonstrating that his tan spread further than his neck. Chestnut hair above dark, smiling eyes and a row of even white teeth flashed in her direction.

"How come everyone in this city knows who I am?" Beatrice asked.

He laughed. "I think there may be one or two who are still in ignorance. Jaime Rodriguez. I'm the editor of *El Periódico*. Pleased to meet you."

Beatrice half-rose to shake his hand. "Likewise. So you're Ana's boss?"

He shrugged and leaned his head to one side. "The word 'boss' implies I have some control over what she does. That is the total opposite of the case. But as I guess you know, she's an excellent investigative journalist, so I can live with that. She tells me you're helping her on that missing accountant story."

Beatrice stiffened. "Missing accountant *and* missing journalist story. Are you not concerned about your employee at all?" She reined herself in, recalling Ana's words. *Tell no one.*

"May I?" With a grin bordering on wolfish, he relaxed into the seat opposite and looked her in the eye. He was undeniably attractive, in that slightly rough, French actor sort of way. And close up, it appeared his eyes were deep blue. Beatrice smiled back.

"It's not unusual for a journalist to slip off the radar when they get close to cracking a story. Sometimes because their hours are irregular, sometimes because they're working undercover and can't take the risk of contacting the paper, sometimes because their minds are on other things. I trust Tiago's judgement and I think he'll be back with a fantastic exclusive in a few days."

Determined to stick to the party line, Beatrice ignored the sudden urge to put the man straight. Instead, she focused on his smile. Teeth that white surely couldn't be natural. She wondered how he did it.

"You must wonder what kind of undisciplined shop I run, Detective Inspector Stubbs. I guess the Metropolitan Police must be more rigid, no?"

"Hi, Jaime. You met Beatrice, then?" Ana returned to her seat and began stacking the photocopied papers into a neat pile.

He fixed his deep blue eyes on Beatrice. "I have had the pleasure, yes." He turned his attention to Ana. "So, any developments?"

Ana shook her head. "Not yet. We spoke to the girlfriend and now have to go through everything she gave us – this lot. I'm taking it home, OK? And I plan to visit the accountants' office tomorrow, but I'll keep you informed."

Jaime laughed. "That'll be a first. I must get on. Good luck with all the research." He waved a hand at the uninviting stack of documents. "Hope to talk to you again, Detective Inspector Stubbs. Can I give you my card?"

"Thank you. Here's mine. And please call me Beatrice. I'm off duty. Nice meeting you, Jaime."

With another flash of teeth, he wandered away. Beatrice

noticed the black cowboy boots complete with faux spurs and the tight-fitting jeans. Jaime was one of those men with an impossibly small bottom.

"Beatrice Stubbs! Were you just flirting with my boss?"

She met Ana's incredulous expression with a look of outraged innocence.

"Don't be ridiculous. Just because I enjoy some civilised interaction with an aesthetically pleasing specimen, you suspect the worst."

"You were checking out his arse!"

"I most certainly was not. And one thing you should learn; making easy assumptions leads to guaranteed failure in the field of detective work. So, out of interest, is he single?"

More photographs of beautiful people. Beatrice's head throbbed and she'd long since lost interest.

"This is Angel Rosado, successful businessman, well-connected and happily married. He and his wife often attend high-profile cultural events, pressing powerful flesh."

"Handsome." Beatrice observed, with little enthusiasm. "And she's very glamorous. Although that's one hell of a nose."

"Yep. Runs in the family. Boom boom." Ana scrolled through more pictures on the gossip website, as Beatrice watched and listened to the commentary. Two solid hours of poring over the scrappy and incomprehensible notes left by Miguel Saez, followed by endless screens of false smiles. Even if she knew who these people were, she'd still be bored. As for the case, a feeling of complete confusion made logical thought beyond her.

"Ana, I think I need a break ..."

"OK, two minutes. This is his sister-in-law again. See how the whole lot are interconnected? There's no branch of the trade without one of them involved. And here he is, Arturo de Aguirre, the patriarch and champion of white Rioja."

Beatrice squinted at the screen. The man's arch expression conveyed immense confidence. "Well, you can see where Mrs

Rosado got her nose from. And this bloke does what exactly?"

"He owns one of the most famous vineyards in the region, Castelo de Aguirre. It's open to the public, maybe we should have a poke around."

"I think that might be a job for me. I planned to visit some Rioja producers. But now, if you don't mind, I need to lie down in a dark room and have a glass of water."

"Are you OK?"

Beatrice considered the question. A vague panicky feeling lapped at her insides, her head pounded and she felt smothered by the foreignness of it all.

"Yes, I think so. Just feeling out of my depth. Miguel's notes in Spanish, his sums, incomprehensible numbers, and all these well-known faces I've never heard of. I wonder how much use I can be."

Ana closed the laptop and went into the kitchen. She returned with a glass of water, ice cubes chinking cheerfully. "I should apologise. I get so into all this stuff, I forget you're not working, you're on holiday. I'm being a bully. Listen, why don't you rest for a couple of hours and I'll make some food. And some phone calls. The only way we'll get any sense out of these figures is by asking an expert. This is where a large family can come in handy."

Beatrice sipped, the cool sensation spreading down her throat and across her chest. She pressed the glass to her forehead, condensation chilling her brow. The itch around her nose and eyes seemed to abate and she looked up at Ana. "Let me guess. You have three highly qualified accountants for siblings and a bank manager for a mother?"

Ana sat on the coffee table, her face concerned. "Do you want a paracetamol? You don't look good."

"I'm fine. Just in need of a rest. Which experts are you going to call?"

"All right. No, the immediate family are no good. I'm an only child and my dad is a professor of Celtic History. He's worse at maths than I am. My mother, when she was alive, couldn't even work out percentages. But I do have plenty of cousins, all of whom have done better in the professional sphere than me. Armando's not only a partner in a Porto accountancy firm, but he loves a mystery. I'll scan this stuff over to him and see what he makes of it."

A breeze brushed over Beatrice's face, a soothing feeling. She wanted to ask Ana more questions, particularly about her mother, but they would keep for later. And anyway, she was still talking.

"Then tomorrow, I'll visit the accountants, check in with Milandro and you can do the tourist thing and take a nose around the Aguirre estate."

"I'm not sure it's a good idea for us to split up. If what happened to Tiago was intended as a warning ..."

Ana hesitated. "I know. I'll be careful. If it makes you feel any better, I'll call the paper and let them know what we're up to. Don't worry about me, I can look after myself."

Beatrice frowned into her water. For an intelligent girl, Ana could be absurdly naïve.

# Chapter Twelve

To: beastubbs@ttl.com
From: Matthew.Bailey@exeter.ac.uk

I shall begin, as is only polite, by thanking you for your previous. However, please do not think for one moment that I am ignorant of the reasons why you chose to explain via electronic correspondence. More of that in a moment.

Firstly, I found much about your communication cause for relief. Your tone sounds cheerful, optimistic, inspired and engaged, just as a tourist should. If your intention was to engender a jealous rage by detailing your culinary experiences thus far, you succeeded to such an extent that my eyes seem to have changed colour permanently. Tanya's journalist friend sounds delightful and very generous in allowing you to stay in her apartment. Both Tanya and Marianne asked me to pass on their regards.

Yet the cautious curmudgeon in me has found much of interest and concern between the lines. For the first week of your extended holiday, we spoke daily on the telephone. Yesterday, you chose to substitute our conversation for a one-sided email, with the casual aside: 'too much to tell you over the phone'. It may well be the most efficient method of informing me of the significant changes which have occurred since our last chat, but also ensures I cannot interrupt.

A further worry is your decision to abandon your plan for relaxation and 'battery-charging' to become involved in an investigation. The fact that it is under the auspices of journalism rather than crime is a semantic distinction. You are working, Old Thing, while on holiday. I only hope Hamilton doesn't find out.

I have typed and deleted the following sentence three times: You know best. Unfortunately, our experience shows this conceit as fundamentally flawed. I trust you understand that I am not talking about the Pembroke incident. Not even I could be that crass. In a more general sense, we have agreed that you function best with your support mechanism intact. While I respect and admire your judgement and professional brilliance, sometimes, Old Thing, you make the worst imaginable decisions for yourself. I hope you understand my unease as concern rather than mistrust.

All that remains for me to say is that I wish you a wonderful adventure in Vitoria, be it culinary, advisory or artistic. I would feel vastly reassured if we could find a way of conversing in the next few days.

Beatrice, be careful. And please call James.

With love, affection and considerable exasperation
Matthew

# Chapter Thirteen

It took less than a minute for Beatrice to decide that she loathed at least eighty percent of her companions on the wine tour. Unreasonable it may have been, but an undeniable fact. A thundercloud loomed over her outlook, driven by her worry for Ana along with a general sense of isolation and loneliness. Not only that, but Matthew's email had hit its target. He should be here. When she'd made the decision to travel alone, with the aim of considering her options, she thought it was best. Now, she missed his anchoring effect and light touch on the tiller. How he'd love this autumnal light, the vivid landscape of seasonal tones, the epicurean delights, her snide observations on other travellers and most of all, he'd love the wine. But he wasn't here. All her own fault, which only made it worse.

The ill-matched bunch waited in the assembly area, a lumpen assortment wearing the universal uniform of the tourist. Turquoise anoraks, puce bum-bags and lime rucksacks, elasticated waists and bulging pockets of all-purpose beige trousers with an abundance of zips. The party, to which Beatrice contributed her own sour expression, created a startlingly ugly contrast to whitewashed walls, oak barrels and a panorama of vineyards through the window. She hated to be part of such a group, and hated herself more for being such an unbearable snob. Perhaps she should leave.

"Good morning, everyone. My name is Claudia and I am

your tour guide today. OK, how many English speakers?"

Most raised their hands, excepting three superior-looking ladies with steely hair and pastel suits, the Italian foursome and a young couple who could not stop kissing and giggling. Beatrice wondered if they'd even heard the question.

"*Qui parle français? Español?*"

Claudia, after much discussion, agreed to conduct the tour in English, Spanish, Italian and French.

She led them outside and began her spiel. The sun bounced off the white walls of the Tourist Centre, as the visitors listened to the history of the Castelo. The two Italian couples continued to talk amongst themselves, pointing out objects of interest to each other as if nothing else was happening. Claudia raised her volume and switched to Spanish. The young couple paid no attention, whispering, goosing and squealing while the poor guide ran through her speech. The Frenchwomen began to scowl and tut, the sun caused Beatrice's eyes to water and her irritation reached breaking point. This was a waste of time. She would leave, forget the money she'd spent on the taxi and admission fee and go back to Calle Cuchillería.

"Claudia?" A stentorian voice echoed around the courtyard, silencing the Italians and drawing everyone's attention upwards. Even the dry-humpers took their eyes off each other for a moment. Arturo de Aguirre surveyed them from a stone balcony above. He exchanged a few rapid words with the tour girl and disappeared. Her strained expression evaporated and she broke into a genuine smile.

"Ladies and gentlemen, we have luck. Señor Aguirre, the owner of the vineyard, will join us. This is not usual."

The truth of that statement was visible in her face. Her anticipation affected everyone, so that as Aguirre rounded the corner, a spontaneous patter of applause greeted him.

"*Kaixo. Ongi etorri*! Welcome, *bienvenue, benvenuti, bienvenidos, velkommen*." He turned his attention to an oriental pair. "*Mabuhay*."

They nodded and smiled. He'd clearly done his research on their party.

He continued with an expansive gesture. "Sadly, that is the extent of my Tagalog vocabulary. Claudia is far more talented with languages. We're so lucky to have her. And yet, four translations make the tour hard work not only for your lovely guide, but also for you. So let's split the group. I will take the English speakers, Claudia, the rest. Come, everyone!"

He did not translate, leaving their tour guide to relay the reason why most of the party was departing. Beatrice assessed the individual striding ahead. The photograph in the gossip magazine had captured his essence. Arrogant, confident and with such force of personality, compliance seemed compulsory. She could still leave and call that taxi, if she wanted. But in the interests of research, it might be better to persevere. She hurried after the rest of Aguirre's acolytes in the direction of the vines.

Long rows of richly coloured foliage stretched into the distance; copper, amaranth, gold, carmine and rust, the breeze and sunlight creating an illusion of flames rippling across the fields. Towards the end of the ordered lines, workers moved back and forth, tending the plants. As the party descended stone steps from the terrace to the vineyard, Beatrice raised a hand to shield her eyes from the sun and caught her foot on the step. She stumbled and lurched into the young man in front.

"Hey up, steady on." He caught her arm, restoring her balance. "You all right there?" His head was shaved and he wore a white T-shirt stretched over a muscle-bound body. Normally the sort of man Beatrice would avoid.

"I'm so sorry. It's these bloody flip-flops. That and not looking where I'm going."

"Can't blame you. One hell of a view, in't it?" He stood beside her and they gazed out over the sweep of ridged vineyards and distant mountains.

"It is," Beatrice agreed. "Imagine waking up to this every

morning."

"Beats the back end of Bolton Gasworks, all right. Can you see that church? Over there, on the top of that hill."

Beatrice's eyes followed the direction of his finger. "Oh yes. Looks like something from a tourist brochure."

"Or a spaghetti western. Come on, we're getting left behind." He held out his hand to guide her and she took it, the kindness of the gesture overcoming her pride.

"Do you really come from Bolton?" she asked.

His eyes creased with amusement. "Somebody's got to. Yeah, I'm a Bolton lad, but I don't live there anymore. Got a place in London."

"Whereabouts? I live in the East End."

"Nice. My flat's in the Docklands. I don't spend much time there. I'm in the army so it's only for when I'm home on leave. You can't knock the Docklands for convenience, but it's got a bit pretentious."

"I know what you mean. Same round my way. Gastro pubs instead of boozers, Italian delis instead of Billingsgate and you could walk the length and breadth of Hoxton in search of a pickled egg." Her foot met soil and she released the man's hand.

The rest of the party awaited them at the top of a row of vines, so they picked up their pace.

"I'm Kevin, by the way."

"Beatrice." They shook hands. "Thanks for the help."

Ana's patience was wearing thin. The receptionist at GFS had assured her that the CEO would be out to meet her in about ten minutes. That was over half an hour ago. She replaced the Financial Times in the rack and approached the desk.

"Sorry to bother you. You said Señor Alvarez would be here soon?"

The woman, whose forehead seemed to be laminated, tilted her head in an expression of artificial surprise. "I said he would be here as soon as he gets a spare moment. You had no appointment and he is a man with many demands on his time."

"I understand that. I'm just wondering how long it's likely to be. Can you give me a rough estimate?" Ana gave her brightest smile.

"I doubt it." The forehead obviously couldn't do frowns either.

Ana maintained the smile as she retook her seat. She'd wait it out. She had to. After drawing a complete blank at the police station, she couldn't go back to the paper empty-handed. Anyway, he couldn't stay in there much longer; it was almost lunchtime. Even Ana's stomach was rumbling, despite what she'd put away at breakfast. A sense of guilt tugged at her, in the knowledge that Beatrice's tetchy behaviour yesterday and this morning was wholly due to Ana. The poor woman only wanted a relaxing break, but she'd been bullied into working for free. Well, their agreement was until the end of the week. Two more days and then Ana would be on her own. And she'd got nowhere.

Her hollow promises to Tiago's mother rang in her ears. Yes, she would come to the funeral. Yes, no matter what the coroner said, she'd try to find out what happened. Yes, of course she would pray for them. Her eyes pricked as she recalled the devastated woman's attempts at controlling her grief.

This was bullshit. The one thing Ana didn't need was any more thinking time. Alvarez could stuff it and Ana would find the information she needed some other way. She got to her feet. The receptionist watched her approach, picked up the phone and asked a question. She listened for a second and replaced the receiver.

"I'm sorry, but it seems you're out of luck. Señor Alvarez has left for a lunch meeting. Why don't you try some other time? Perhaps when it's more convenient for our managing director."

Ana knew there would be no convenient time. "Is there anyone else I could speak to? Someone who worked with Miguel Saez? There must be someone here who knew him."

The receptionist shook her head. "It's a busy time of year, I'm afraid. Might I suggest you call ahead next time, and I'll see what I can do?" She slid her hand back to the mouse and stared at the screen. Ana suppressed her parting shot and left quietly.

The lunchtime rush created the usual jam of vehicles, all searching for the elusive parking spot. Thank God for the Vespa. Ana unlocked it and retrieved her helmet under the seat. From the open window of a passing blue Mercedes, a cigarette butt traced a long arc to the gutter at her feet. Ana glanced at the driver, but only a hand and forearm were visible. She just registered a white shirt with rolled-up sleeves and a missing forefinger, before the car turned the corner. What a tosser.

Whilst the beauty of the region left her slack-jawed with awe, Beatrice wasn't sorry to return indoors. The sun, even in October, still contained substantial force. Crouching low under the vines, she'd admired the texture of the trunk, twisted and fibrous like the ropes of a mighty ocean liner, and relished the shade.

Aguirre talked them through the harvesting process, emphasising the length of time from the earliest September ripeners, such as the Viura grape, to the latest in November. He encouraged them to taste a grape from the vine and pointed out the baskets and padded trucks used for transporting the fruit to the press house. The middle-aged British couple plied him with questions, while the Danish family and three Bolton boys limited themselves to respectful nods. The two Danish children, no more than thirteen, behaved impeccably. Their interest in wine must have been on a par with Beatrice's in Disneyland, but not once did their attentive demeanour slip.

En route to the wine press, Kevin introduced her to his companions.

"This is Beatrice, who tried to nut me between the shoulder blades back there. Beatrice, meet Tyler and Jase, two of me oldest mates. It's Tyler's fault we're here, 'cos he's getting married in three weeks. This is his stag weekend."

Beatrice shook hands with the two men. "Pleased to meet

you, and congratulations, Tyler. I'm aware a stag weekend is supposed to entail alcohol and entertainment, but I'd always assumed something racier than a wine tasting."

They all laughed and Tyler shrugged with a weary grin. "There's eighteen of me mates and family arriving in Bilbao on Saturday. But it were only us three fancied seeing summat more than the inside of a bar."

Jase took over. "So we come out a week early, hired a car and headed to Rioja country. What about you, Beatrice? You one of them pilgrims?"

"Good God, no. My interests are far more secular. I'm on holiday, using Vitoria as a base to explore the region's food and drink. The only pilgrimage I'm likely to make is to the altar of fine wine. Talking of which, we're holding everyone up."

Aguirre's smile as they approached the elevated walkway remained as broad as ever, although Beatrice detected a tension in the jaw, as if he were grinding his teeth.

"Ah, finally, our stragglers. So, if you'd like to gather round, I'll explain the process and let you watch in peace for a few minutes. First, the grapes are de-stalked before entering the press. The machine squeezes out the grape juice and here at Castelo de Aguirre, we allow the juice to rest with the skins for two hours, to allow maximum flavour. After the pressing and resting, the juice is extracted to vats for the fermentation process to begin. Why don't you spread out and have a look?"

Beatrice was about to follow Kevin to a vantage point at the end of the platform when Aguirre intercepted her. "Probably the best spot is at this end. Come."

His arms were spread in an open gesture of demonstration, although Beatrice couldn't help feeling as if her getaway were blocked. She allowed him to guide her away from the others with the distinct impression she'd been corralled.

Even the Vespa couldn't avoid every jam. Especially when the traffic was bumper to bumper. Ana rested her foot on the ground and waited as a vegetable truck, beeping its monotonous alarm, reversed into a delivery bay. Radios competed from open windows and the smell of roasting chestnuts teased across the stationary traffic, reminding Ana of her stomach. The café opposite the office always did decent *pintxos* so that would be her first stop. A sudden impact jerked her forward, causing her to slide off the seat and bang her knees against the chassis. The bike heaved sideways as her foot left the ground and she struggled against its weight. Once stable, she twisted in her seat to yell at the thoughtless driver behind.

Rather than the apologetic mother or impatient taxi-driver she expected, the occupants of the blue Mercedes were four men, all wearing sunglasses and staring blankly at her.

"What the fuck! Look where you're going, arsehole!" She twisted over her shoulder to see if the Vespa had sustained any damage. The Mercedes blasted its horn, making her jump, and was joined by several others behind. The truck had gone and the road was clearing. She flipped them the finger, revved and took off down Calle Postas, furious and shaken.

Macho dickheads! Dressed up like Reservoir Dogs and having fun by picking on a woman on a Vespa. She should have taken the number of the Merc. Too late. After dodging in and out of the lanes on Calle de los Herrán, it was nowhere to be seen. Her adrenalin levels began to settle as she took a right, muttering insults in three languages.

A squeal of tyres made her glance in her mirror. The Mercedes tore onto Calle de Olaguibel, gaining fast. The liquid heat of her anger solidified into an icy fear. She felt exposed and precarious on the Vespa, against the malevolent weight of the approaching car. They couldn't do anything, not out in the street, surely? Without indicating, Ana took another right turn and accelerated well over the limit towards the park.

They were right behind her. The Vespa had the edge on standing starts, but it would never outrun a vehicle with that horsepower. It pulled level with her back wheel. Ana's hands, sweaty and tense, reached for the brakes. She had to slow down. One nudge at this speed would send her flying over the handlebars. But if she slowed, they could draw level and broadside her. Lights changed ahead and Ana leaned to the right, braking hard. A group of teenagers sauntered over the pelican crossing to Parque di Judizmendi. The nose of the Mercedes inched closer until the wheel arch brushed Ana's calf. A half-curse, half-gulp escaped her and she made a decision. As the lights turned amber, she swung the bike up onto the pavement, spun around and tore over the crossing after the kids. She hit the squeaky little horn, which parted the group, allowing her to squeeze through and into the park itself. With one eye on the mirror, she rode as fast as she dared across to the other side, out onto Calle Errkatxiki and turned left. A supermarket car park seemed the perfect place to rest, to have a few shaky tears, but she kept going to Avenida de Santiago, which would take her almost all the way home.

# Chapter Fourteen

It was good to be back.

Until today, Luz had resented the enforced separation from Tunçay, finding fault with everything at Castelo de Aguirre; her sisters seemed boring, her mother shallow and her father insufferable. Not only that, but her return barely registered as significant, because everyone was focused on Thursday's birthday party. The Birthday Party. Her nephew, Ramón, would be one year old, and the celebrations planned were worthy of The Last Emperor. Only her little brother, Basajaun, seemed pleased to see her. Probably because she was the only one who had time to play with him, listen to his excitable chatter and construct hugely complex Lego empires.

But early on Wednesday morning, her mother knocked on her door. Luz was awake, reading *The Pelican Brief*, in an attempt to improve her English.

"Coffee." Marisol took the book from Luz's hands and handed her a cup. She read the title and gave it back with an approving smile. "Good idea. Reading should never be an idle pleasure for an intelligent mind. Now, Basajaun has gone to school, the marquee and catering people will want to set up, so I thought you and I could go into the city. I want to buy you some beautiful things. Maybe a new dress for tomorrow? And after we've given the credit card some exercise, we'll have lunch. You can choose where."

Luz looked up at her mother under her eyebrows. She wanted to refuse, to tell her that she knew exactly the purpose of the outing, and that no matter how much they spent on a dress, Luz would not be groomed and paraded in front of eligible suitors like a prize poodle. But a morning away from the Castelo with her mother's full attention was an opportunity not to be missed.

"All right. But I don't want anything colourful. Ideally, I'd like something black."

Marisol opened the blinds. "Why not? Shall we get your lip pierced as well? I mean, if you want to buy into the nihilistic student uniform, you really should do it properly. Now, I'm going to check which car we can take, and I'll see you outside in twenty minutes. Put your hair up and wear those earrings your grandmother left you. Strapless bra and comfortable shoes but bring a pair of stilettos in your handbag." She smiled. "Today, we are shopping professionally."

Two pairs of amazing heels, a silver choker, a cocktail ring and now the dress. Marisol should have been a lawyer. She knew exactly how to make you think you'd won, while she came away with every box ticked. It was black, yes. A halterneck prom dress, with diamante detail and a circle skirt. Despite herself, Luz stared at her reflection, entranced. Her mother had always had an eye. All the Aguirre girls had the classic pear shape. But this dress suggested a cleavage, while minimising her substantial hips. She twirled, imagining Tunçay's face.

"What do you think, my darling?" Marisol's voice carried pride, admiration and the slightest wobble. Luz couldn't resist.

"It's perfect, Mama. I love it."

Marisol held her face and kissed her on both cheeks before grasping her hands. She had tears in her eyes. "My baby girl. Look at you. Such elegance. You do have real poise, Luz. Your father will just burst with paternal pride when he sees you."

Luz doubted that, but chose not to break the moment. "Thank you."

"Now change, quickly. I'll pay and then we have one more stop before lunch. No outfit is complete without the right foundations. Just one moment ..." She ducked behind Luz, took out a marker pen and drew a line on her back where the dress ended. She was an expert, no question.

"Black, yes, and a flesh-coloured one but we'll take toupee tape so there's no danger of slippage. Visible underwear ..." Marisol shuddered and the assistant nodded with absolute sincerity.

"Is that everything?"

"I'm not sure. Luz, why don't you choose some things for yourself? There are some fabulous sets here. Look at this one, blush pink with either a thong or Brazilian to go with it. I'm sure you're getting to the age when you appreciate beautiful underwear. Or perhaps you know someone else who does."

Luz spotted the conspiratorial look between her mother and the assistant. The smiles. The understanding. It would be so easy to play along.

"No one apart from my room-mate. And she favours sports bras, so there's not much point. Shall we go? My stomach is rumbling. I missed breakfast, you know."

"It's only half past twelve, my sweet. And even if you don't see the need right now, perhaps you might be glad of some quality items soon enough. I'm going to look at pyjamas for Basajaun. You choose and put them on my account. See you in a minute."

The assistant and Marisol melted away, as if by an agreed signal, and Luz felt like a mouse facing a cube of cheese. If she took it, she was trapped. If she refused, her mother, with feline patience, would get her claws in some other way. So she might as well have some decent knickers. Those black high-legs reminded her of paintings by Lautrec. If they had a matching bra in her size, a private version of the can-can might be just the thing. Luz picked up the lacy panties.

By the end of their lunch, during which Luz demolished a full *Marmitako* and her mother picked at a Caesar salad, Marisol had still not pounced. They chatted about the law course, Basajaun, the imminent party, Luz's room-mate, the guests invited for tomorrow, local gossip and the advantages of small breasts for an ageing décolletage. Over coffee, the conversation became more intimate, Marisol sharing her concerns about Inez's marriage and Angel's impotence. Luz enthusiastically defended Angel, who did not fit the typical arrogant money man Aguirre preferred to cultivate.

"And I bet if you two stopped looking over their shoulders and putting on the pressure, it would happen. Sometimes, I wonder if you realise how much your children feel more like puppets than individuals."

Marisol's teaspoon stopped its circular motion and her eyes locked onto Luz.

"That's a strange thing to say. I fought with your father for months so that you could go to university. I thought, maybe I was naïve, I was trying to give you independence."

"I know. You did fight for me and I'm sorry if that sounded ungrateful. I love being there, I'm happier than I could have imagined, but I keep asking myself, am I really free?"

The waiter brought the bill and Marisol tossed the credit card onto the silver platter without checking.

"Free. That's an interesting word. How was your lunch?"

Luz blushed. "If you mean ..."

Marisol's face hardened and she shook her head. "As you grow, my dear, spoilt, little girl, you will realise that no one is free. The hawk, soaring over the fields at will, is chained by his need to find prey. The bat, roaming the night while the world sleeps, is driven by a need to survive. You have no such biological urgency. You have never had to fend for yourself. But you are part of the system. We all find ways of surviving."

Luz rolled her eyes at the rhetoric, but didn't hesitate. "Why can't I find my own way of surviving? What if I don't want to be a submissive brood mare like Paz? I can be a useful member of society, a lawyer, a professional who can earn her keep. I'm not ungrateful, it's just I have to be my own person."

Neither spoke again until they left the restaurant and headed for the car.

"Mama, thank you for lunch and all the shopping. I'm sorry."

Marisol reached out to kiss her on the cheek. "It was a pleasure. I don't get to spend enough time with you. Today was important to me." She pressed the fob and unlocked the vehicle. "But I am keen to hear about the boyfriend."

Luz opened the back door and stashed her bags. She didn't speak until her mother started the car.

"It's complicated."

"Most things are. But is he worth the pain?"

Luz turned to her. "How did you know? Please tell me the truth."

The Jaguar pulled out of the underground car park and into the afternoon sun. Two nuns crossed in front of them and Luz watched her mother nod at them piously, then break into a smile.

"You're glowing, my darling girl. Your family evidently bore you to tears, you can't wait to get back to Burgos and I haven't seen your eyes shine like this since you were six years old and we bought you that puppy."

"Bear. I loved that dog."

"He was a favourite with all of us. But he doted on you. People change when they fall in love. With a dog, with a cause, with a person, no matter. So either law is proving the love of your life or you've met someone. I suspect the latter."

"You can't tell anyone. Especially not Papí."

Marisol checked her rear-view mirror, her smile fading. "You'd be surprised, my little Luz, how much your father cares for your happiness. I think he'd be happy to hear you had someone special in your life."

Luz turned to look out of the window. It was a lie. Her father would only accept one of his own choices. Even if Luz had met a good Catholic boy, whose father was well connected, whose honour was beyond reproach and who loved her like Romeo, he would never pass. Luz had seen the list of her possible future partners. She despised every last one.

"He wouldn't, Mama. Even if I told him that there's no future for this relationship, he'd still disapprove."

Marisol slowed the car and glanced at her.

"Why? What kind of man is he?"

Luz laughed at the suspicion in her voice. "He's the most honourable, devout and loving man I know, and I'm not good enough for him."

"Is he married?"

"No. Don't worry, I'm not that stupid."

They drove on in silence until Luz blurted it out.

"His name is Tunçay. He's a Turkish waiter and a Muslim."

As the road straightened, opening up the landscape, they both instinctively looked up to see the first view of the Castelo. On so many occasions, the sight had filled Luz with pride, anticipation, impatience and even reluctance, but today was the first time she experienced dread.

Her mother began talking, facing directly ahead. "One thing you will learn from studying a subject such as law is the art of compromise. You are still young, and you should enjoy this time while you have no responsibilities. Celebrate your time with your waiter, making sure to live every moment to its fullest. Later, when you have to face the reality of adulthood, when you must use your head over your heart, when your decisions are practical rather than romantic, you will have some beautiful memories to sustain you."

Luz watched her mother's face, which seemed to shift between soft comprehension and hard certainty. "Do you have some beautiful memories?"

Marisol smiled without taking her eyes from the road. "Yes. And some of them after I married your father." She indicated left, into the driveway of the Castelo.

Luz gazed over the estate and spotted her father leading a group of tourists into the visitors' centre.

Marisol frowned. "What the hell is he doing? He's not supposed to do tours today because we've got enough to do! It's Claudia's job to look after visitors."

"Mama? You won't tell him, will you?"

"No, I don't think that would be wise. And you must give nothing away either. Be the good girl you always have been, give him no reason to suspect. You still have time, Luz. Don't waste it by challenging your father. Now, I'll take your shopping upstairs while you check the bathrooms in the visitors' centre. Toilet paper, air freshener, you know what to do. Then tell your father to come up to the house."

"I will. Thank you, Mama. For everything." She kissed her mother's cheek.

Marisol touched her finger to Luz's lips, half an affectionate gesture, half a reminder. Luz understood.

# Chapter Fifteen

"Hey, Beatrice, I reckon you're in there." Kevin sidled up as Aguirre led the party back to the assembly point for tasting. And naturally, shopping.

Jase wiggled his eyebrows and could not suppress a grin. "Play your cards right and you could be going home with more than a plastic cup. He couldn't keep his hands off you."

Beatrice laughed at their semi-salacious teasing. "He is a gentleman and took pity on me, as an older lady on her own. I have to say, he really is a fascinating speaker. Didn't you think?"

"He were all right. But we didn't get the personal touch, see? 'Look at this, Ms Stubbs. Would you like to stand here, Ms Stubbs? This is a superlative view.' Old Aguirre is on t'prowl." Kevin's impression was remarkably accurate. "Well, Beatrice, keep your hand on your ha'penny, that's all I'll say."

Tyler nudged her with an elbow. "I suppose we're dumped now you've hooked yourself a Latino, hey? Typical woman. Three handsome blokes, all fit as a butcher's dog, but no. She's had her head turned by a more expensive vintage."

The lads' protective loyalty amused Beatrice and distracted her from the obvious question. Why would Arturo de Aguirre go out of his way to be charming and solicitous to some dowdy old trout? Unless he knew, or wanted to know, something.

The tour, the sunshine and one glass of white Rioja had finished the Danes off. The British couple headed straight for the shop, so only Beatrice and the boys were graced by the presence of their host. Kevin and Tyler kept exchanging knowing looks, but Jase, with good manners and genuine interest, engaged the man in conversation, allowing Beatrice to make her own assessment.

The man had a presence you could not ignore. His voice sent vibrations through the wooden furniture, his expansive inclusion of everyone worked its charm on even the most suspicious and his anecdotes and incidental facts about the wine made the small group feel fortunate for his insight. Yet, for all his magnetism, it seemed his eyes were drawn to her. She sensed his gaze as she sipped, laughed and checked her watch.

"Señor Aguirre, I need to get a taxi back to Vitoria. Do you happen to have a telephone I could use?"

Tyler put down his glass. "Beatrice, we could give you a lift, if you like. It's no bother. We're staying in Vitoria."

Aguirre beamed at them. "Vitoria? Perfect. I have to collect some items from the city this afternoon. Ms Stubbs, I would be happy to drive you myself. And then, perhaps you and these young gentlemen would allow me to invite you for *pinxtos* in one of our most famous bars. An insider tip, I think you'd say."

He didn't wait for agreement but beckoned the barman to give instructions.

Beatrice ignored all three of the smug expressions surrounding her. "Excuse me, gentlemen. I must just visit the ladies' room."

Stone steps in flip-flops demanded careful concentration, but when a figure crossed the flagstones and disappeared in the direction of the toilets, Beatrice stopped dead. Why was Ana here? She hurried down the steps and opened the door. Immediately, she realised her mistake. The girl placing a bouquet of sweet peas in a vase in front of the mirror had long dark hair, a slender figure and a pleasant smile, but that was as far as the resemblance went. Ana's fine features and glowing skin were absent, replaced by a broad forehead and sallow complexion. Her nose stamped her unmistakeably as Aguirre's daughter, clear as a cattle brand.

Beatrice returned the smile. "*Buenos dias.*"

"*Buenos dias.* I think you're one of the English party, no?"

"That's right. The tour was most entertaining."

The girl's smile seemed to fade a little. "Yes, my father is a great ambassador for Rioja. The UK is our biggest export market, you know."

"So I hear. I'm not surprised. It's a wonderful wine. You must be very proud of him."

"Wonderful, yes. Well, I mustn't detain you. Have a nice day, Ms Stubbs."

"Thank you. You too."

Only as she was washing her hands and inhaling the perfume of the sweet peas did it occur to Beatrice to wonder how the girl had known her name.

She checked her watch as she ascended the steps to join her companions, quite unnecessarily as the growls in her stomach were already announcing lunchtime. The lapse of concentration proved unwise. Her foot didn't clear the step, the flip-flop caught the edge and tipped her forwards onto her knees, and the bridge of her nose connected painfully with stone.

She cried out. Pain shot through her face, her eyes watered and she tasted blood.

"Oh my God! Are you okay?" The girl rushed down the stairs and turned Beatrice to face her. "Let me see." She removed Beatrice's hand from her face and winced. "You have a nosebleed. Come, we need to get ice on that before you get a black eye. These steps! One of these days, someone will sue. Come, can you stand?"

The kitchen, illuminated only by a pale blue fly-killing fluorescent, was a cool and silent oasis of stainless steel. Beatrice sat on a stool, holding kitchen roll to her face while the girl dug in the fridge for ice. Her whole head throbbed, her teeth ached and her knee was already stiffening.

"The ice must be upstairs, behind the bar. Put this on for now while I get some." She handed Beatrice a bag of frozen spinach. The cold went from relief to agony in seconds, springing fresh tears to add to the mess on her face. She kept up the pressure for as long as she could stand it, and then removed the spinach. Again, relief for an instant, before the pulsing pain returned, spreading across her face and into her head.

Loud voices came from outside the door. Aguirre's daughter sounded shrill and determined, although Beatrice couldn't understand a word. The door opened and Aguirre strode across the floor, followed by his daughter.

"Ms Stubbs, I am horrified by this. To have such an accident, here, at the Castelo! I insist on taking you to the hospital personally. I will ensure you get the best treatment, all at my expense. What a terrible thing to happen!"

The girl offered Beatrice ice wrapped in a tea towel, guiding it to her face. The pain, metallic and relentless, forced her eyes to close.

"Keep it on, Ms Stubbs, even if it does hurt. You can go to the hospital, if you want. But I have studied first aid. I can check if it's broken in ten seconds. If it's not, there's no point in going to hospital. You just need to keep it clean and cold and get some rest. What do you think?"

"Luz! Don't be ridiculous." Aguirre's tone bordered on menacing.

His daughter's calm voice held a hint of stubbornness. "It's up to Ms Stubbs."

A voice came from the doorway. "That would be the best solution, I believe. Good afternoon, Ms Stubbs. My name is Marisol de Aguirre. I'm Arturo's wife. I'm so sorry to hear what happened. It must be very painful for you. Luz is right, you should keep the ice on to minimise the bruising. If you will allow her to check, she can either get medical help or simply clean you up and drive you home."

The word 'home' worked like a talisman. "Yes, I think that might be best. You do it, Luz. But please don't hurt me ... I have a terribly low pain threshold."

Luz put her hand on Beatrice's. "It will hurt. But as I said, only a couple of seconds."

The woman spoke again. "We will give you some privacy. Come, Arturo."

The door closed, Luz lifted the ice pack and Beatrice whimpered.

By the time Luz had applied butterfly stitches to the cut, cleaned Beatrice's face and found her a T-shirt to replaced the bloodied twin set, the men had gone. On the bar sat an envelope containing a note of heartfelt regret from Aguirre and his wife. Propped next to it was a napkin with Kevin's number scrawled across it. He'd also written the name of their hotel, and 'Let us know how you are' with three kisses. Beatrice tucked both into the carrier bag containing her soiled clothes. Once belted into Luz's Peugeot, she replaced the ice pack against her face.

"How are you feeling?" Luz turned to her as she started the engine.

"Stupid, mostly. With a pounding headache. I need to lie down in a darkened room for a few hours, I think."

"Good idea. I could find no signs of concussion, so a sleep should be just what you need. Which hotel are you staying at in Vitoria?"

"I'm staying with a friend. In Calle Cuchillería. Do you know it?"

"Very well. It has some great bars." She pulled out of the estate and onto the main road. "Is that why you're here? To visit a friend?"

"No, I'm on a sabbatical from my job. Trying to decide if I should take early retirement. So I thought a holiday in Spain and Portugal would be a good way to start."

"Definitely. What do you do?"

Beatrice hesitated. "I'm a detective with the Metropolitan Police in London."

Luz took her eyes off the road to look at Beatrice, her expression hidden by her sunglasses. She turned to face front.

"That sounds like a great job. I admire people like you. It must be fantastic to know you are making the world a better place, every day. That's exactly why I want to work in law. I know your job can't be easy, and neither is pursuing the legal profession, but you are helping people, directly. Why do you want to retire?"

Beatrice considered her response while watching the lush colours of the landscape undulate into the distance.

"You're right. It's not always easy to see it, because I spend most of my time exploring the darker end of society. But yes, we do make a difference. And that's why I'm thinking about retiring. Because I'm not sure I'm good enough."

"Hmm. I'm not sure I'm good enough either. To be honest, law was not my best subject. The important thing for me is that I have passion. I want to help people, fight for them so they get what they deserve. I want to understand their problems and try to do something right. So I will work and work until I am good enough. You should put that ice back on unless you want to look like Rocky."

Beatrice did as she was told. "I wonder why you don't want to follow in your father's footsteps and take over his successful business. He has passion too."

Luz's tone turned acidic. "Yes, a passion for making money. My father is a great showman, Ms Stubbs. Behind the scenes, it's a different story. Now, where are you going after you leave Vitoria? Have you worked out your itinerary?"

Despite her pain, Beatrice recognised the whiff of an opportunity rapidly followed by a changed subject. But she was too tired to care.

The aftermath of adrenalin left Ana sick and light-headed. She shoved her helmet under the seat and locked the bike. The muscles in her legs felt as if she'd been sprinting and her hands shook like she'd been mainlining caffeine. She hesitated. Maybe she should go into the office, talk to people, seek comfort in companionship. Beatrice might not be back for a while. But the draw of her own balcony, her bright, optimistic flat and some peace to think this through won her over and she headed down the street.

Unusually, the constant movement of passers-by and chatter billowing from the bars irritated her. A fleeing child shot into her path. Rather than grabbing him and returning him to his mother, she side-stepped and powered on. The sun beat down, her clothes scratched at her skin and the lure of her cool, empty flat shimmered like a mirage ahead.

She unlocked the front door with a sense of reaching sanctuary and rested her forehead on the cool marble while she waited for the lift. She never usually bothered but today the creaking ascent was exactly what she needed. Had she opted for the steps, her soft footfalls may not have warned the men waiting above. Maybe she would have spotted the shadows looming over the stairwell. The smell of smoke might well have alerted her to her welcoming committee. And then she could have run, fled back out the door, escaped into the cat's cradle of intersecting streets and alleys, and lost her pursuers.

The lift ascended with stately grace, giving Ana several moments to breathe deeply, feeling her tension recede. A satisfying clunk announced her arrival on the fourth floor. She yanked open the doors and stepped outside. Her senses, already sharpened from her earlier encounter, screamed alarm signals. The smell of black tobacco and body odour, the sound of shifting feet and the shapes moving in her direction pumped a chemical reaction to danger and she jerked back into the lift, knowing as she did so, the futility of such a move.

Four of them, two older, two younger. The thick-necked younger one reached out his hand as if to cup her arm. The gesture served two purposes; invitation and threat. She came out of her own accord. One of the older men had a missing finger. Ana wasn't surprised.

She raised her voice. This was one occasion when nosy neighbours could prove useful.

"Right. I've had enough of this. What do you want? I should report you to the police for harassment. I know it was you in that ..."

Thick-neck smiled and guided her forward to her own front door with his right hand on her back and his left jabbing a blade under her ribcage.

The greying, saggy-faced older man spoke with a weary bluntness. "Let us into the apartment and keep your mouth shut."

She spent several seconds fumbling for her keys, still hoping a neighbour might intervene; perhaps an enquiry would float down from an upper floor, an act of casual curiosity could rescue her. The other young meathead took her bag, snatched up the keys and had the door open in seconds.

Thick-neck slid his arm around her waist and looked down the neck of her shirt. With a shit-eating grin, he jerked his head towards her apartment. "Ladies first."

He shoved her into the hallway. She turned to face the four men as they approached. Missing Finger was smoking. The saggy-faced guy indicated the door and the meathead, still holding her bag, locked it. Thick-neck stood openly leering at her.

Missing Finger spoke. "Ana, go back to Portugal. That's an order."

Ana found her voice. "Fuck you."

He exhaled a foul cloud of smoke in her direction. "Funny you should say that. To be honest, it's all the same to me. Go back to Portugal, stay here in Spain. I don't care. But the boys ..." he looked at the two thugs. "The boys would prefer it if you stayed. Because if you disobey me, they will be responsible for your punishment. And it seems your minds are running along the same lines."

He lowered himself into an armchair and without taking

his eyes from her, nodded his permission. The saggy-faced one folded his arms and leant against the wall as the two thugs, practically salivating, approached her.

# Chapter Sixteen

Calle Cuchillería swarmed with activity. Everyone was dressed up, made up and ready to be seen. Couples, families and groups of young men strolled past the bars and cafés, stopping to greet friends, kiss cheeks and shake hands every few paces.

Luz had repeated her instructions regarding painkillers and herbal teas several times, apparently reluctant to let Beatrice go. Eventually, after extracting a promise of a phone call the following day, she got back in the car and left. Beatrice made her way to Ana's flat, passing restaurants and street vendors emanating aromas which would normally cause an inevitable delay. Today, however, she needed her bedroom, a cup of tea and a mirror to check the extent of the damage.

The lift seemed even slower than before, but four flights of stairs was out of the question. The ice pack, now soggy and uncomfortable, dripped onto the lino by her feet. Eventually, the lift released her to do battle with Ana's apartment door. This time, the door won. Each time the lock seemed to give, another barrier prevented it from opening. Defeated, Beatrice rang the bell and waited. After a full minute of silence, she rapped on the wood, already rehearsing her apology. She was reaching for her mobile when she heard a bolt withdrawn.

The door opened. Beatrice stood back to allow an ugly, grizzled individual to come out. Unsmiling, he stared at her and passed by. He was followed by a hefty farmer-like man in a white shirt, who jerked his head in acknowledgement, and two lumps practising Elvis-type sneers. They moved down the stairs, the last two throwing aggressive looks back up at her. Beatrice rushed into the apartment, locked the door and followed the sounds of vomiting to the bathroom.

Twenty minutes later, after opening all the windows to get rid of the smell of smoke, Beatrice perched on the edge of the sofa and listened to Ana's story. A sense of panic escalated as all her previous perspectives shifted and shattered. The unencumbered freedom of the scooter became vulnerability, people's friendly assistance twisted into sly observation and the sense of solidarity engendered by their collaboration dissipated like the steam off her tea. They were no safer than a pair of kittens on a six-lane motorway.

"So after you shook them off in the park ..."

"I made a massive mistake. I came home."

Beatrice stomach convulsed. "Oh my God. They were waiting for you. Did they hurt you at all? Ana? Did they hurt you?"

Ana drew her top lip into her mouth and shook her head.

"No. They came in, made some unsubtle threats and told me to go back to Portugal. If not, I have to take the consequences."

Her tone was casual but Beatrice observed the girl's demeanour. Legs crossed, or more like wrapped around one another like pipe-cleaners. Her arms crossed her chest, gripping shoulder and elbow, in an attitude of defensiveness and fear. Beatrice felt as if she'd swallowed an ice cube. She slid off the sofa and moved closer to Ana. A memory surfaced, of watching a children's counsellor interact with a frightened teen. She allowed the recollection to guide her movements and didn't attempt to touch Ana, kneeling instead beside the armchair.

"Ana, what did they do?"

The girl shook her head, rubbing her upper arms as if she were cold. "Nothing. You turned up and rang the doorbell, thanks be to God. If you'd been any later ... oh, let's not talk about it. There's no real harm done."

"Of course. I don't want to push you."

A silence expanded into the space between them. Beatrice felt foolish, kneeling on the floor in sympathy, but instinct told her to wait a few more seconds.

Ana's voice, when it came, was tight. "They didn't hurt me. Just gave me a taste of what would happen if I refused to leave. Bit of manhandling to let me know who holds the power, that's all. It was enough."

"I'll make some more tea and then perhaps we should consider our next steps." Beatrice's knee protested as she rose, so she used the armrest to help herself upright. She was surprised to feel Ana's cold hand cover hers.

"Beatrice, I've been honest. No rape, no violence, just some inappropriate touching and heavy threats. Now will you do me the same courtesy and tell me what really happened to you?"

"I fell up the steps. Honestly. These bloody stupid flip-flops tripped me and I smacked my face on a lump of stone. Clumsy, yes, but sinister, no. What happened here frightens me far more."

Ana looked at her, nodding slowly.

"You're right. You don't need this bullshit. Look, you're very good and you've been generous with your time. I really appreciate all your help, but I've held you up long enough. I'm going to take a break and return to Portugal, so it might be time for you to move on with your trip. We've reached the end of the road."

Beatrice sat in her room, or rather Ana's guest room and acknowledged her duty. Her conscience, which she'd been able to drown out by constant activity, took full advantage of the meditative silence. *Call him.* She'd left it far too long and apart from anything else, it was bad manners. With a glance at the clock, she picked up her mobile.

"Beatrice! How lovely to hear from you. I'm so relieved you called."

Bubbles of unanticipated pleasure fizzed upwards, countering the leaden pull of homesickness. She missed him. She needed him. Why had she waited so long?

"James, you're very kind. Rather than reprimanding me for missing our last session, you sound as if you're actually pleased to hear from me."

"I most definitely am pleased to hear from you. Although I should say that I have another client due in about ten minutes, so a full consultation will not be possible right now."

"Oh, I didn't expect one. Phoning you out of the blue and expecting you to have a free hour would be downright rude. No, it's just a quick call to tell you I decided to take the sabbatical after all. Which is why I missed my last appointment. I'm in Spain at the moment and plan to travel around till I get fed up."

He took a few seconds to respond. "I see. I hope you have a relaxing and contemplative holiday. Can I ask what you had in mind regarding our ongoing treatment?"

With a grimace, Beatrice knew she should have thought about that. She hadn't and James knew it.

"Well, I was wondering if we could have chats over the phone, instead. We've done that before, remember."

"I do remember. That's certainly possible. I have a couple of practical concerns, but they can wait. I have the feeling this is more than a courtesy call, Beatrice. Is there anything you'd like to talk about?"

Seconds ticked past as Beatrice considered her reply.

James prompted her. "Any indications as to your state of mind are always welcome."

"My state of mind? I'm watching an abyss open up. This situation is complicated and not entirely relevant, but it makes me feel helpless. Exactly the problem I was facing before. I will never be able to protect all of them, so what's the point? What is the point of any of this? Right now, the world seems callous, James. Just selfish and brutal in pursuit of its own interests. On top of that, institutions which supposedly stand for truth and justice and honour are infected with the same individualistic point-scoring as everywhere else so I really don't know why I bother feeling any obligation to do my duty."

"I may have misunderstood, but I thought you were on holiday. Whom exactly is it your duty to protect? Have you adopted a colony of Catalonian cats?"

Beatrice laughed, acknowledging James's accurate analogy. "Not cats. But I offered to advise on a missing persons' case. I tell you what, James, it's no fun working a line of enquiry as a civilian."

"Which leads me to ask, why do it? I understood the offer of a sabbatical was to take a break from your routine, to use the time to reflect and consider your future."

Again, Beatrice dug deep for an honest response, but time ran out on her.

"Beatrice, I'm sorry, but my next client is due. And I think we need more than a few minutes to unpack what you've just said. I have a slot on Friday. Could you call me at eight-thirty?"

"Yes, of course. Sorry to hog your time like this."

"Please don't apologise. I'd rather know how you are than not. Between now and Friday's conversation, I'd like you to think about three things. What is the aim of this sabbatical? How is your current choice of action furthering that aim? How would Matthew and Hamilton react if they knew? And how does that affect you?"

"That's four things."

"You can have the last one for free. Half past eight UK time on Friday, okay?"

"Thank you James. It's kind of you to fit me in. I'll try to be better by then."

"You don't need to be 'better'. Just honest."

He made it sound easy.

A tap on the door pulled her from a fretful doze. Still fully dressed, she lay on top of the quilt, trying to recall her peculiar dream when the tap came again.

"Hello?"

Ana's voice came through the wood. "Sorry to wake you, Beatrice. Can I come in?"

"Of course. I'm decent." Beatrice swung her feet to the floor and rubbed her face.

The woman who entered the room was wholly altered. The tense, haunted creature had disappeared, replaced by a determined expression in jeans and a leather jacket.

She smiled as she came into the room and stood with her hands on her hips in front of Beatrice. "I heard you on the phone before. Have you made arrangements to leave?"

A warm flush crept up Beatrice's throat. "No, I suppose I should ..."

"Good. We might need to rethink this. I had a couple of calls while you were resting. The police went public with the identity of the body this afternoon. Jaime, bless him, called me first to break the news. The story runs tomorrow."

"And cause of death?"

"Accident. No mention of the mutilation. So we know the police are hiding the truth. But more importantly, Armando got back to me. Seems Miguel Saez was onto something. Come on, we're going to *El Papagaio* to eat lunch and create a smokescreen."

# Chapter Seventeen

"Ana! Beatrice! Finally!" Enrique's pleasure at their arrival seemed heartfelt. He clapped a hand to his chest. "Oh Beatrice! Your face!"

"I tripped up some steps. My own fault for wearing ridiculous shoes."

"You poor woman. On your holiday as well. Where have you two been? I haven't seen you all week."

"Sorry Enrique. You know how it is." Ana's smile disappeared so fast it might not have even been there. The girl was quite a performer.

Concern rippled across Enrique's face. "Have you news of Tiago?"

Ana nodded, her face scrunched up she covered her eyes. Right on time, Beatrice put an arm around her shoulders and pulled a sympathetic face. Enrique hurried from behind the bar, shielding them from the inquisitive stares of his other customers.

"Come, sit at the back, it's quieter. I'll bring drinks."

Ana looked up, her eyes glistening, her forehead creased. "Tiago's dead, Enrique. He had an accident and fell. I just heard this afternoon."

All animation and colour drained from Enrique's face. "*No puede ser*! Not Tiago? When was this?"

Ana shrugged as if the timing was an irrelevance.

"You need something for the shock. Sit, sit." He rushed back to the bar, snapping an order at a young waiter, who tore himself away from the TV and trudged through to the back.

Beatrice dropped her voice. "That was amazing. You convinced me completely."

"It wasn't only an act. Tiago was one of the sweetest, gentlest men I ever met. I'm going to miss him."

Shame burst over Beatrice like prickly heat. "Ana, I'm sorry. I didn't mean to be so insensitive ..."

"It's fine. I've not yet cried for him, so I may as well take the opportunity to grieve when it's most useful. See? Not entirely heartless but always practical. Here he comes."

Enrique set a bottle of red on the table with two glasses. On his upper arm, he wore a black armband. He tapped it, met their eyes and nodded with theatrical woe.

"Today, you are my guests. You will drink a fine Rioja, eat the best I can offer and say goodbye to our friend."

Ana gave him a weak smile. "Thank you. It's a double goodbye, in fact. I'm leaving Vitoria. The loss of Tiago ... I can't explain it. I just want to go home for a while."

Enrique shook his head. "For me, this is a second blow. The tragic death of that fine young man and now you, one of my favourites, go back to Portugal. Today is a sad day. Very sad for all of us."

He returned to the bar, maintaining his pained air even as he continued to serve his curious clientele. His explanations involved lots of head-shaking and sorrowful glances in the direction of their table.

Beatrice poured the wine. "How does he know that 'home' means Portugal?"

"Everyone knows where I come from. I speak reasonable Castilian, but if I get stuck, I simply use Portuguese with a Spanish accent. They call it my *Portañol*. He's not given us anything new by that."

"Hmm. Did he react as you imagined? He learns of an

acquaintance's death, provides food and puts on an armband. I appreciate the offer of sustenance might be a cultural trait, but I find it very peculiar that he asked no questions."

Ana sniffed the wine, nodding. "Me too. That's not normal behaviour. Every time I've interviewed someone even loosely connected to an unexpected death, the first thing people want is the details – how. Enrique asked only one question – when. Why would it matter when Tiago died, unless it was Sunday night and so connected to *El Papagaio*?"

The young waiter approached bearing a heavy copper tureen. He placed it between them and lifted the lid. "*Paella, señoras. Buen provecho!*"

The golden rice, studded with prawns, clams, peas, mussels, peppers, lemon wedges and chicken sat in a bath of fragrant stock. Beatrice looked across at Enrique. Despite her suspicions of his various sins such as lying, dissembling and ham acting, she acknowledged his gift with a happy grin. The tragic lines fell away from his face and he blew them both a kiss before placing his hand on his chest, shaking his head and adopting his grief mask once more.

The waiter served a portion each, brought a breadbasket and returned to his spot to watch the football. Determined to devote at least four of her senses to the feast in front of her, Beatrice lent Ana her ears.

"Your cousin. What did he say about the accountant's books?"

Ana kept her head down, but a slow smile crept across her face. "What do you think of the wine?"

With exaggerated respect, Beatrice lifted her glass to the light, wafted the rim under her nose and finally took a careful sip.

"Magenta and ruby, fading to a cerise rim. No hint of tawny. Nose, a riot of summer fruits with some leather, earth and French oak. Textured and creamy with structured tannins which do not dominate the end palate, leaving us with caramel and burnt toast. A deeply satisfying glass. I suggest paella as the perfect accompaniment."

She dug her fork into the steaming mass and was about to lift it to her mouth when she caught Ana's gesture. Holding the bottle by the neck, Ana twisted the label to face Beatrice.

*Castelo de Aguirre Gran Reserva 2009*

Beatrice began to eat. Ana began to talk.

"Do you know how much Rioja is produced every year? I'll tell you. The region produces just under 200 million litres of red, over 100 million of white, with around 15 of rosé. It used to be around 300 million of red and very little else."

This much Beatrice knew. "So white is on the up. Largely due to Aguirre and his operation. Are you not going to eat?"

"I'm in shock, remember. I'll grieve here and get a kebab on the way home. It does smell gorgeous, though. Force a couple of mouthfuls down me and don't take no for an answer."

An elaborate Kabuki performance ensued, after which Beatrice felt she'd earned a part in any major mimed soap opera. Ana, for her part, affected great reluctance and misery while making enthusiastic noises of enjoyment.

Ana: (drops head onto fist) Jesus, these prawns taste like a fishy bicep. Pass me another, would you?

Beatrice: (opens pleading palms) Wait till you get to the clams. Melt in your mouth. Do you want some bread? (offers breadbasket, squeezes hand)

Ana: (shakes head sadly) Is the Pope Catholic? Tear me off a chunk and pass it over.

Beatrice: Grief steals the appetite but the bereaved often take to drink. Do you want a top up? It really is a divine wine.

Ana: (wipes away fictional tears): For authenticity's sake, I suppose I can't refuse.

Enrique and his punters proved an attentive audience, observing and remarking on each gesture with less than covert analysis. Many heads joined Enrique in the regretful shake.

"Right, so Miguel's figures focused on exports. Our friend," she tapped the bottle, "is the leading exporter of white Rioja.

His marketing pitch makes a massive deal of the Viura grape. Apparently it forms 80% of every bottle of Aguirre white."

"Exactly what I heard on the tour. He grows almost exclusively white grapes as the Control Board permits a greater density per hectare than red."

Ana focused on Beatrice, her eyes sharp. "Do you remember the numbers?"

"No. And you look far too cheerful. Now dab your eyes and tell me."

Ana pressed a napkin to the bridge of her nose and talked almost as quickly as if she were speaking Spanish.

"No wine-grower can produce more than seven thousand kilos of grapes per hectare. Not if they want the official Rioja seal. Aguirre has just under sixty-five hectares. So his maximum output can only be around ninety million litres. Most, but not all of which is white. And out of the total yield, most vineyards sell two thirds to the domestic market. The figures Miguel found at Alava Exports showed that Aguirre's vineyard exported seventy-three million litres. Not simply white Rioja, but Viura."

"Numbers aren't my strong point. But it seems the bloke sells more of his stuff abroad than he does at home. So his worst crime is disloyalty?"

Ana dropped the napkin but kept her hands in a prayer gesture over her nose and mouth. "More like fraud. He also sells fifty-eight million litres in Spain. Numbers aren't my strong point either, but I can add seventy-three to fifty-eight. Comes to more than his maximum yield of ninety-one. Someone's getting shafted, Beatrice, and I doubt it's the Spanish."

Beatrice remembered the spotlight and handed Ana a tissue while considering the implications. She imagined the outrage of her favourite connoisseurs if they heard.

"So while you go to Portugal, should I go back to the police?"

"I'm not going to Portugal and you're not going to the police. Come here to me and listen. I've delayed you long enough. Go on holiday. I'm more grateful for your help than I can say, but I can't ask you for more."

"Without that first sentence, I might have agreed. I'm not comfortable leaving at this point. However, since I'm your guest, you could always throw me out, onto the street, like an unwanted old moggy ..."

"If you make me laugh, our performance is knackered. Thing is, I really don't want you to go, but I can't think of any good reason to keep you. If you would hang on a few more days, though, I'd be more grateful than you can imagine."

Beatrice reached for her hand, this time for a genuine reason.

Ana squeezed back. "Thing is, we have to get out of my apartment. For our own safety. Perhaps Jaime would let us stay at his place."

"There's a thought."

Ana's eyes crinkled. "You'd better behave yourself, mind. As well as being easy on the eye, he's a decent bloke and has some useful contacts. You know what, we could really do with comparing the export wine to the stuff Aguirre sells here. Do you know anyone in the wine trade?"

"As a matter of fact, I do. And he would just love the thought of offering his expertise. I'll give Adrian a ring when we get back."

"Great. Shit." Ana's shoulders shook, her face crumpled and she held out her arms. "Enrique's coming. Give me a hug."

# Chapter Eighteen

"Oh my God! What the hell happened?"

"It's fine, Jaime. My nose became intimately acquainted with some stone steps. I fell over. Nothing broken but I know it doesn't look pretty."

As if remembering his manners, Jaime leant in to kiss Beatrice. He smelt of coffee and cigarettes, a surprisingly attractive combination. She offered both cheeks and inhaled.

"Welcome, Beatrice. I'm very happy to see you again." He searched her face. "Are you sure you're all right?"

"Yes. Really. Probably because of the painkillers. It's very kind of you to put us up. I was quite prepared to book a hotel, but I must confess, I feel far safer here. It's awfully good of you."

"Not at all. I'm glad I could help. I told Ana on the phone, I'd rather know you were safe. For me, it's a pleasure to have guests. A boring bachelor doesn't often receive visitors, so this gives me a chance to practise my cooking. Have you eaten?"

"We had lunch, but that was a while back. And I'm sure Ana's still hungry. Where has she got to? She was only supposed to pay the taxi driver."

With that, something crunched into a wall followed by a foreign expletive. Beatrice and Jaime walked back along the corridor to find Ana wrestling with Beatrice's suitcase, plus her own two bags.

Jaime shot Beatrice a wicked grin. "Here, let me take that.

Otherwise you'll damage the paintwork."

Ana thrust the handle towards him. "Bugger the paintwork. Your lift is out of order. And so are you, Beatrice Stubbs. I swear to God that case is even heavier than before. What the hell have you got in there?"

"Inappropriate shoes, mostly, and a few souvenirs. The Guggenheim had the most wonderful pottery."

"You're travelling round Spain dragging a suitcase full of crockery?"

They followed Jaime into his flat, a large gloomy space with minimal furnishings and a surfeit of electronics. But it was clean and tidy and smelt of furniture polish.

As if he'd read her thoughts, Jaime said, "I'm afraid the place was a bit of a mess. So I've been cleaning since you called. You should come around more often. Now, are you hungry?"

Ana dropped her bags inside the doorway. "I could eat the leg of the Lamb of God and come back for its tail. Beatrice, how about yourself?"

The sun set, filling Jaime's apartment with golden-pink light as they sat around the remains of roast chicken in sherry sauce. He listened to the whole story with careful attention. Like Ana, he seemed initially suspicious of the explanation for Beatrice's puffy eyes and butterfly stitched nose, but accepted it after Beatrice repeated her tale twice. He offered his unconditional assistance, asked dozens of questions and smoked several cigarettes. The only time his composure wobbled was when he heard the truth about Tiago. He placed his hands over his eyes and seemed to wrestle for control. Eventually, he lifted his head.

"You should have told me. Tiago should have … oh shit, this is such a mess. Ana, this isn't some scoop about dodgy politicians or footballers having underage sex. If what you say is true, Tiago was killed for chasing this story. And you two carry on as if …" He lit another cigarette, shaking his head.

"Jaime, listen …"

"No, Ana, just shut the fuck up for a second. Sorry, Beatrice. But you must understand how dangerous this situation is. If Tiago was murdered, whoever did it wants the story as dead as he is. We have to be extremely careful. Neither of you should be seen in Vitoria. If there's any further investigation to be done, we'll find another way. The paper can't afford to make an enemy of Arturo de Aguirre, but nor can we afford to lose an exposé like this."

Lit up by the rose-coloured sky, Ana's eyes blazed in the autumn sun. "If it is fraud, it is on an industrial scale, and will have repercussions all the way along the chain. This will go national and probably international. We'd better be prepared to take some heat."

Jaime stretched his arms above his head, which, Beatrice noted, tightened the muscles across his chest. His shirt, made of some heavy cream material, strained at the press studs.

"I'm ready for that. The paper can handle it." He relaxed his stretch and pointed at them with his cigarette. "But you two, as individuals, are far too vulnerable. Now listen to me. Both of you. I want you to promise that neither of you will do anything, say anything, or call anyone without telling me first. We need to work as a team and that means no individual risks. OK?"

They promised.

He gave them a quarter-smile. "*Vale.* Now, I'd like to take a coffee. There's a nice café at the end of my street, if you ladies would like to join me."

Beatrice still found this habit very odd. Heading out into the streets at the time she'd normally be donning her pyjamas.

"If you don't mind, I think I might stay here and lie down a while. Today has been rather hard work and a beast of a headache has begun."

Jaime's deep blue eyes were full of concern. "Of course. You look really pale. Ana can take the guest room, but I've put you in my bed. I'll sleep in the study. Don't argue, there's a sofa where I often fall asleep if I'm working late. The bathroom is through the door on the left."

"You do look peaky, Beatrice. Will I get you some more painkillers while we're out?"

"No need, thanks. I have some spares in my bag. I'll see if I can sleep it off before taking any more. Jaime, you're extremely kind and I'm very grateful."

"Don't mention it. I hope you sleep well, Beatrice, and feel lots better tomorrow." He bent forward and kissed her forehead.

She sat on Jaime's bed, listening to the sounds of them leaving the building. Beautiful eyes, great cook, generous personality and the softest lips. Why on earth was he living alone?

# Chapter Nineteen

Rain lashed the panes as if someone were repeatedly hurling a bucketful at the window. Adrian stood with his hands on his hips, frowning at Boot Street. The view outside was a colourful blur, as umbrellas bobbed along the pavement like petals floating downstream. A piquant waft of *jamon iberica* from the meat platter on the table caused him to inhale and close his eyes. The doorbell rang. Even though he'd been waiting impatiently for over an hour, it startled him. He buzzed his visitor into the building and unlocked the flat door.

Wet patches darkened the shoulders of Matthew's mud-green jacket, his hair dripped down his face and his shoes oozed water onto the hall carpet. He looked every inch like an eccentric English university professor and smelt like a spaniel fresh from the river. Adrian shook his head as he reached for Matthew's suitcase.

"No umbrella?"

"Left the wretched thing on the train. I'll take my shoes off out here."

As Adrian returned with two bath towels, Matthew wiped the water from his face with reddened hands. Affection overpowered Adrian's annoyance and concern for soft furnishings.

"You need to get out of those wet things. Immediately."

Matthew nodded. "Yes. I don't want to catch a cold."

"Not only that, but the whiff would overpower any kind of

accurate tasting."

The miserable expression lifted. "Oh, you managed to get some then?"

"Did you doubt I would? Now, go and change and I'll make you a hot toddy."

Some time back, a *Color Me Beautiful* consultant had identified Adrian as winter. His colouring, sharp and distinctive, apparently allowed him to wear bolder hues; black and white, berry and jewel. The system intrigued him, so he read up on it and reorganised his wardrobe accordingly. Customers who came through the door of the Hoxton Wine Emporium were mentally assigned a season in under ten seconds. Adrian took no formal training in the science of complementary tones, merely employing natural good taste and excellent instincts. He was rarely wrong.

Matthew, despite having all the fashion sense of a goat, had also discovered his true palette. Moss, rust, olive and taupe, the colours of a kitchen garden, complemented his chocolate eyes and warm skin as he sat opposite, sipping from a Villeroy & Boch mug. The lemon juice, honey and Aberfeldy did the trick and Matthew glowed with enthusiasm while Adrian explained how his Spanish ex-boyfriend had arranged for a case of Castelo de Aguirre white Viura to be delivered direct from Rioja country.

"He's the perfect one to call, because his current squeeze is a trucker who works the continental routes. Paolo's tastes generally run to rough trade, you see. I must have been an exception. Anyway, the trucker picked up a case en route and it got here in less time than it took you to travel up from Devon."

"Well done. And please express my gratitude to Paolo and his timely trucker. So if the goods are here, perhaps we should perform the experiment?"

"Why not? And if our results are conclusive, we can call Beatrice back this afternoon. Are you feeling better?"

Matthew stood. "Thoroughly restored, thank you. Just

curious and a little peckish."

"I can meet both those basic needs. We have a selection of Spanish meats, a quality Manchego, roasted peppers, chilli almonds and a baguette fresh from the oven. I went for the terroir concept. But rather than sully our buds beforehand, shall we taste first?"

Matthew rubbed his hands together. "Superlative plan. I assume the wine is chilled?"

Adrian gave him an arch look before leading the way to the kitchen.

On the central island lay a white linen napkin, six Riedel wine glasses, two water glasses, two ballpoint pens and two brand-new notepads purchased that morning at Paperchase. Adrian's preparations, as ever, were thoroughly thought through.

Matthew seated himself on a breakfast stool and adopted a certain critical air. For his part, Adrian was unconcerned. In certain fields, such as wine and musical theatre, Adrian remained the uncontested expert. Even more so since opening his own emporium. Matthew took off his glasses to read the label on each bottle, observed the extraction of all three corks and studied the elderflower-coloured liquid as it rose to a third of the way up the glass.

The pair began a practised routine. Each lifting their first glass to the light, they studied the colour. Adrian replaced his on the napkin and wrote a brief description. Pale, more hay than straw, vaguest hint of green? Matthew raised his to the window, tilting it at various angles a moment longer before turning to his notebook. By which time Adrian was assessing the bouquet. Holding the stem so as not to affect the temperature, he swirled the wine around the bowl, using minute revolutions of the wrist. He passed the glass under his nose, on the inhale. Some lemon, green beans, and blossom. Cut grass? He pressed his nose deeper into the bowl. Camomile, apricot and asparagus.

He set down the wine and wrote detailed impressions on nose.

Lastly, the attack. He rolled the liquid around his mouth, giving each taste bud its chance. Elegance, some honey, a whisper of apple. Pleasant acidity, light and dry. The taste developed depth, revealing more of the fruit as green apple, balanced by a floral sweetness. After swallowing, the mouthfeel lengthened into a spice. Baked apple?

He returned his attention to Matthew, who finished scrawling in tiny handwriting and looked up with a smile. "We'll compare later, of course, but that was a wholly pleasurable experience."

Adrian bowed his head in acknowledgement. "That was the original. The Aguirre white Rioja sold in Spain. Now for the exports. I have two samples; one from my own supplier, Imperial Wines and another sourced from Grapemeister."

He poured them both some water, they drank and began again. The routine followed the pattern exactly until Matthew took his first sip. Adrian, still trying to define the exact nose, had fallen behind and when Matthew placed his glass back on the napkin as if he'd been poisoned, Adrian's first reaction was offence.

"Oh, please, Matthew. I accept you might not like it quite as much, but this is a product from my own shop. I chose to stock this so it can't possibly be as rank as that expression of yours makes out."

Matthew wasn't listening, instead pulling the napkin from around the neck of the bottle and examining the label once more.

Adrian took a sip, rolled the liquid around for three seconds and swallowed quickly so he could speak.

"That could be a supermarket blend-in-a-box! There must have been a mistake."

"A little harsh, but it is far from the same wine."

"Matthew, I take my choice of stock seriously. There is no way I would have selected this. I never buy on mere strength of name. I taste. I go there and taste."

Matthew steepled his hands under his chin. "Right. One

more to go. And if the gap between the two remains as startling, we may need a whistle to blow."

Adrian returned from his office with a print-out and stood in front of Matthew, raising his eyebrows in enquiry. Matthew glanced at the paper, gave the thumbs-up and returned his attention to the telephone, through which he reassured Beatrice.

"Absolutely. I think you could say we learnt our lesson last time, Old Thing. Yes, I know and we're only coming over to act as consultant oenologists. Just for the weekend, that's all. I have to get back to Exeter and Adrian's colleague has only agreed to cover till Monday. But we are both convinced our expertise will be beneficial ..."

Adrian held the print-out in front of Matthew's face, pointing out the flight times before indicating his watch.

"Ah. Now, it seems we really have to step on it if we're to make these flights. Sorry? No, no, Adrian has arranged a hotel, but perhaps you'd like to make a dinner reservation? We'll be with you by teatime. I'd lean to seafood this evening, but if you have ..."

Adrian sighed and flapped the papers.

"Must dash. See you this evening. Jolly well looking forward to it. Bye for now."

The doorbell rang.

Adrian picked up his hastily packed suitcase. Fortunately, his skill at packing for a mini-break was honed through practice. "That'll be the taxi. An extravagance, I know, but it's still raining. Come on, Matthew, Beatrice needs us."

# Chapter Twenty

Beatrice needed to calm down. She'd taken her mood stabilisers every day, but because of the irregular routine of the past week, her timing was all over the place. And now, she was like a hyperactive child. Even knowing that this phase would inevitably be followed by a dip, she couldn't summon up any sobering anxiety. The most frustrating thing when she felt sociable, extrovert and animated was spending the majority of the day alone.

By the time Beatrice woke, Jaime had already left for work. Ana was pacing the kitchen, speaking Spanish on her phone. After helping herself to coffee, Beatrice's first priority was to check the damage to her face. Her left eye was swollen and the colour of an overripe damson. The right looked far from normal but no worse than if she had a stye in it. The bridge of her nose had bled in the night, leaving a dark dried crust around the stitches. She looked bloody awful, but apart from a constantly throbbing face and a very stiff knee, she felt fantastic.

Ana made a series of phone calls to arrange meetings for the following day and then dressed herself for Tiago's funeral. Black suited her; the sadness in her eyes less so. Jaime returned to pick her up at ten, as the funeral was taking place in Tiago's home village, near Pamplona. In a narrow black suit with shoestring tie and messy hair, Jaime looked like an extra from *A Fistful of Dollars*.

He flashed those astounding teeth and took her hand. "Be careful, Beatrice. I think it would be better if you stayed here till we return. Remember, no risks."

She saw them off with a sigh. Probably the only occasion in her life on which she actually wanted to go to the funeral of a complete stranger. Matthew and Adrian were due to arrive in Bilbao at three o'clock, but then she had to wait for the bus to deliver them to Vitoria.

Five hours and nothing to do. Jaime's apartment was the average single male's abode, purely functional and unless you liked video games, a little depressing. Like a student's flat. For the editor of a newspaper, he didn't seem to have much in the way of books. She mooched about, idly examining the few framed cuttings which she couldn't read, opening kitchen cupboards, looking out over the city from the second floor balcony and checking out the wardrobe. Denim, leather, embroidered shirts, cowboy boots; she wondered if he might be into line-dancing. Telling herself she was looking for something to pass the time, she decided to take a peek at Jaime's study. She found it locked, to her surprise and immediate guilt. *Why would he lock it, unless he didn't trust ... oh.*

Time to go out. She'd stay on the main streets, potter about in the city, keeping her head down and later find somewhere to have lunch. That could hardly be seen as breaking her promise to take no risks. Her mood lifted still further as she collected her handbag, checked she had the key and headed out into the streets.

But she'd forgotten about her face. Everywhere she went people stared, or winced, or gave sympathetic smiles; she certainly was drawing attention to herself. After a while, she began to avoid eye contact until she realised that keeping her focus on the ground would be counter-productive to remaining alert and thus safe. Her optimism for the day soured and the low sun seemed unnecessarily bright, so she gave up. The only useful thing she managed was to buy a pair of trainers and sports socks to protect her feet. Just as she turned back towards the apartment, an idea occurred. Sunglasses. They worked wonders, reducing the staring and softening the glare. Why did it take her so long to think of these things? Half an hour later, she'd purchased something suitably Jackie O which didn't hurt her nose. By which time her headache had returned.

The walk back was not as easy as she had imagined. She'd over-estimated her familiarity with the layout of Vitoria and found herself going in circles around every country in South America. Calle Argentina, Calle Chile, Calle Ecuador, and when she eventually found Calle Bolivia, it was not the place she had left that morning. She felt like Patrick McGoohan. Disorientation, heat and her throbbing nose combined to turn stress into a growing panic. She followed the street again and noticed that Calle Bolivia was not a dead-end, as it first appeared. A footpath led through to another street, also called Calle Bolivia. Beatrice still wasn't exactly sure where she was, but her instinct told her to turn right. As the road curved around, she recognised the building ahead. She'd been gazing at it that very morning, from Jaime's balcony. She lifted her eyes towards the block across the road, seeking Jaime's apartment. She wasn't the only one.

Two men stood outside the apartment block, also looking up at the second floor. Beatrice stopped. She couldn't see them clearly, but the matching hefty physiques, shades and dark suits seemed familiar. She slipped behind a tree to observe the situation. Everything fell away; the heat, the pain in her face, her dry mouth, the slick moisture of her hands on the carrier bag, as her training and experience kicked in. She focused on each detail. One of the men walked up to the door and rang one of the buzzers. He waited, listening, while his colleague kept his head tilted back, watching the apartment.

If these were the muscle-bound Rottweilers who had so frightened Ana, where were their handlers? Possibly watching her watching them? Beatrice scanned the street, her pulse rapid and her breathing short. A dark blue Mercedes, Ana had said.

Most of the cars were white, with the odd silver or red vehicle. Further along, some darker colours stood out, but they were too far away to be distinguishable. The doorbell ringer returned to the street and a grunty conversation ensued. They turned and swaggered in the opposite direction to Beatrice, glancing backwards and upwards with ostentatious suspicion. She followed, with extreme caution, using trees, vans and advertising hoardings as cover, until she saw them stop beside one of the darker sedans; a Mercedes.

Of course. Anyone returning from the city would come up the street that way, passing the Mercedes first. Simply due to her erroneous sense of direction, Beatrice had come the other way. She started to retreat, pausing to check she had not attracted attention. The pair of thugs stood smoking and waiting, keeping their attention on Jaime's building, talking to the occupants of the car. Beatrice turned the corner and started to speed-walk while dialling Ana's number. Straight to voicemail. The clock said eleven-fifty. They were probably already at the church. She left a message and looked around, wondering what to do next. Alone in a city where she knew no one.

Almost no one.

The napkin was a little worse for wear from being stuffed at the bottom of her handbag, but the number was legible. Beatrice kept walking as she dialled.

"Hello, is that Kev? This is Beatrice, the clumsy woman you met on the wine tour. Just wondering what you're up to today? Do you happen to have any plans for lunch?"


The Artium was an inspired idea. Cool, quiet and displaying so much of interest on the walls, Beatrice's face barely attracted a second glance. She pottered around for over an hour before the lads arrived, and had only seen a fraction of the vast collection. Yet one thing had already made an impression. The glaring gap between 1936 and 1940. It wasn't the only glaring gap. Her knowledge of the Spanish Civil War was gleaned from writers such as Laurie Lee and Jessica Mitford. The Artium's extensive library would be able to set her straight, but Beatrice hesitated.

Past experience had taught her the danger of comprehending history. Knowledge with the aim of learning lessons was all well and good, but exploring a tragic period in a nation's past, coupled with excessive empathy, could be devastating. One of her worst black holes since 'the incident' had occurred after visiting the *Umschlagplatz* in Warsaw. All those first names carved onto a white wall, representing 300,000 individuals transported from that very platform to the Treblinka gas chambers. The horror and enormity of scale penetrated her bones. She was unable to speak for three days, while Matthew paced corridors, called doctors and tried everything to stop her tears.

No, not the library. *Because history is more than dates and artefacts. History is human.* Instead, she chose to explore the gift shop, a place bright and lively enough to distract her from the welling blackness inside. She bought presents for both Matthew's daughters, for Adrian and for herself, but nothing seemed exactly right for Matthew. So just before two o'clock, she paid and left the shop, with a vague sense of guilt, as if she'd forgotten something. Flashbacks, gloom in beautiful experiences, self-flagellation … the patterns were familiar. A mood swing now was the last thing she needed. The sight of three strapping chaps standing underneath the enormous chandelier made of lightbulbs gave her a fillip.

"Hello Kev, Jase. Hello, Tyler. It's very good of you to come and meet me at such short notice."

Kev gave her a broad smile. "All right, Beatrice? Good to see you again."

"Yeah, we wondered how you were getting on," added Jase.

"Bit worried old Aguirre might have kidnapped you," Tyler grinned.

Beatrice looked at each of them in turn. "It's lovely to see you all. And even better, not one of you has winced or gasped or shown any kind of reaction to the mess I've made of my face."

Kev shrugged. "We've seen a lot worse than that. Right, where's this restaurant?"

A strange sense of disconnect came over Beatrice as they got experimental with the menu, encouraged each other to taste their dishes and laughed at Tyler's anecdotes. The three men appeared completely relaxed, with not a hint of awkwardness towards her, but she could find out precious little about their profession. Each time she asked a direct question, one of them would gently lead the conversation elsewhere. So far, she had established that they were stationed in Afghanistan, they'd met while on training and they all came from the Manchester area.

"And your fiancée, Tyler? Is she a Mancunian?"

"Oooh, no. Good job she can't hear you. She's from Birkenhead. It'll take her years to get over the shame of marrying a squaddie from Stockport."

"But what happens after you get married? She won't go with you to Afghanistan, surely?" Beatrice asked.

"No, no. But after this tour of duty, I'll get stationed somewhere else, most like. Don't mind where so long as it has smaller insects. Hey, Jase. Tell Beatrice about that scorpion you found."

And once again, the conversation carried her away. She didn't resist. The waiter cleared their plates and Beatrice expressed her compliments on the garlic soup. Since arriving in Spain, she had dined exquisitely everywhere she went and collected enough recipe ideas to last her months. Jase and Tyler excused themselves to have a cigarette outside, while Kev and Beatrice ordered coffees.

Beatrice tried another, blander query. "How much longer are you staying in Vitoria? If you don't mind my asking."

Kev nodded, as if considering the question with care. "We're off to Bilbao on Saturday to meet Tyler's crowd for a weekend of mayhem. Listen, Beatrice, don't get us wrong; it's not like we're being evasive. Well, I s'pose we are, but not to be rude or owt.

It's not easy to get people to understand, but we're on active duty. We're part of a peacekeeping force in the most dangerous country in the world. The past isn't pretty, and God knows what the future holds, so we'd rather just talk about the here and now. Immediate plans, that's about as far as we can go. Might not make much sense to you, but for us, that's the way it is."

Beatrice gazed at him, noticing for the first time how his eyes seemed much older than the rest of his face.

"As a matter of fact, it does. To me, it makes perfect sense."

# Chapter 21

The usual frisson rippled across the crowd as Aguirre and Marisol descended the steps to the ballroom. The huge French windows opened onto the terrace, which today was covered by a marquee in primary colours. The sun playing on the canvas gave the scene a sense of vibrancy and warmth, the latter assisted by outdoor heaters. Beyond the marquee, circus performers threaded their way between a bouncy castle and a petting zoo, face painters and a puppet show. Most children seemed to be running from one attraction to the other, rarely standing still for long.

The majority of adults remained indoors, sipping champagne, observing one another and occasionally glancing towards the garden with indulgent smiles. The colours indoors were no less splendid. Like an exotic aviary, the plumage made up of vibrant dresses and designer suits. Aguirre affected not to notice the covert glances and the overt stares as he took in the room, nodding at acquaintances, smiling at friends and ignoring his mistress entirely. Marisol had an unerring sense of which women caught his attention, so he had learnt not even to make eye contact. Nevertheless, his Polish beauty's platinum hair refracted light in his peripheral vision, along with chandeliers, diamonds and envious eyes.

Paz turned to look over a bare shoulder, waving her fingers in a half-greeting, half-beckon. She and Angel were talking to the handsome young CEO of Tortuga Construction, Simon

Vasconcellos. A clever move, as Aguirre had him on the shortlist for potential partners for Luz. Of whom there was no sign.

Kisses and handshakes exchanged, small talk performed and Aguirre was already bored.

"And your sister?" he asked Paz, scanning the room with impunity and resting his gaze on Klaudyna, who was laughing at some frivolity. She held his gaze for a second, before focusing once more on her companions.

Paz shrugged, without breaking the flow of her monologue to her mother, a speech so familiar Aguirre could have delivered it himself. Immigrants – the scourge of Spain. Angel answered in her stead, apparently relieved to have an excuse not to listen.

"Luz isn't feeling so good. Inez has gone up to see her."

Aguirre frowned. "She's sick?"

"I doubt it. More like chronic shyness," Paz interrupted and immediately returned to her theme. "Which in turn leads to social unrest and a destabilising of the whole country merely for the sake of a minaret!"

The construction magnate's eyes were glazing over. Marisol moved with grace and speed.

"Paz, my darling, how many times must I tell you that politics interests no one but politicians? It's a good job my other daughters are less opinionated. Señor Vasconcellos, I hear you are an art lover. Did you see the piece in the hall? We picked it up at auction and I find it so intriguing. It's through here. I'd love to hear an expert's opinion."

Aguirre watched his wife do what she did best and congratulated himself on his excellent judgement in marrying her. More beautiful candidates had scored poorly in the social arena, sexier possibilities had unimpressive backgrounds. Marisol, average-looking at best, beat them all with her blend of charm, contacts and determination. And for the losers, Aguirre was generous with his consolation prizes.

A silver shift and blonde hair shimmered past, a magnet for attention. Aguirre directed his eyes at Angel.

"Any news on the German supermarket contract?"

"I think," Angel glanced at his sister-in-law, "we've been banned from talking shop. Today is all about Ramón. Inez and Paz insist."

"You see, Angel, another classic example of how you are failing as a husband. A woman never tells me what I can and cannot discuss in my own home."

Angel's posture gave everything away. He recoiled, feigned amusement and attempted to hide his blush. Such a stupid man. The arrival of Guido, his other son-in-law, diverted his attention.

"Since when is *pata negra* an 'amuse-bouche'? This catering company is run by a pretentious goat's arse! Where did you find these people, Arturo?'

An equally stupid man. Proud of his oafish disrespect and ingratitude, assuming his nationalistic hubris will mitigate any offence. A baboon. But at least this baboon wasn't firing blanks.

Aguirre rolled his eyes. "Tell me about it, Guido. Your mother-in-law attended some charity do and came back singing the caterer's praises. I decided to give them a try. Pretentious, indeed, but I have to say she was right about the quality. After all, we wouldn't want that bunch of cowboys who did your garden party, would we?"

And balance restored.


Across the lawn ran a gaudy troop of small boys, yelling at the top of their lungs. Basajaun was right in the middle, his features obscured by markings. Face paint, but at this distance, Luz had no idea what he was supposed to be. She smiled at their noisy enthusiasm, at the balloons, the stilt-walkers and the bubble-machine and wished she could join them. Just take off this dress, clean her face, drag on her jeans and run and laugh and play until she was exhausted.

She should join the party. She looked exactly as she'd hoped. Classy, groomed and a little bit sexy. But if he wasn't there to see her, what was the point? She tugged at the Cartier diamonds in her earlobe. Tonight, she was a show pony, with no other purpose than to be admired and offered up to whichever poor devil her father had chosen. For a second, Luz considered her potential suitor's lack of freedom. For as an Aguirre-in-law, his hands would forever be manipulated by invisible strings. In many ways, Tunçay was lucky. She should go.

A knock at the door made her start and snatch up her lipstick as an excuse.

"Come in. Almost ready."

It was not, as expected, her mother, impatient and shrewish, but her oldest sister.

"Hi Inez. Sorry, my make-up took ages. I'm just on my way."

Inez closed the door. "Relax, I'm not on sheepdog duty. I just fancied a few minutes peace. Talking of which, guess who's on the warpath again. Ranting to Vasconcellos about Spain's loss of identity to Islam, blah, blah, bloody blah."

"She should shut her mouth. She has no idea what she's talking about." Luz blushed, aware her vehemence might arouse suspicion.

Inez didn't notice, picking up pieces from Luz's jewellery box and placing them against her neck. "I know. He's quite a looker, actually. Tall, big brown eyes and dirty blond hair."

"Vasconcellos? Bland. Looks like a catalogue model. I suppose he's the recipient of my batted lashes today?"

"Yep. But you might get off lightly. Mama will be watching Papí and he'll be watching his Polish slut."

"He's lining up a new mistress? What happened to the Brazilian model?"

"Luz, you are so out of touch. He's been banging Klaudyna Kulka ever since our garden party in June. Is that dress new? It suits you. Flattering up top."

"Thanks. Yours is fabulous. I love all the pleats."

Inez sat on the bed, her eyes sly. "Yes, I'm hoping the pleats come in useful, in fact."

Abandoning all pretence at make-up, Luz turned to her sister. She'd seen that expression of cunning triumph before.

"What is it? Tell me."

A smile spreading across her face, Inez reached into her Hermès handbag and brought out a plastic bag. She unwrapped something from the tissue paper and waved it in a figure of eight in front of Luz.

A jolt of delight hit Luz as she realised what she was seeing. "Oh my God, are you pregnant?" she whispered.

Inez shrugged. "Nothing's certain till I've seen the doctor, but the test says yes."

Luz jumped to her feet and hugged her. "I'm so happy for you! You and Angel, I mean, you've waited so long. And I'm going to be an auntie again. Oh, make it a girl, will you? Paz is having another boy ..."

"That doesn't surprise me. If I didn't know better, I'd say Paz *was* a man."

Luz laughed, a little shocked. "So you must give me a little niece, so I can buy her beautiful things and play princesses."

Inez laughed and squeezed her sister's arms. "I'll try. Now listen. No one knows, not even Angel. I want confirmation before I tell anyone. And try and keep Mama away from me. She's stressed as hell at the moment, but I swear she can smell when something's going on. I don't want her to guess, I want to surprise her and Papí. I can't wait to see their faces."

"And Angel's!"

Inez took Luz's place in front of the mirror and tilted her head left and right. "Yes, you're right. I guess it will come as a bit of a surprise to Angel. Listen, they'll ring the gong in about five minutes. We should get down there. I'll go first and keep your Vasconcellos entertained till you arrive. He'll need rescuing from Paz by now."

She slipped out the door and blew a kiss.

Luz took one last look in the mirror then decided she didn't care. He could like what he saw or not. It made no difference.

She had no interest in him and would tell him so.

Aguirre worked the room, expressing admiration and pleasure everywhere he went, but kept Klaudyna and Marisol in his peripheral vision. His impatience at his youngest daughter's absence grew along with his geniality. He glanced at his watch and across at his wife. Eyes as bright as a lighthouse, Marisol picked up Aguirre's intentions, excused herself and ascended the stairs. When the housekeeper appeared at his elbow to ask if she should sound the lunch gong, he hesitated, but then spotted Luz skulking along the wall in the direction of the garden. He instructed Carmina to wait fifteen more minutes. The dress Luz wore was spectacular, undoubtedly chosen by Marisol, but the guilty look and withdrawn posture showed it at its worst. He moved as fast as his status allowed, kept his focus on her and broke into a huge smile as he cut off her escape.

"My beautiful little girl!" he boomed, attracting attention from every corner. "No, no longer a little girl, an elegant woman. Look at me!"

"Papí," she moved to kiss his cheeks, partly to hide her embarrassment, he noticed.

Aguirre turned to the nearest party; a judge and two executives from the TV station who cast approving looks at his daughter. On cue, the producer nodded. "They grow so fast, don't they? She'll be breaking hearts soon, I'll bet."

Aguirre acknowledged the compliment with a modest bow of his head.

"Come, my little jewel. There's someone I want you to meet." His hand firmly on his daughter's elbow, he smiled at the ingratiating faces.

"Papí, I thought I'd find Ramón first. I haven't said ..."

He dropped his voice. "You should have thought of that earlier. There's only quarter of an hour before the gong. Didn't you see what time it is? And I'd like you to escort Señor Vasconcellos to the buffet. Your duties are firstly to our guests."

He steered her back in the direction of their group. Luz pulled her arm from her father's grasp but continued walking in the right direction. No more than Aguirre expected. Had it been Inez, a full-blown row could easily have erupted. But Luz was gentler, more malleable and always did as she was told.

According to family tradition, Marisol would escort the most senior male figure, today a French count in his eighties, while Aguirre charmed one of the influential ladies. His daughters had instructions to target some useful contact or other and the rest could fend for themselves. He expected nothing of his sons-in-law. Angel was positively dangerous when he opened his weak mouth. Guido, slow-witted and dull, would find someone with whom he could argue football. Perhaps his third son-in-law might break the pattern by being rich, well-connected *and* intelligent. Aguirre waved Vasconcellos over.

"Simon, let me introduce my daughter, Luz. The jewel in our family crown. She lives up to her name, a very bright girl. Bright and beautiful."

Luz offered her hand which Vasconcellos took but pulled her closer to brush both cheeks with his lips.

"Miss Aguirre, it is a pleasure. I've heard so much about you." His smile was generous. Hers was half-hearted.

"Oh but you haven't heard the best. Luz is a great aficionado of fine architecture. I'm sure she would appreciate your views on that Calatrava project we discussed earlier. Excuse me one moment."

He wove a path to the dining room, resisting a look back until he reached the open doors. With some satisfaction, he noted Vasconcellos bend his head to listen to Luz, who was explaining something with great earnestness. Aguirre sighed. If only she could smile a little more and talk a little less.

His eyes swept over the room, checking all was as it should be when his attention was caught by Marisol, standing motionless on the staircase. In a second, he knew something was wrong. She stared across the room, her jaw set and lips pinched. Aguirre followed her sightline, almost sure the object of such livid focus would be his beautiful Klaudyna, and began rehearsing denials. He frowned when he realised her furious glare was directed at her youngest daughter. Oblivious, Luz continued to lecture poor Vasconcellos.

Aguirre slid through the crowds, exuding purpose so as not to be derailed by favour-seekers, until he reached Marisol.

"What is it?"

She fixed her stare on him and he noticed her fists were clenched.

"Marisol?"

"Come with me. We need to talk."

# Chapter 22

The bus arrived five minutes early. Beatrice was already waiting. She found a free spot on a bench between a chap in a business suit and two teenage girls and settled down to wait, anticipating Adrian's reaction to her bruised face, Matthew's thoughts on today's close shave and both their impressions of Ana and Jaime.

When Beatrice called her from the museum, Ana had returned to the apartment with Jaime and reported the coast clear. Of the 'welcoming committee', there was no sign. They agreed on meeting at the hotel for dinner and strategic planning.

She shifted around and crossed her legs. A twinge in her knee made her grimace. She started to give it a gentle rub when her phone rang. She didn't recognise the number but answered anyway.

"Hello?"

A woman's voice. "Hello, is that Beatrice Stubbs?"

"Yes. Who's this?"

"It's Luz Aguirre. From the vineyard. I just wanted to ask how you are after yesterday's fall."

"Oh, how kind of you to call. I should have called you to say thanks, but there's rather a lot going on, you see. I'm fine. Surprisingly well, in fact. Your first aid was extremely efficient."

"I'm pleased to hear that. My parents would like to send you some flowers, by way of an apology. I know you're staying in

Calle Cuchillería. Could you tell me which apartment?"

Uneasy about sharing Ana's address, Beatrice stalled. "There's really no need to apologise. If I received flowers every time I tripped over, I could start up a business."

"They insist. Personally, I think those steps are lethal. So I think they're lucky to get away with nothing more than a flower basket."

"I suspect the insistence comes from you rather than them, but a flower basket is always welcome. The thing is, I'm moving to the Hotel Valencia, which is in the centre. Do you know it?"

"Yes, I do. My sister had her wedding reception there. It's very grand."

"Is it? Oh, good. I like a bit of luxury."

Luz laughed. "I hope you have a lovely stay and the flowers lift your spirits. It was a pleasure to meet you, Mrs Stubbs. Get well soon and enjoy the rest of your holiday."

"Thank you Luz, and good luck with your studies."

It could be genuine, of course. A gesture from a nice, well-mannered young woman with a conscience. Or it could be an Aguirre-induced way of finding her. Happily, she hadn't needed to lie, but nor had she given too much away.

After an alarming start, the day had exceeded expectations. A hushed hour in front of Miró, Gargallo, del Rivero, Brossa and Nagel, the delicious lunch of fresh pintxos with a glass of rosé and pleasant company and a feeling of having averted a trough had brought Beatrice to almost a kind of equilibrium. Now a friendly gesture from the Aguirre family and her two favourite men in the world were imminent. All well with the world.

Someone cleared his throat, pointedly. Beatrice realised she was bouncing up and down on her buttocks, so forcing the other occupants of the bench to bounce with her. She desisted and held up her hands.

"Sorry."

The suit, the teenagers and an older woman with a laundry

bag smiled at her evident impatience. Certain behaviour was universally understood and forgiven.

Seconds later, the bus arrived. Choosing to stick with the sunglasses to minimise the shock factor, Beatrice hurried to meet them.

Adrian spotted her first, but was diplomatic enough to point her out to Matthew while he claimed their bags.

"Beatrice!" He embraced her cautiously. "I've been rather worried about you. Are things really all right? Are you?"

"I am now. It's actually wonderful to see you, Matthew. Oh dear, I really am getting to be a sentimental old bat. It's not even a fortnight since I left."

"An eventful fortnight, by all accounts," Matthew said, his smile not quite eradicating the frown of concern.

"Hello, Beatrice! Hardy Boys reporting for duty!"

Beatrice beamed. Adrian, crisp as a stick of celery, wore a green linen shirt, off-white trousers and carried something resembling a cricketer's holdall. He held out his arms as if for a hug but grabbed her shoulders.

With maximum drama, he dropped his voice to a funereal pitch. "I think we'd best get it over with. Let us see your face."

Beatrice sighed, and with a shrug, removed her sunglasses.

Adrian dropped his bag and clapped both hands over his mouth. Matthew's eyes roved over her, finally meeting her patient gaze. They were attracting quite some attention in the bus station, everyone drawn to such a spectacle.

"Tell me again, and I promise to believe you. This was an accident."

"It looks horrific, I know. But the culprit was a useless pair of shoes, as prosaic as that. Matthew, and as a matter of fact, you too Adrian, should both be aware of my clumsy streak. We do have things to worry about, but I assure you, this isn't one of them. Now come on, let's get to the hotel. There are some people I want you to meet."

Despite the promised grandeur, the superb location, fine food and perfectly matched wine, the meeting was not going well. Matthew had taken against Jaime. Beatrice wasn't sure precisely why. Perhaps Jaime's casual dress: jeans, an open-necked shirt and a bandana round his neck instead of a tie, had offended him. It might have been Jaime's familiar way of flirt-teasing, or maybe he'd caught one of Beatrice's admiring looks at the editor. One thing was for sure, Matthew was unimpressed.

"I have to say I disagree, Jaime. Hard evidence is exactly what Adrian and I have flown here to provide. We have bottled proof that the export wine is something other than what it says on the label. And as two people investigating this racket have already met with a sticky end, I think it wisest to take what we have to the police. Now."

Matthew's measured tones sounded calm and reasonable. One would have to know him extremely well to detect the undercurrent of hostility in his voice.

Beatrice chipped in. "The thing is, Matthew, we've already tried to get the police to take this seriously. We know for a fact they suppressed the coroner's findings about Tiago. His death was recorded as an accident and thus no investigation will be forthcoming. Not only that, but the detective we spoke to immediately contacted London to call me off."

Matthew fixed her with a frown. "How do you know that?"

"Hamilton rang me and bawled me out. Told me to stop interfering." She returned her attention to the pork fillet on her plate, avoiding Matthew's incisive stare.

Ana took over. "In a way, Matthew, you're right. We have proof that someone, somewhere, is ripping off the British public. But we don't know which link in the chain is responsible. Or whether, which I think is more likely, the whole process is corrupt. We need to find out a little more about where this is happening and then we can point the finger in the right direction."

"Sounds fair enough to me," said Adrian, topping up Jaime's glass. "And I quite fancy a nose round the vineyard. Why don't we see what we can find out tomorrow and then have a rethink?"

Jaime smiled at him. "Thank you. Yes, I agree. With information from the DOC, the wine expert's insights and the background of the vineyard, we should have a clearer picture by tomorrow evening."

Matthew shook his head. "Jaime, Ana, forgive my being blunt, but I am concerned you are chasing a story. Whereas I see this as a criminal investigation, which should be carried out by the professionals. The *local* professionals." He glanced at Beatrice. "Dabbling in a case which involves two dead men seems at best foolhardy."

Ana put down her fork and gazed at Matthew. "One of those dead men was my best friend. The police won't investigate why someone hacked off his nose, so I will. I want to take them enough evidence so they are forced to act. And at the moment, I haven't got it. Couldn't we work as a team, as Adrian says, for one more day?"

Everyone paused; forks hovered, glasses stopped midway to lips and all eyes rested on Matthew.

He sighed. "No one should do anything alone. We must stay in pairs, or all together."

Ana gave him a brilliant smile and the meal resumed.

Jaime nodded. "I agree with Matthew. No need to worry about me. I'm going to be at the office, surrounded by people. Ana and Beatrice should go to San Sebastian together. You can take my car. And Adrian and Matthew could join an official tour of Castelo de Aguirre."

Ana's eyes widened. "Your car? Seriously?"

"I know. Trusting you with my pride and joy, I must be out of my mind." Jaime took a sip of wine. "But if I can't be there myself, it's the least I can do. Just be careful, OK?"

Ana grinned. "Trust me. I'm an excellent driver. Adrian, can I get a top-up there? I've a throat on me tonight."

Matthew caught Beatrice's eyes. He smiled but she knew there was trouble brewing. And what was worse, she knew she deserved it.

# Chapter 23

The police arrived as Tunçay was spooning yoghurt onto a plate of corn fritters for the party on table six. Three burst through the serving doors, two of whom carried guns. Another two appeared from the back door, also armed. The kitchen, normally filled with shouts and clatter, had never heard noise like it. All the gunmen were shouting, making it impossible to hear any clear instructions. Tunçay put down the yoghurt and raised his hands in the air, just in case.

The only man without a gun marched up to the chef, Mehmet.

"Immigration Office. I want to see your papers. Now." In chef's whites, there was nowhere to keep documents, so Mehmet went to the cloakroom to fetch his coat. The whole time, two gunmen kept their weapons trained on him. His documents, of course, were legal and valid, which seemed to disappoint the officer. He repeated the process with everyone, glaring at each man as if he'd caught them stowing away in the back of a truck, rather than trying to serve starters for a party of nine.

Tunçay put it down to paranoia at first, but as the seconds ticked by, he knew the officer was taking twice as long to scrutinise his own work permit and passport as he had the others. He lifted his head to stare at Tunçay. Everyone watched and all four guns pointed his way.

"How do you pronounce this?" he barked, stabbing his finger

at Tunçay's name.

"Toon-Jai Kilij."

"Where are you from?"

"Turkey. Sinop, on the Black Sea coast."

"Why are you here?"

"To travel. To learn Spanish and ... everything."

"When are you going home?"

"About two in the morning, I expect. We have to clean the restaurant after ..."

"I mean when are you going back to Turkey?"

"I ... I don't know yet. I have plans to travel and ..."

The man threw the papers onto the stainless steel counter in Tunçay's direction and walked back through the swing doors. Holstering their weapons, the police officers followed, casting aggressive looks at anyone who raised their eyes. Tunçay collected his documents with shaking hands and looked up at Mehmet. Normally, Mehmet took the title of the scariest person in Tunçay's life, but today he'd been reduced to the status of victim by a different kind of bully.

"What was that all about?"

Mehmet scooped the corn fritters back into the deep fryer. "I guess the old bastard didn't get laid last night and needed to release some testosterone. Put some more yoghurt on that plate then get these to table six. They've been waiting almost twenty minutes."

The last comment contained a reproach, as if Tunçay had neglected his duties in favour of being hassled by Immigration.

He dressed the starter and once the golden patties were reheated, balanced the plates and bounced his way back into the restaurant, already rehearsing his apology in Spanish. The police had gone, but Deniz the barman signalled his concern with a pointed look at the staff table. Two men sat with Bulent, both wearing dark suits. This was not unusual, as Bulent had various business activities in addition to the restaurant. But the shifty glance he gave Tunçay was certainly out of the ordinary.

Dumping the plates with a distracted 'Sorry', Tunçay leant over the bar to Deniz.

"Who are they?"

"No idea. Don't think Bulent knows them either, but I'd say his balls are in his throat. The ugly one with the wrinkles sat down, took Bulent's cigarette out of his mouth and stubbed it out on the tablecloth. So I'm pretty sure they're not from the church."

"Which is the ugly one with the wrinkles? They both look the same to me."

A bell rang from the kitchen and Tunçay hurried away.

At nine-fifteen, Tunçay took a break. Desserts had been served, so there would be a lull until coffee. He held up his Marlboros and indicated the door, just to let Mehmet know, and pushed out into the night air. The alleyway stank of urine and bins and greasy fumes pumped out by extractor fans. Still, it was quiet. He lit a cigarette and inhaled, holding his breath for just a second, before blowing a thin jet of smoke towards the sky. Tonight, he wouldn't need to perform the elaborate post-cigarette ritual of teeth-cleaning and breath-freshening. Luz wouldn't be back until Sunday. It was bad enough in a normal week, not knowing when he'd see her again, but a guaranteed absence of four days made him miserable.

She was missing him too, if the several text messages per day were any indication. And he certainly liked the idea of her new underwear. Sunday. A day off, no work on Monday, and his sexy Spanish chica all wrapped up in black lace and ribbons. Time just didn't move fast enough.

The door opened behind him. Tunçay didn't bother to turn around, knowing Deniz would be hoping to scrounge yet another smoke.

"Ah, there you are."

Tunçay had never seen Bulent in the kitchen, leave alone outside the back door. He dropped his cigarette and straightened up.

"Sorry, just taking a quick break."

"It's fine. It's all calm in there. No need to rush back. Look, have one of these." He offered his silver case, which Tunçay had often mocked behind his back as affected.

"OK, thanks."

"Turkish tobacco. I never smoke anything else." Bulent flicked open a Zippo and the whiff of lighter fuel made Tunçay feel momentarily nostalgic.

They smoked in silence, Tunçay struggling to think of something cool and Mehmet-like to say. Bulent sighed and ran a hand over his thick black hair.

"I'm sorry about this, Tunçay, but I have to let you go. The police were here tonight looking for illegal immigrants."

"What? I'm legal. You know that."

"Yes, I know that. The problem is you have made some enemies somewhere. I don't know who, but these are powerful people. Powerful enough to get the police to search my premises every single night until you leave my employ and return to Turkey."

Tunçay couldn't see Bulent's expression, but his tone was serious and regretful. This was not a joke.

"Bulent, you have the authority to fire me. It's your restaurant. But to make me go back to Turkey? That's insane."

"On the contrary, young man. That would be the wisest course of action I can think of. You're right to say my authority extends no further than this restaurant. But my concern for you goes far beyond that. I can't make you leave this country. If I could, I would. Because if you go of your own accord or if you go under my persuasion, at least you'll go alive."

The Bond baddie routine was too much. Tunçay burst into snorts of laughter.

"I'll get my stuff. You know, you could have planted a can of chick peas in my jacket or something. Most bosses would have the balls to tell me I'm not good enough instead of inventing all this bullshit. What about my wages?"

Bulent caught him by the shoulder. "If you ever had any respect for me, please take this seriously. You're a good man, and a good waiter, in fact. I'm sorry to lose you. Mehmet will be mad as hell. You're the best we have, according to him. Here. This is five hundred euros, which should cover your wages this week and buy you a last-minute flight to Turkey. Go, Tunçay. And I wish you happiness, health and peace."

He walked away, down the alley to the main street and around the corner.

Five hundred euros. He stared at the pool of light where Bulent had disappeared. A compliment from Mehmet. Something he'd always craved but now it came too late. Two silhouettes crossed the light and stopped, turning to look at him. A tiny glow indicated a cigarette. Powerful enemies.

Confusion gave way to temper which caved in to fear. Tunçay stormed into the kitchen, grabbed his jacket and walked out through the restaurant, aware of Mehmet's silent gaze.

He didn't say goodbye.

# Chapter 24

Brilliant sunshine enriched the terracotta and sand of roofs and spires, the sky offered a royal blue mantle as backdrop and a cacophony of horns echoed up from the streets below. With a towel wrapped around his waist, Adrian stepped onto the hotel balcony to appreciate the view. The air smelt fresh yet autumnal, containing a reminder. All is ripe and the time is now. He stretched, wincing slightly as his back muscles complained. By heaving Beatrice's suitcase out of Jaime's flat and up the steps to the hotel, he was sure he'd done himself a mischief. One day, he would have to teach her the art of capsule packing. The phone rang.

"Hello?"

"It's me. Matthew and I are on our way down to breakfast. Are you fit?"

"Not quite."

"Well, hurry up and put a skirt on. Change of plan. Full briefing before I leave, which is in half an hour."

"Give me five minutes. See you down there."

Adrian shook his head as he replaced the receiver. Her joy and relief at their arrival had soon reverted to the usual bossy exasperation. He smiled and began the task of choosing a suitable ensemble for the day. An ensemble which was unlikely to include a skirt.

Beatrice looked like hell. The black bruising around both eye sockets, the swelling of her eyelids and the little bits of crusted blood between the stitches wrenched at Adrian's heart. He almost wished someone had done it on purpose so he could hate them. But he, like Matthew, was familiar with her lack of coordination. She seemed unbothered, launching straight into her instructions as Adrian sat down.

"I don't think there's anything to be gained from visiting the vineyard again. You should go to Alava Exports. Take a look at another link in the chain."

Adrian shrugged. "Fine with me. Could you pass the coffee?"

Beatrice shoved the cafetière towards him.

"Ana has made you an appointment for eleven. You're posing as British wine buyers, which won't be too onerous a challenge, I shouldn't think. Ask as many questions as you can about Alava Exports' numbers. See if you can get a feel of which vineyards have a sizeable share of the market and how much. Don't limit yourselves to Viura or even to white. Be enthusiastic, be professional and be curious. But also be bland. The proprietor, Angel Rosado, is Aguirre's son-in-law, so will be alert to any excessive interest in the Castelo de Aguirre output. Matthew, you have toast crumbs on your tie."

Matthew looked down. "That's not toast. That's croissant."

Adrian poured coffee into the white china cup. "The white Rioja story is big news, though, so it won't hurt to make some general enquiries."

"He's right. If we ignored the phenomenon, it might look even more suspicious," said Matthew, picking pastry flakes from his woollen tie.

Beatrice twisted her wrist to see her watch. "Yes, yes. What I mean is, just try to be subtle. Underplay everything. We're treading on thin ground. I have to go or I'll be late. Be careful. Far more careful than ... you have ever been."

Adrian appreciated her sensitive circumnavigation of

unpleasant memories. "We will. What time will you be back?"

"No idea. Ana's meeting someone from the *Denominación de Origen* Control Board at midday and I'm lunching with that wine writer at two, so if all goes smoothly, we'll be back by tea-time. Now I really must go. First I have to call James, then Ana's picking me up."

Matthew frowned. "Picking you up with what? Not that ghastly moped?"

Beatrice stood and hitched her handbag up her shoulder. "It's not a moped, it's a Vespa. And that's strictly for city driving. Jaime lent us his car to get us to San Sebastian, remember? We're going to have a whale of a time. It's a soft top BMW, you know, in powder blue."

Matthew stirred his coffee. "Hardly *Easy Rider.*"

Adrian smoothed over Matthew's obvious snipe by deliberately misunderstanding the reference. "No, it'll be more like *Thelma and Louise* meets *Sideways*. Have fun and be careful."

"It's you two I'm worried about. Remember what I said. Be subtle. See you both later." She kissed Adrian's cheek and patted his shoulder. "Look after him." She reached down to embrace Matthew. "Stay out of trouble, you old coot."

With that, she hurried away towards the lifts.

Matthew yawned. "She does worry so. Now, shall we have another croissant and discuss how to approach this?"

Adrian reached for the coffee with a grin. He'd got it all worked out.


The huge warehouse appeared unwelcoming and unattractive after the charms of the city. Two olive trees in faux cut-off wine bottles either side of a large welcome mat indicated the visitors' entrance. Adrian and Matthew slammed the taxi doors shut and, with a wave, the driver sped off in the direction they had come.

"I had no idea you spoke Spanish so well," said Adrian, as they surveyed the building. "How come you let Ana and Jaime do all the ordering last night?"

"Sometimes it's better not to let on how much you understand. You never know when it will come in handy."

"They *are* on our side, Matthew. You don't like Jaime much, do you?"

Matthew squinted at him. "I'm yet to form an opinion. Anyway, Spanish isn't all that different to Italian. You should hear my Greek. I sound like a native, if I do say so myself. Shall we go in? Only I find this sun awfully strong."

Adrian accepted the change of subject and began walking across the dusty drive. "I think I'd like Greece. You should invite me sometime."

"And Greece is guaranteed to like you. Are we all set?"

The receptionist behind the marble desk greeted them with a perky smile as they walked into the air-conditioned foyer.

"Bailey and Son, Fine Wines? You are right on time. Mister Rosado will be with you in one moment. Why don't you take a seat? Help yourself to coffee. Could I take your business cards to add you to our system?"

Adrian tensed, but nodded. He held out a hand to a blinking Matthew. "You did bring our business cards, Dad?"

Matthew ran a hand across his hair. He patted his pockets, looked in his briefcase and sighed. "I must have left them at the hotel. I'm sorry, young lady. Perhaps my son could let you have our details by fax later this afternoon."

Adrian rolled his eyes and addressed the receptionist. "I'll email you by close of play today. And your name is ...?"

While Adrian entered the details into his phone, he noticed two things. Matthew pulling out a handkerchief and taking off his glasses to polish them, and the lift numbers descending. Professor Bailey was wholly in character and ready to make his debut performance. The lift doors opened.

"Good morning. My name is Angel Rosado. You must be Mr Bailey, and son."

He extended his hand and gave his full attention to Matthew, so Adrian took the opportunity to pass judgement. Slicked-back hair and so cleanly shaven he looked waxed, Angel Rosado was polished to perfection. The cut of his suit and fall of the navy fabric made Adrian covetous. His lemon shirt would not favour many complexions, but on Rosado, it heightened the tan and emphasised the whiteness of his teeth. Black brogues, a Tissot watch and a fresh trace of Miller Harris; this man dressed the part.

Greetings exchanged with Matthew, he turned to Adrian. "Mr Bailey Junior, I presume?" His hazel eyes met Adrian's, the mildly patronising smile evaporated and they shook hands. Cool, professional and firm. And Adrian knew.

# Chapter 25

At eleven minutes past eight, Luz opened her eyes and made a decision. Having debated her promise to stay for the weekend versus her will to get on with her own life, Maria Luz Dolores Santiago de Aguirre opted for the latter. She would take a train back to Burgos, the first available, and tonight, she'd go to the restaurant, wearing her new dress. She couldn't wait to see Tunçay's face. Especially when she told him what she was wearing underneath.

Her duties performed, her family appeased, she had no reason to stay. If possible, she'd avoid her father, say goodbye to Marisol and leave a present for Basajaun. She badly wanted to kiss him and hold him and tell him she'd see him soon, but his heartbreaking sobs whenever she left were more than she could take today. Just the thought of his tearful blue eyes made her bite her lip.

After a hot shower, she dressed in her old jeans, a navy jumper and black leather biker boots, an outfit to infuriate her father. She searched for her phone to check train times but couldn't find it anywhere. The Castelo clock chimed nine. Hunger gnawed at her, as she'd only picked at the buffet yesterday. Maybe breakfast first, then trains.

He would be in the vineyards. He always toured the estate after breakfast. She would be in the breakfast room, nibbling on toast and fruits, reading a magazine. Basajaun, if the gods were smiling, would be at school. The usual sounds floated through the house; sounds which, as a child, she had spent hours decoding. In the car park stood her mother's Jaguar, but the Range Rover was missing. She smiled. As she expected. Time to venture downstairs, grab some food and say goodbye.

Her smile contracted as she opened the door to the breakfast room. Her father's head rose above the newspaper.

"Good morning, Luz. I wondered when you would finally rise. Please sit down. While your mother is out, we need to talk. Coffee?"

With a nod, Luz sank into the chair nearest the door. He filled a cup and pushed it towards her with a cold blank stare. She knew that look. He was about to read the riot act. She'd ditched Vasconcellos as soon as she was able and retreated to her room, claiming a headache. Instead, she'd checked her emails, made some calls and sent more than one lewd message to Tunçay. In her father's eyes, she'd neglected her duties.

Luz added sugar to her cup and stirred. She didn't care. He could rant and rail and threaten till his arteries burst, but she was no longer under his control. And poor old Simon Vasconcellos could find some other strategic alliance. She slugged the espresso in one. All she had to do was listen, appear contrite and she could get out of there. Back to Burgos.

"You are not going back to Burgos."

She jumped, dropping her cup into the saucer.

"Your studies are officially at an end. I called the university this morning to withdraw you from the course. You are to stay here with us, until your mother and I resolve this situation."

Luz shook her head and opened her mouth but he had no intention of stopping.

"What? You expected to go back? How could you be so selfish? How long did you think you could continue like this? Our agreement was for five years. Five years in which you would study law. Which, incidentally, already put you at risk. You would have been twenty-seven by the time you completed that course, which is very late to marry. I should never have allowed myself to be persuaded. In retrospect, I was the stupid one." He stood up and faced the window.

Luz blinked. "You cannot stop me going back. I have to finish ..."

"I think I made myself clear. It is finished. Your mother has gone to collect your things and finalise any outstanding arrangements. And how did you propose to deal with your current situation? I doubt you even thought that far. I still can't comprehend this. My own daughter. To bring such shame on me, on all of us. How, Luz? How could you be so stupid?"

The caffeine buzzed around Luz's bloodstream, making her feel simultaneously wide-awake and as if she were dreaming. She kept her eyes on her father's thunderous face as she grasped the enormity of his words. He wanted to destroy her. He wanted her back on her leash. She'd always known her freedom would be short-lived, but to snatch it away already? He was right about one thing. How could she be so stupid? Her mother had unlocked the information and handed her father the key. By trusting Marisol, she'd signed her own jail sentence. She should have known. They weren't parents. Parents were people who loved you and wanted nothing more than your happiness. These two were debt-collectors.

Luz got to her feet. Shaky and cold, she made a decision. Her voice was steady.

"I am leaving now. I am going to Burgos and I will complete my studies. All I ever asked from you was financial support. But I can live without it. I can get a job and pay my own way. I am twenty-three years old and an adult. I thank you for all you have done, but I need to be my own person. You no longer tell me what to do."

Aguirre exhaled a humourless laugh. "Go to your room, Luz. You aren't going anywhere but I want you out of my sight. Tomorrow, you will travel with your mother to Bilbao, to see a specialist. We have to deal with this situation as soon as possible."

He took out his mobile and began composing a message.

Luz exploded. "Situation!? What is the matter with you? I'm in love. That's all! I'm not mentally ill, you arrogant, domineering arsehole! I know there's no future in this and to be honest, wouldn't even want to bring him into such a family. He deserves better. But you will not manipulate my relationships! Not now, not in the future. I am never going to marry some chinless prick because it suits your empire-building. I will NOT be bullied by you. Not anymore. And if you try to interfere ..."

The door opened. The housekeeper peered in.

"*Señor*? Your car is ready."

"Good. Please make sure my daughter eats something. She's becoming hysterical."

Without another word, he left the room. The housekeeper took one look at Luz's face and followed.

The urge to smash something, to hurl something, to wreck his hermetically sealed world bubbled up like lava. She clenched her chunky little espresso cup in her hand and aimed for the window. Beyond the glass stretched acres of vineyard, a quivering palette of Van Gogh colours which represented so much more than grapes. She replaced the cup on the saucer. Smashing his window would be an irrelevance to him, merely proof that his daughter was undisciplined and immature. If she really wanted to cut the cords, to remove his influence, she would have to go much further.

The housekeeper was still lurking outside the door when Luz emerged.

"I'm sorry, Carmina, I'm just not hungry. In fact, I still have a headache. Maybe it's best if I have a lie-down in my room. Papí's right. I got a bit over-emotional. Do you know where he's gone?"

The relief on the housekeeper's face showed she'd been prepared for a battle.

"The airport. He's going to Madrid. He has meetings today

and a television interview this evening. We're all going to watch it." She gave a proud smile. "He wants you to stay indoors till your mother gets home. I think a rest will do you good. Do you need anything?"

Luz shook her head, tempted to check the front door to see if the old bastard had locked it, but she stuck to her role and made her way quietly up the stairs. Halfway up she stopped.

"Carmina, which channel is the interview?"

"EITB. Eight-thirty."

"Great, thanks. So he'll be back very late this evening?"

"No, he's not coming back until tomorrow. He has a room in the Hotel Ritz, you know, all paid for by the TV station. He's a real VIP, your father!"

Luz smiled and continued upstairs. Father in Madrid, mother in Burgos. Looked like she had some time on her hands.

Her laptop was missing from the bedside table, where she'd left it last night. And the reason she couldn't find her mobile phone? Because it wasn't there. Luz called it twice from the phone in her room, before she realised it was probably ringing in the depths of Marisol's handbag. Her mother had made it as difficult as possible to contact Tunçay. A clean break, she would say, you'll soon forget all about him. Why hadn't she memorised his number instead of relying on technology for everything? She clenched her fists in frustration and glared at herself in the mirror.

A clean break. Yes. She inhaled deeply. Tunçay wasn't expecting her till Sunday. He might send her a text or two, but by this evening she'd be with him in person. The priority now was the break.

Clean, yet irreparable. She rummaged in her bag for her pencil case. Inside were two memory sticks, one partly filled with notes on EU Food Safety legislation for her second-year project. Notes she could afford to lose.

Back in the corridor, she checked the window. The only

vehicles now on the forecourt belonged to the caterers, the event managers and a cleaning company. The household was busy restoring order after the party. If nothing had changed, the spare key to her father's office would be in his bedside table. A creature of habit, he never expected an enemy within.

Her parents' room was pristine. The bed had been made, the rugs vacuumed and the flowers changed. Just as if they lived in a hotel. Luz padded up to the Emperor-size bed and opened the cabinet on her father's side. Several business books, an English-Spanish dictionary and a tube of haemorrhoid cream. In the drawer lay a notebook, various ballpoint pens, a box of tissues and a set of keys. She released her breath. The only obstacle now would be the password. He always used the same system, so all she needed to know was how to spell it.

At 11.22, Luz plugged her memory stick into the USB port and saved the Alava Export files, copies of relevant emails, Excel accounting sheets and personnel details of people who never appeared on the payroll. She printed everything out and also emailed them to herself as attachments. Then she flicked through her handbag until she found a card. She checked the email with great care and sent everything to that address. She wrote nothing in the body text. Even if she had no opportunity to explain, any half-decent brain could work it out. And this recipient's brain was above average. Luz cleared the browser history, shut down the machine and rifled through the drawers for cash. She collected 270 Euro. Then she listened at the door for over two minutes. Satisfied, she locked the office, returned the keys, slipped back to her room and prepared to leave. She shook her head with a smile. KLAUDYNA. How could *he* be so stupid?

She emptied her room of everything valuable. The dress, the heels and the diamonds she took. Sentimental gifts from her mother and sisters she left behind. Unless she could sell it, it was of no use to her. The suitcase, stuffed with clothes, jewellery, watches, paintings and shoes, weighed three times as much as when she'd arrived. She heaved it down the stairs, stopping frequently to check no one was around, and dragged it through to the library, the least used room in the house. This place had been her sanctuary as a teenager. When she tired of her sisters' incessant bickering or her father's continual booming oratory, she would nestle into the wing-backed chairs and let the words fly her far away. And should she hear approaching feet, there was always the door into the old conservatory, where she could hide behind any number of potted plants or rattan sofas. The newer, larger 'Wintergarden' had taken prominence so that now, only she and the staff ever used this largely forgotten room.

It was approaching one o'clock. She had to get out before her mother returned. Luz watched the activity in the courtyard and chose her moment. A cleaner threw the last bags of rubbish into his two-seater pickup and wiped his hands on his overalls. Luz broke cover and approached, checking the name on his badge. Raoul.

"Hi, my name is Luz Aguirre. You've done a great job."

His eyes widened and he spoke with a Mexican accent. "You're welcome. I hope the little boy had a good party."

"He loved every minute. Raoul, can I ask you where you're going now?"

The guy's eyes widened further. "Where I'm going? To the dump and back to the depot in Vitoria. Is there something else you want me to do before I go?"

"Yes, kind of. You see, I ordered a taxi, but it's late. I need to get into the city fast. Could you take me? I'll pay you, of course."

His head retreated into his neck, like a tortoise. "In this van? *Señora*, it's dirty and it stinks."

Luz jumped into the passenger side of the cab. He wasn't wrong. It was filthy and it stank of rotten oranges.

"Seventy Euro to take me to the city. See that door over

there? Behind it is a big suitcase. Can you bring it over here and throw it in the back?"

"*Señora* ..."

"If you don't argue and just do it, I'll make that a hundred. Come on, Raoul, I'll be sure to tell my father how kind you've been."

# Chapter 26

Just hearing the phone ring soothed Beatrice. She sat on the windowsill of her hotel bedroom, staring out at the streets of Vitoria, but visualised James's office: cream and white upholstery, light wood and James himself, legs crossed, quietly exuding peace.

"James Curran?"

"Beatrice Stubbs, checking in."

"Beatrice, hello, you're punctual. Thank you for calling."

"Thank you for finding the time. I realise we should have discussed ongoing treatment before I left. It just all happened in a bit of a rush. But I am taking my mood stabilisers and feel mostly OK."

"Good. The medication is essential. Think of it as the scaffolding around your treatment. Whereas the building work within rests on the foundations of CBT. Are you still maintaining your journal? Or mood diary, if you prefer to call it that?"

"Not really. I mean, I'm keeping an eye on the swings, and just avoided a trough, but I'm not recording my emotional state on a daily basis. I'm not really in any sort of routine, you see."

"I appreciate that. But when you do find yourself with a couple of minutes to spare, such as just before you go to sleep, that would be an ideal opportunity to make a note of your mental outlook. Now, two things you've said already raise questions in my mind, but first, can we return to the points I asked you to consider yesterday?"

"Yes. I have thought about them." No matter how much effort she put into James's exercises, Beatrice always felt as if she were back at college, busking a tutorial on a subject she had but skimmed. "You asked the aim of this sabbatical. It wasn't my choice, to be truthful. Hamilton refused my resignation and this was his idea of a compromise. Three months away, then if I still wanted to resign, he would accept it. So in a nutshell, the aim is to find out if I really want to retire."

"If you're not sure if you want to retire, why did you resign?"

"Because I don't feel up to the job. I have endangered other officers and civilians, either through omission or incompetence, so shouldn't be in the position of Detective Inspector."

James remained silent for several seconds, prompting Beatrice to second-guess him.

"So your next question will be 'Why are you getting involved in another investigation when you don't feel competent?' Well, that wasn't actually by choice either. A friend of a friend needed some help, so I sort of rolled up my sleeves and pitched in."

"Interesting. So the situation in which you find yourself is not of your choosing. You are powerless, at the mercy of stronger wills. Forgive me if I find that image difficult to reconcile with the Beatrice Stubbs I know as my client."

In the seconds that elapsed before Beatrice composed a reply, she recognised a pattern so familiar she almost bored herself. A flare of anger at James's disrespectful tone. Infuriation at his lack of faith in her. A moment of considering a different therapist. Acknowledgement that he only ever treated her with less respect when she did likewise. Acceptance of a failed smokescreen. She was dissembling, refusing to face reality and James knew it.

"As for Matthew and Hamilton, the former joined me last night. He and Adrian have come to lend their wine expertise. And Hamilton would sack me if he knew. He's already told me not to interfere."

"Do I need to help you unpack the implications of this, or can we move on?"

"Let's move on. Fourth question. What was it again?"

"No, I'd prefer you to elaborate on two phrases you used at the beginning of this call: 'mostly OK', and 'avoided a trough'. Are they connected?"

"I suppose. I've spotted some features of rapid cycling – giddy bouts of elation, followed by over-sensitivity, an urge to recall maudlin memories, increased sexual attraction, and a tendency to extrapolate. You know, seeing one incident as reflective of what is rotten with the whole world."

"So the avoidance of a trough took what form exactly?"

"Umm ... calling you. Seeing Matthew. An awareness of other kinds of coping strategies. I feel much more grounded. Back on track sort of thing."

"Beatrice, I apologise in advance for what I am about to ask. But I believe I would be negligent in not doing so. I would like you to take five minutes to think. I will stay on the line, but I don't want you to speak until I tell you the five minutes are up. During those five minutes, you are going to think back to the months leading up to your attempted suicide. I want you to tell me the patterns you and I uncovered together, how one state of mind can give way to another and the impact those months had on you. Please be honest."

Before he'd finished speaking, the domino-effect began. Her heart rate increased, self-pity provoked tears, fear invoked resentment and her mind flailed around for a means of escape. She switched the phone to speaker, placed it on the table and put her hands over her eyes, blocking out images of what came afterwards and focusing on what went before. The circles, the cycles. Bad days, bad weeks, followed by a determination to help herself. New starts, excessive optimism, inappropriate behaviour. Three steps forward, four back. And the gradual comprehension that it would never get better. She could never evade this black demon permanently. She would fight this battle for the rest of her life unless she withdrew from the fray. The clarity and the horror of that moment emptied her of all emotion and her practical side took over. Make it painless, with as little mess as possible, organise the paperwork and get it over with.

James's voice came from the mobile. "That's five minutes. Beatrice, I know that was a deeply unpleasant exercise and I am sorry for the pain I caused. When revisiting those months, what did you observe?"

Beatrice blew her nose and picked up the phone. "Patterns. I keep thinking I can fix it myself. I keep thinking I will get better and be able to manage on my own again. But I never really managed. Not always when I was hyper and definitely not when I was depressed."

"Can we take that one step further? When you're in a cycle, regardless of direction, how would you assess your decision-making capabilities?"

"You're talking present tense, James."

"And you're talking past. Are these patterns obsolete or something we still need to address?"

Beatrice stared at the palm of her hand. Lines she'd been born with, scars she'd added.

"No, not obsolete. I recognise paranoia and a certain amount of displacement activity."

"So we come to question four. Is your current choice of activity furthering the aim of your sabbatical, or are you seeking any opportunity to evade serious thought?"

"Why would I call you if I was trying to avoid thinking? Every single time we speak, I end up crying. I'm doing my best, but it bloody hurts, James. You bloody hurt. I know this is good for me and it is working, I suppose, but it's not easy."

"Beatrice, I think we can consider a milestone passed. Normally when you rail against the painful nature of therapy, you cite your age as a reason for sympathy. This time, you have taken responsibility. A story, if you have time. A child born with a malformed right foot. The big toe was missing and therefore so was his balance. Nevertheless, the child learnt to walk, even run, after a fashion. But he expended so much effort, compensating for that missing digit. Medicine advanced and surgeons were able to fit him with a prosthetic toe. Once he got used to it, he could do twice as much with half the energy. It didn't take him long to adapt, as he was only nine. You have a few years on him, but I'd like to think of what you and I do together as an artificial, but not uncomfortable, improvement to your life. Perhaps we can re-imagine Cognitive Behavioural Therapy as Curran's Big Toe."

Still sniffing, Beatrice expelled an involuntary laugh. "Do you use that line on all your clients?"

"No, because none is so determined to repel my assistance as you. Now, could we look at some exercises for you to try and arrange a follow-up session as soon as convenient?"

James. Inextricably linked with tears and tissues. Maybe he was right. It was simply a question of balance.

# Chapter 27

By the time Ana found a parking spot in the shadow of the Good Shepherd Cathedral, Beatrice was feeling guilty. Absorbed in dissecting her own behaviour, the usual reaction to a conversation with James, she'd made barely any conversation with Ana on the journey. But her companion seemed similarly introspective.

They made directly for the seafront and wandered the wide promenade. Both gazed at the spread of sand and sea as the bay curved away. To her left rose a hill, covered in greenery, and to her right another, featuring some impressive architecture. Natural sentinels protecting the harbour. On the beach, dogs hared after one another, chased balls, splashed in the surf and barked. At the base of the sea wall, two bare-chested men worked on a sand-sculpture, their shirts spread out to catch coins from above.

"What do you say to a snack and something to drink first?" Beatrice asked her transformed companion.

Ana's hair was pulled into a tight bun and her face heavily made-up. She wore a dove-grey trouser suit with flat brogues. Her earrings were silver studs. She checked her watch, still radiating unease and tension.

"You've got plenty of time, so go ahead. I'll give it a miss. I'm going to take the scenic route to the meeting, just in case."

"You don't still think we're being followed? I thought you were convinced we were clear?"

"I am convinced. Those how-to-shake-a-tail tricks were very useful. Specially as I'm not even sure it was a tail. But you can't be too careful. Now listen, I don't think this guy's likely to give me more than an hour of his time, so I might come and lurk in the background while you talk to the Lopez woman. I won't join you, just be there to keep an eye." She opened her briefcase and withdrew a pair of black-rimmed glasses. In a second, her soft, luminous beauty developed an incisive edge, a metallic precision which could both intimidate and impress.

"I didn't know you wore specs," commented Beatrice.

"I don't. They're just glass. I used them a fair bit when I was younger, in an attempt to make people take me seriously. I thought glasses and DMs gave me an attitude."

"Did it work?"

"Sometimes." She applied plum lipstick, using her phone screen to check her reflection. "But it turns out blokes *do* make passes at girls with glasses. That's when the Doctor Martens came in handy. How do I look?"

"Somewhere between a columnist for the Financial Times and Belle du Jour. Either way, quite scary."

Ana laughed, straightened up and scanned the street. People crossed back and forth to the beach; holidaymakers, old folk, workers taking a break from the office. Children's laughter carried over the sound of the traffic. Beatrice felt a pull towards the water. Perhaps an ice-cream and a wander along the sand. She had ages yet.

Ana picked up the briefcase. "Right, I'm off. Wish me luck. And I'll join you at Casa Mimo just after two. You're sure you know where to go?"

"Lord, you do fuss. Yes. I wrote everything down. The directions, your instructions, the line of questioning we chose and even your recommendations as to what to eat. I'll be fine. Good luck, be careful and don't talk to strangers."

Ana grinned and strode off in the direction of the river. Beatrice crossed the road and spent forty minutes just people-watching. Unfortunately, people-watching, no matter how joyful, tended to put her into a fug. An affliction she couldn't shake, like being unable to appreciate a film because you can see through the flimsy sets. All these smiling faces, scampering paws, affectionate gestures and abandoned squeals of delight simply reminded Beatrice of how this moment was soon to be nothing more than a memory. One to be recalled, perhaps, beside a hospital bed, in a snowy graveyard or on a therapist's couch. She got up and headed for the old town.

On arrival at the restaurant, the waiter showed her to a reserved table near the back. It was a relief to sit down. Traipsing around the city streets was illuminating but tough on the feet. Not only that, but as preparation for a pretentious lunch, she had denied herself any kind of pre-lunch snack. In short, she was hot, tired, aching, hungry, and in a foul mood. Now, rather than enjoying her food, she could fully expect to be patronised and belittled by a snotty bloody wine expert. She ordered a glass of Rueda and a bottle of mineral water and hoped the bread basket would accompany her aperitif.

"Ms Stubbs?"

Beatrice looked up with a start. The tall woman standing at her table wore a black dress beneath a leather jacket, sunglasses and her short hair was dyed a shocking pink. She held out a hand. "I'm Isabella Lopez. Nice to meet you."

Beatrice got to her feet and recovered herself. "Nice to meet you too, Ms Lopez. Please, have a seat."

The dramatic creature smiled and hooked her handbag over the back of the chair. She sat, eased off her jacket and removed her sunglasses. "What happened to your face? You look more like a cage fighter than a journalist."

"At my age, that's actually a compliment. I fell up some stairs and hit my nose."

Isabella shrugged. "It happens. Are you waiting for long?"

The waiter arrived with the drinks. "Just long enough to

order a drink. What would you like?" She remembered she was talking to one of the most famous wine experts in the region. "Or maybe we should decide what to eat first, so as not to queer your palate?"

"Queer my palate?" An enormous smile spread across her face. With a laugh, she reached behind her and pulled a gold-covered notebook from her bag. "I have to write that down. What a fantastic expression!" She looked up at the waiter, still beaming. "*Una cerveza, por favor.*"

"Beer? Oh, I assumed you'd want wine. I suppose that's a stereotypical assumption you get all the time?"

"I do want wine. But I'm thirsty and beer is the best solution to that problem. Now, you must call me Isabella and can I call you Beatrice? You see, Beatrice, people do make assumptions about wine writers, but why wouldn't they? There is probably more bullshit written about wine than any other subject I can think of. Except modern art, perhaps. So it's no surprise that people expect us to be pretentious, precious snobs. Many of us are. But there are a few, and I include myself in this particular circle, who write about wine because we love the subject. It is a fascinating field which you must already know, as a food writer. Which magazine do you write for?"

Stunned by the torrent of rapid-fire information, it took Beatrice several seconds to remember the persona in which Ana had drilled her. "*Contemporary Cuisine.* We're independent, offering unbiased advice on quality food and drink all over Europe. We feature a different country each issue, which is why I'm researching Spain. It seemed to make sense to start in San Sebastian, and talk to the experts first." Her speech sounded rehearsed and unnatural, but Isabella was nodding.

"Of course. Where else? Have you tried any of the Michelin three stars yet? Who have you seen so far? Arzak? Andoni? Berasategui? When did you arrive?"

"Two hours ago."

That dazzling smile stretched across her face again as she

thanked the waiter for her beer. He seemed pleasantly surprised by the reactions to his presence. Isabella took a long draught and smacked her lips.

"So I am the first? Perfect. You could not have made a better start, Beatrice, and you will be glad. I'll order for us today, and make a list of where else you should go and in which order. We're going to start with the equivalent of fish and chips. Today, you'll eat everyday Spanish food. Nothing special. But wait till you see how special it is. Then you will try an asador, visit one of the vineyards, perhaps one of the less famous ... what are you drinking?"

Without waiting for an answer, she picked up the glass and sniffed. "Good choice. In fact, visiting the Rueda region is a great idea. They're overshadowed by the Rioja country, especially in recent years, which seems unfair as one of the finest wines ..."

"Yes, I wanted to ask you about that. You see, Isabella, the truth is, I'm more of an expert on food than wine. Which is why I chose to start my research with you. But should we order first, do you think? I've not eaten since breakfast."

Isabella obviously heard the urgency in Beatrice's tone and hailed the waiter. She rattled off instructions, underlined by emphatic hand gestures, and the waiter obediently wrote it all down. Then, finally, he brought the bread.

Beatrice grabbed a small roll and began buttering. Isabella studied her.

"Not too much bread. We have a feast ahead of us so you must not ... what was it ... queer your palate." She laughed and picked up the wine list. "This is fun for me, you know. To introduce someone to our food, our wine, our culture. You said you had a question."

Beatrice swallowed but before she could speak, Isabella flowed on.

"About Rueda being overshadowed, wasn't it? Mmm, that wasn't always the case. Their whites, verdejo and sauvignon blanc, have always outsold those of Rioja and built a well-deserved reputation for excellent wines. White Rioja used to be made the same way as red, in small barrels, aged for years. But then came stainless steel tanks, allowing vinification at low temperatures. Very successful move. Clean, fresh and the fruit to the fore. But the New World Chardonnays did it better. So white Rioja, once again, became the bridesmaid."

The roll had gone and Beatrice eyed the basket. At the risk of getting told off, she sneaked a slice of dark brown seeded stuff and asked another question to distract her pink-haired companion. "So what changed? How come it's the trendy wine of the moment?"

"Yes, that's what we all want to know. The truth is actually quite simple. It's a combination of a new style, smart marketing and one influential vineyard. That bread is very heavy so I suggest you only have one piece. So first, the new style. Rather than ageing it in barrels, the wine was only fermented in oak. That's what gives the stamp of old school quality to a modern wine. This showed the grape, mostly Viura, at its best. Mixed with Malvasia, the new white Rioja has a depth and richness, orange along with lemon, giving it a subtle edge over the competition. Ah ha! *Mejillones tigres!*"

An hour and a half later, Beatrice could take no more. Her appetite satiated, her notebook was as full as her stomach. She wrote the wine information in the front and details of the meal in the back, so she could gloat to Matthew later. She was also a little tipsy, in a pleasantly soft, at-ease-with-the-world sort of way. Isabella was still talking. In fact, she hadn't stopped.

"... lost his grape grower's card as a result. So no, it would be impossible to sell your wine as anything but what it is. As I said, the Control Board performs strict tests, both sensory and in the lab. If the wine is sub-standard, it cannot be called Rioja."

Beatrice saw Ana slip through the front door and take up position on a bar stool. She took a slow scan of the interior but did not acknowledge Beatrice.

"So if the wine is confirmed as meriting the Rioja label, what happens next?"

"That's up to the vineyard. They choose a winemaker and distributor and decide how much they want to sell and where. Do you want dessert?"

"Yes, but possibly sometime next week. Thank you for choosing such an amazing selection. I can honestly say that was one of the finest eating experiences I've ever had."

Isabella flashed her teeth once again. "Just a normal everyday snack for us, you know."

"So if a wine went out into the world labelled as Rioja, but actually contained something else, that could only happen at the bottling stage?"

Isabella's smile faded to be replaced by a look of puzzlement. "It's highly unlikely. I mean, the wine that leaves the vineyard has been quality tested and bears the guaranteed official label. Each bottle carries a stamp and a number. Impossible to fake."

Beatrice nodded and made a note. Nothing was impossible to fake, but Isabella Lopez had certainly narrowed the scope. At only one point in the chain could another wine find its way into a Rioja bottle. After paying the surprisingly reasonable bill, Beatrice stood and offered her hand.

"Isabella, you have been more help than I can say. Thank you so much."

Isabella brushed her hand away, took her by the shoulders and kissed her on both cheeks. "It was a pleasure to meet you. Thank you for lunch. Please don't forget to send me a copy of the article. I would love to read it. Have a wonderful stay!"

"I won't forget." This lying lark got easier the more you did it. Not even a blush this time. Isabella turned and waved as she left, with one last burst of that incredible smile.

Ana came over and slid into the recently vacated seat. "You've lipstick on your cheek."

Beatrice dabbed at her face with a napkin. "How was your meeting?"

Ana shrugged. "Not sure. False. He was so cagey and asked more questions than he answered. I've a feeling he'd been primed. How was yours?"

"Excellent. I had seafood, the most astonishing ham, black pudding, little fishy kebabs and green beans with garlic, those Gernika peppers and three different kinds of wine to match."

Ana started to laugh. "So while you were sampling the local goodies and getting drunk, did you make any progress at all?"

Beatrice shoved her notebook at Ana. "All in there. I am a consummate professional."

Ana pushed it back. "And a lush. Come on, you can tell me all about it in the car. It'll keep you awake. Do you need the bathroom before we go?"

"You treat me like a wayward child. Actually, I think I do. Back in a minute."

# Chapter 28

On the outskirts of Miranda de Ebro, the Range Rover turned into a newly developed housing estate, passed a group of gardeners planting shrubs along the roadside and rumbled into the underground car park. A navy Maserati was the only other vehicle in the extensive space.

Marisol checked her make-up and switched her phone to silent. She took the lift to the penthouse floor, as instructed. The door to the show apartment stood wide open and she heard classical music – Ravel's *Bolero* – playing within. Floor-to-ceiling windows filled the space with light. She locked the door behind her, turned and saw what lay on the dining table. A black cat mask, complete with ears and whiskers.

A note read: *Put this on. Take everything else off. Except your heels.*

She sighed. Masks. Of course. They'd done striptease, handcuffs, feathers and ice cubes; next on the list had to be masks. Why was the sexual experimentation phase always so predictable? Next, it would be role play or body paint.

She did as she was told, taking the time to fold her clothes carefully on the chair. She glanced out the window. Even if there had been anyone around, no one could see this far up. She walked to the bedroom, her skin responding with goosebumps to the cool breeze.

The room was empty. She stepped further in, to check the ensuite. Two hands caught her hips and pulled her backwards. She gasped as his lips met her neck and she felt the hairs on his chest tickle her back. The momentary adrenalin of fear transformed into an erotic charge of need, causing her breath to grow ragged. His hands moved up, cupping her breasts and pinching her nipples as she arched back against him. He kicked the door closed and turned her to face the full-length mirror.

A second electric charge shot through her. Most of his body was hidden by hers, but he towered head and shoulders above her, even with her heels. Dirty blond hair spiked over the devil mask disguising his eyes, but his mouth was visible, lips parted as he breathed into her ear. His hands moved with the grace and confidence of a master conductor, coaxing an orchestra of moans, sighs and whispers.

"Oh yes. Oh God, yes. Please, Simon, please."

Towels. Marisol smiled as she stepped dripping from the shower. He'd even remembered to bring towels this time. The man who thought of everything. Her body glowed as if in agreement. She dried her hair and reapplied her make-up, her mind already on the next phase of the day. When she returned to the living room, he had set the table for a picnic, with bread, cheeses, grapes, tapenade and red wine. He'd even brought a tablecloth and glasses. Still naked, he offered her a grape.

"Let me get dressed first."

"No, I want to watch you eat as you are."

Marisol put on her underwear. "If I do that, we both know what will happen and I'll have to shower all over again. How late is it?"

"Only two. We have plenty of time, and I know so many ways we could spend it." He gave her what he obviously thought was a smouldering look.

"Not today. Too much to do." She zipped up her dress and checked her phone. No messages. Relieved, she sat at the table and cut herself a slice of Manchego.

Vasconcellos watched her, his pretty features swelling towards petulance. "I arranged it so there would be no viewings today. We can stay here as long as we want. Anyway, I thought he was in Madrid until tomorrow?"

"He is. But I have other problems to deal with." She plucked a handful of grapes. "One of which is your ex-future wife."

"My ex-future wife – how does that work?"

Marisol took a sip of wine and studied the naked man opposite. Beautiful, needy, reasonably smart, potentially powerful, eager to please, very rich and a seriously good fuck. It was a damn shame to let him go. He'd have made an ideal son-in-law. Still, dropping him as Luz's intended meant their affair could continue for longer. Every cloud …

"You're not going to marry Luz. And before you ask, no, it's nothing to do with us. The stupid little bitch is pregnant."

"No way! Luz, pregnant? Jesus. I didn't even know she was seeing someone."

Marisol decided to limit what to share. This kind of gossip was practically hard currency and Vasconcellos would not always be in her thrall. It would be tough to find her daughter any kind of match now, but if the full details emerged, it might be impossible.

"You aren't the only one. Arturo and I only found out by accident." She sighed. "It's inconvenient, but not a major problem. This morning I took her out of university, tomorrow I'll take her to my specialist in Bilbao. All over and forgotten by Monday. Then I'll start the search for someone older, equally wealthy but slightly more desperate than Vitoria's most eligible bachelor, Simon Vasconcellos. On the bright side, you and I can continue to enjoy each other's company for a while longer."

His concerned expression softened into a smile, then his focus shifted and he gazed at the tapenade. Marisol waited a few moments, aware the vague expression on his face could mean anything from digestion to deep thought. Finally, she got bored, wiped her fingers with a napkin and emptied her glass. If that got no reaction, she'd glance at her watch. He reacted. Turning to her with an intense blaze in his eyes, he reached for her hand.

"So your daughter loves another man. For my part, I wish her joy. Why don't you find the baby's father and see if he wants to marry Luz? Life is short and hard enough, so when an opportunity for joy arises, she should take it. Maybe they'll be happy together. Happier than she and I could have ever been. What kind of marriage is it when two people swear vows to one another while both are in love with someone else? Yes, that's right, in love with someone else. I love you. So this is not just a chance for Luz, it's one for the two of us. Leave Aguirre and be with me, Marisol. I can give you everything you want and more. I've never in my life loved a woman the way I love you. I don't think I ever will. This is *our* chance."

Marisol removed her hand from his grasp and reached up to stroke his face. Their eyes locked and she saw the conviction, the determination, the foolish belief that love could conquer all.

"Simon, you wonderful, sexy, thoughtful man. Listen to me. You will thank me for the rest of your life for saying this. No. I will not leave Arturo. For someone born as beautiful and privileged as you, it is impossible to understand how some of us need to constantly shore up our positions, strengthen our defences, prepare for enemies where we least expect, and ceaselessly work to maintain our status. I will never leave my husband for you and there will come a day when you'll be grateful I did not. Nor will Luz marry whichever opportunistic little shit rutted her. She will do the correct thing and stand by the family. Because she is an Aguirre. And so am I."

Vasconcellos stared at her without moving. Marisol stood up, brushed off any crumbs and picked up her phone.

"Thank you for this afternoon. You're amazing. And if you're free next Thursday, I'm attending a charity lunch in Santander. We could book a hotel and experiment a little. I was wondering … would you like to see me in my uniform?"

His eyes changed. She walked round the table and kissed

him deeply. He kissed her back with such craven desire her resolve weakened and she found herself reaching beneath the tablecloth.

Ten minutes later, the Range Rover emerged from the underground car park, nosed out of the driveway and turned in the direction of Vitoria. The driver didn't look back.

# Chapter 29

"Oi. I need to get a coffee. Do you want to come in or stay here?"

Beatrice jolted awake and stared out at the car park. "Where are we?"

"About twenty minutes from Vitoria, but I'm flagging and I need some caffeine. You can carry on snoring if you like." Ana unclipped her seatbelt and reached in the back for her briefcase.

"Yes," Beatrice yawned. "That might be best. I'll sit here and keep an eye on things."

Ana withdrew her purse and shoved the briefcase behind her. She shook her head with a laugh. "Three glasses? You're a cheap date. Back in five minutes."

Her hair loose, the jacket discarded, Ana looked much more like herself as she strode towards the entrance of the motorway services. Beatrice adjusted her position. Creaky and sticky and rather puffed-up, she needed a shower and a lie-down under cool sheets. She dragged her bag from the back seat and checked her phone. 16.24. No messages. So presumably Matthew and Adrian had nothing to report. Well, she'd be back at the hotel by five-ish and a full report could be delivered over dinner.

A car reversed towards her from the space opposite. Ana had a habit of parking backwards, presumably to make a quick getaway. That girl really would make an excellent police officer.

Beatrice watched a family return to their Opel Corsa, the children's whiny bleating audible. Too much sugar, bound to be. Why, she wondered, did motorway service stations all over the world attract exactly the same kind of washed-out, tetchy, badly dressed people?

Still, the journey had been worth it. Not just for that lunch, but her and Ana's information tallied exactly. The fraud could not be perpetrated from the Aguirre estate. The Control Board lived up to their name and even Aguirre's influence would not be sufficient to endanger the name of Rioja. So it had to be Alava Exports. Filling an approved bottle with another product made no sense, so they must be making fake labels for sub-standard bottles. Unless something else happened between approval and bottling. Did Aguirre bottle his own produce, or was that part of the Alava Exports service?

Beatrice picked up her phone again to call Matthew. 16.36. The phone rang before she could press a button, startling her into losing her grip. She snatched it up again. Ana's name on the display. Probably enquiring as to drinks preferences.

"Yes? Five minutes, I think you said. You've been in there almost quarter of an hour."

No response. Beatrice checked the screen. Full signal. She pressed the phone to her ear, peering at the main building.

"Ana? Are you all right? Ana? Ana!"

The phone went dead. Beatrice scrabbled to release her seatbelt while redialling Ana's mobile. It rang and rang and went to answer phone. She looked around the car park again. The bland, boring functional car park had shifted into something with shadows, anonymous vehicles and hidden eyes. She got out of the car and went round to the driver's seat. The keys dangled from the ignition. She yanked them out, locked the car and hurried towards the service station, pressing Ana's number again. No reply.

The automatic doors opened, releasing a smell of chips, coffee and fried onions. Beatrice glanced at the café, her eyes scanning and dismissing each dark-haired female in seconds. The shop, full of shouting teenagers; and the toilets, with the inevitable queue of false smiles and sharp eyes were all devoid of anyone resembling Ana. Beatrice hurried back to the main concourse and took several deep breaths, while her eyes assessed each passer-by.

Stop panicking. Ana pressed the number by mistake. Her phone is at the bottom of her bag and she can't hear it. Beatrice shook her head at her own reasoning. Ana keeps her phone in her pocket and answers on the first ring like a gunslinger. Her briefcase is still in the car. Which is locked. Where right now, Ana will be standing outside, frowning and holding a take-away coffee.

Beatrice ducked her way through a crowd of German bikers, but even before approaching the car, she knew Ana wasn't there. She tried the phone again. Her head, muddled and hot, nagged at her. She'd forgotten something. Her eyes lifted and she saw it. A large black SUV had stopped directly in front of their vehicle, blocking their exit. Two thickset men, the driver and front-seat passenger, turned to stare. The tinted back windows gave nothing away. Blood pumped in Beatrice's ears as she unlocked the car and sat in the driver's seat. A pointless exercise, as she couldn't drive. Her phone beeped. Beatrice jumped.

The message was from Ana. Short and to the point.

GO! NOW!

A car horn made her start once again. A Dutch motorhome behind the SUV expressed its impatience. The black vehicle drove forward, at about two kilometres per hour.

Beatrice looked back at the screen. Go? Where? Her hand reached for the keys. Everything was wrong. The handbrake, the gearstick, the seatbelt and there was no bloody clutch pedal. An automatic. It was insane. She rarely drove in Britain, so to take a strange car onto the wrong side of Spanish roads whilst in a blind panic was pure madness. The SUV turned left at the end of the row. They'd be back, she knew it. In as much time as it took to circle the car park. Beatrice started the car, as Matthew's voice surfaced from a half-forgotten memory.

"It's like riding a bike. You never really forget how to do it. Now, check your mirrors and indicate. Off we go."

Pulling out smoothly, without a single kangaroo jump, Beatrice followed the path the SUV had taken. Her right foot tensed, ready to brake as she cruised out of the service station and back onto the motorway. She checked all three mirrors every ten seconds as her thoughts followed a circular swooping pattern. She'd left Ana. On Ana's instructions. But was it really Ana? She should turn back. No sign of the SUV. She should call the police. The traffic was terrifying. She'd left Ana. Still no sign of that car. Or those men. She kept going. She'd left Ana. The speedometer bobbed around just below ninety kph. She stayed in the slow lane, a healthy distance behind a large truck. A blue motorway sign informed her that she was thirteen kilometres from Vitoria. A flash of lights made her check her rear-view mirror. The SUV was speeding down the fast lane, intimidating vehicles in its path by flashing its lights and driving dangerously close.

Beatrice fought back her panic and tried to think logically. The men were after her, that much was clear. The question was, why? Did they mean to crank up the level of threat so she and Ana would do as they were told and leave well alone? Or was their intention to get rid of them more permanently, in the same way as Tiago? The tension in her shoulders developed into a pain as she saw the vehicle indicate and slow to pull in behind her. They couldn't run her off the road, not with this many witnesses. They would have to get her onto some deserted back road, which was not going to happen. One alternative was to follow her into the city and grab her as she left the car. In which case, she would have to stop somewhere public. The grille filled her rear window. They were so close she couldn't even see the occupants. If she were to brake ... and that gave her an idea.

On entering the centre of Vitoria, Beatrice had no idea which way to go. The traffic stopped at a set of lights, with Beatrice on the inside lane and her pursuers directly behind. Her hands were still shaking. She looked for the handle to unwind the window. It was missing. Her heart skipped until she realised this was a slightly more modern car than Matthew's ancient VW Golf. She depressed the button and the glass rolled down. An elderly man with a stick stood waiting for his Scottie dog to finish sniffing a tree trunk.

"*Scusi? Pardon! Donde é policia?* Emergency! *Policia?*"

The old chap and his dog both looked up. The dog lost interest instantly, but the man continued to stare. Beatrice checked the lights. Still red. The old man. Still staring. With great deliberation, he pointed up the street to her right. He raised one finger and indicated a left with the opposite hand. The lights changed and an immediate blast of a horn sounded from behind. The old man continued, by holding up two fingers and indicating left again. He gave the thumbs-up just as she jerked forward from the impact of the SUV driving into her bumper. The old man's jaw fell open.

She accelerated and swung into the right turn without indicating. Her eyes flicked to the mirror. She'd gained a second or two but they were approaching fast. She indicated right and slowed, watching for a gap in the traffic. She had to time it perfectly. A motorbike zoomed past, leaving a space before the taxi behind and Beatrice wrenched the wheel to the left. The taxi blared its horn and the driver stopped to gesticulate out of the window, blocking the path of the SUV. Second left. She hoped to God the old sod had given her the correct directions. The cacophony of horns and voices receded as she followed the curve and she checked the mirror to see how much time she had. Here they were.

She sped past the first left, conscious of the black shape growing in her peripheral vision, and screeched into the next street. He was right. She recognised the street up ahead and the forbidding façade of the police station. She checked the mirror to be sure. Much too close. She took a deep breath, mentally apologised to Jaime and slammed both feet to the floor. Her judgement may have been accurate and the BMW might have halted in time. She'd never know. Because three tons of Mercedes-Benz driving at forty-three kilometres per hour rammed her straight into the wall of the police station.

The airbag released, her seatbelt squashed her ribcage and all the air seemed to leave her lungs. A second of stillness. Then a metallic squeal pierced the silence and a reverse pull bounced her forwards. She banged her face on the steering wheel, bringing tears and blood to her eyes. Bile filled her mouth as she heard shouting. The shattered windscreen collapsed inwards. Her door opened and a man said something she didn't understand. The SUV pulled past, gunned its engines and screeched off down a side street. A fresh volley of yells went up and a siren began wailing. The man released Beatrice's seatbelt and eased her out of the car. She got to her feet, bloodied and shaking, and threw up all over her shoes.

As she submitted to an examination by the police medic, she prepared herself to face Detective Milandro. She knew how he was likely to perceive this situation. The interfering Brit crashes back into his life. Literally. She had to convince him to take her seriously. This was not simply an overactive imagination and excess of alcohol. She needed backup.

To her surprise, the medic didn't breathalyse her. Instead, he squirted some clear gel onto a dressing and handed it to her.

"Keep this against your lip. The bleeding has stopped but this will prevent the swelling. You will have some more bruises. I leave you now. Good luck."

"Thank you," Beatrice mumbled. Once the door closed behind him, Beatrice reached for her handbag. What a mess. Tiny cubes of glass and brick dust lay in every fold of the leather, along with a dark greasy stain all over the bottom. Still, she should be grateful someone had thought to rescue it from the car. Keeping one hand pressed to her mouth, she carried the bag over to the bin, wincing at the pains in her chest and neck. She shook off the debris then dug around inside till she found what she was looking for. Her mobile and a business card. Jaime Rodriguez, Editor of *El Periódico*. With a glance at the door, she dialled.

"Rodriguez? *Diga.*"

"Hello, Jaime. This is Beatrice."

"Beatrice? Beatrice! How's your road trip going?"

His friendly voice offered a sense of sanctuary which swelled Beatrice's throat so that she was unable to speak for several seconds.

"Beatrice? What's the matter?"

She took a deep breath, which hurt. "Jaime, I'm afraid I have some bad news. Ana has disappeared. And I crashed your car." She blurted out the story, managing to stay professional as she delivered the facts.

Jaime didn't waste time. "Where are you now?"

"In Vitoria, at the police station. Could you come? Only I think I might need moral support."

"Give me ten minutes."

Twenty minutes later, she was still sitting alone in the medical room. The shock gradually subsided and all she had to focus on was worry and pain. She called Ana's number every five minutes, but the phone was switched off. Flicking through her address book, her thumb hovered over James, but she decided against. Too complicated. Instead she selected Adrian.

He answered on the first ring. "Aha! You're back. How did it go?"

"Oh Adrian. I am glad to hear your voice. Are you at the hotel? Is Matthew with you?"

"He's just popped to the loo. We're still in Ribera. I'm on the terrace sampling a rosé and admiring the scenery. We've got lots to tell you. When will you be back?"

Beatrice hesitated. "How far are you from Alava Exports?"

"Around a fifteen-minute walk. We were about to pay the bill here and call for a taxi back to Vitoria. We've had a marvellous afternoon. The tour was tremendous, let me tell you. And Spanish men! I had no idea! I fell in love three times today and at least two of these waiters meet with my approval."

"Adrian, listen to me, this is important. Is there any way you can safely observe the Alava Exports site without being seen? I need you to watch for any activity over the next couple of hours."

"Umm, I think so. What sort of activity are we looking for?"

"Anything. The company should be finished for the day, so I want to know what goes on after hours. But Adrian ..."

"I know. Keep out of sight, do nothing, say nothing and just report back to you later."

"I'd be most grateful. Shall we meet back at the hotel at eight?"

"See you then. Oh, how was your day?"

"Horrible. I lost Ana and I crashed the car into a police station."

His gasp was genuine. "Oh my God! Are you all right?"

"Yes, yes. Right now I'm more worried about Ana than anything else."

"We'll come back and help."

"No, you stay where you are. The police are already searching for her. The best thing you can do is keep an eye on that place. But please do it safely. Give my love to Matthew and tell him not to worry. Everything is under control."

"OK, I will. Beatrice?"

"Yes?"

"Do take care."

Detective Milandro opened the door and studied Beatrice.

"How are you feeling?"

Beatrice knew from experience the Spanish detective's bland expression was not to be trusted, but his concern seemed real. "Shaken and bruised but mostly worried. Is there any news of Ana?"

"Not yet. But I have dispatched three teams to search. Your associate is here, from the newspaper."

"Oh thank God."

"I'd like to hear the story again and this time my boss wants to sit in. Would you come with me to an interview room?"

Beatrice got to her feet and took the dressing from her lip. "Of course. Detective, I know I'm a horn in your side, but I assure you I really am trying to do the right thing."

His eyes narrowed, but his lips twitched in an impression of a smile.

"This interview, can Jaime come too?"

Milandro looked at her, his expression neutral. "Are you sure that's what you want?"

She nodded. He shrugged and led the way down the corridor.

Jaime seemed most dreadfully upset. Of course. Seeing the remains of his beloved vehicle being winched out of the wall must have come as a bit of a shock. While Milandro went to find his senior officer, Jaime's hands shook and he looked as if he was about to cry.

"Jaime, I am so sorry about your car. Believe me, if there was any other way ..."

He gathered himself. "I don't care about the BMW. It's insured. And there are more important things to worry about. I'm just thankful you weren't too badly hurt. Even so, you don't look good. You're so pale. Maybe you should eat something? Perhaps some chocolate? Did you take a coffee?"

"I'm fine, really. I know my face is a train wreck, but it's not as bad as it looks. I'm just so worried about Ana. These men, if it is the same bunch, made some very unpleasant threats last time.

They frightened Ana badly. They told her to leave Vitoria."

"But she didn't." Jaime shook his head, a tired gesture.

"No, of course not. She's a journalist. She could no more leave a story alone than a child could a scab. We found out a great deal today and I'm convinced we've been looking in the wrong direction. It's not Aguirre himself who's been ..."

The door opened. Milandro hesitated, his face dark and uncertain. Beatrice's instinct screamed bad news.

"Ana?" she asked, her voice constrained.

He shook his head. "Nothing yet. Patrols have combed the site and alerted traffic police. A general bulletin has gone out across the region. But I just had news from the coroner which makes me very concerned for her welfare. The body of Miguel Saez surfaced this morning, in the lake near Garaio. The coroner suspects foul play. The cause of death was drowning, but his body had been mutilated before he died."

Beatrice clutched her hands together, her eyes fixed on the detective. "Facially mutilated?"

Milandro's eyes narrowed. "Yes. His mouth was slit to his ears."

Jaime retched and staggered out of the door. Beatrice went to press her hands to her mouth but reconsidered. Instead she squeezed her eyes shut. Tiago's nose, Miguel's mouth. And Ana?

She looked up at the detective, unable to voice her plea. He understood.

"We'll find her, Detective Inspector Stubbs. But I think you might need to tell me everything."

# Chapter 30

Tunçay's chest constricted and his dry eyes opened. Shafts of sunlight penetrating the curtains showed the layers of smoke shifting around the bedsit. The connection between the smell of an ashtray and the taste in his mouth repulsed him. He never smoked in his room. It was disgusting. He was disgusting.

He swung his heavy legs off the bed and sat up. Fully clothed, stinking of cigarettes and with a hangover pounding at the door, he needed water. As he got to his feet, his lungs protested and a coughing fit forced him back onto the mattress. It also welcomed in his hangover. He stumbled to the tiny kitchenette and drank three glasses of water in succession, hands shaking and eyes watering. There had to be a word for what his stomach was doing but he couldn't describe it, not in any language.

He opened all the windows, squinting into the low sunshine, and breathed some fresh air, which set off his cough once more. With an extreme effort not to vomit, he collected the empty bottles and full ashtray and tipped them into the bin. The stench of stale lager brought acidic bile to his throat and he stood with his head over the sink for several minutes. The wave receded.

Chill air freshened the room but turned his skin clammy. Tunçay grabbed his washbag and towel and unlocked the door, putting his faith in the power of hot, steamy water.

Forty minutes later, he was dressed, the flat was cleaner and he'd begun throwing his few belongings into his suitcase. Some decisions were clear. He would not leave Luz. But he would leave Burgos. Where to go was another question. Not Turkey. He wasn't ready yet. Maybe he could get a job in Logroño and see Luz at weekends. He needed to talk to her before doing anything, but her phone went unanswered and his texts received no reply.

Maybe he should wait till Sunday and talk to her, face to face. He finished packing and ate a noodle soup. If he didn't show up at the restaurant and kept his head down, he could take action in the next couple of weeks. No need to be hasty. After all, his rent was paid till the end of October. His phone rang.

Mehmet. Tunçay let it ring. What could he say? He was washing up his bowl when he heard something outside the front door. He stopped and held his breath. Nothing. He tiptoed across and looked through the spyhole. Nothing. He unlocked the door and slowly inched it open. On the doormat lay a magazine. Tunçay scanned the corridor. No one. He bent to pick it up. A tourist brochure: *Turkey. A Country for all Tastes.*

He left it there, locked the door and called Mehmet.


"I told you on the phone, the only place I will take you is the airport. You have to get on a plane and leave. Don't piss me about, Tunçay. Listen, I've never seen Bulent scared of anything or anyone before. But this is serious. On the next flight if I have to drag you myself."

"Mehmet, you're not listening. I can't leave yet. I can't. I need to talk to someone and I can't get her on the phone. I need to tell her what's happening. I have to stay until at least Sunday."

Mehmet didn't reply. Tunçay recognised that expression of focusing on the task in hand. Whether it was mincing mutton, shelling fava beans or driving through midday traffic, Mehmet maintained his concentration.

"This is your university girl, I suppose? Yes, don't look shocked, everyone knows. Deniz's mother-in-law lives on the ground floor of your building so nothing is secret. By the way, she doesn't mind the overnight guest but disapproves of you feeding the cat. Listen to me, Tunçay. For your girlfriend, this is a student romance, a bit of exotic while away from home, forgotten as soon as real life starts. You'll get more loyalty from the cat. As soon as she goes back to her family, you'll be dropped. Don't risk yourself for a spoilt little princess. And remember, these people could make life very awkward for Bulent, for Deniz, for all of us."

Tunçay stayed silent until the traffic began moving. "All right, I will go back to Turkey. At least for a while, till things settle down. But I must go to her *residencia* first. If I can't leave her a message, I won't go."

Mehmet cleared his throat with something like a curse, but indicated towards the university. "Which way?"

"Left. Calle Francisco de Vitoria. Do you have a pen?"

Confident, loud laughter filled the open spaces as Tunçay moved through the lunchtime crowds of students. Everyone seemed to have a purpose and a right to be there. He reached into his jacket for the letter and reminded himself of his own purpose. Luz's block was quieter than the main concourse, but he still felt an interloper as he stood in the doorway. Where were the mailboxes? Exposed and nervous, he turned away. He'd call. He'd send an email. What difference did a hand-written letter make? He knew exactly what difference it would make. He turned back.

The *residencia* door was wedged open. Perhaps the mailboxes were inside. Once over the threshold, he made a rapid decision. He would go to her room. Maybe leave the letter with her flatmate. He'd come this far, Mehmet was waiting, he had to act and get out. Her voice seemed to echo in his head, giving him directions as he ran up the stairs. He'd gone two doors past her room before he realised and retraced his steps, breathing heavily.

When he'd recovered his calm, which took longer than his breath, he knocked. The girl who opened the door looked familiar. Rita. The room-mate, the giggling customer, the uninteresting background to so many photographs featuring his beautiful Luz. Her expression was haughty, but curious.

"What do you want?"

His speech facility stalled. "I came because of Luz." He indicated the envelope.

Rita dropped her head onto her shoulder and her smile fell short of her eyes. "Ha! I thought as much. Well, Lovely Lashes, you missed the boat. She's gone. Her mother came this morning to collect her stuff. She's dropped out, the silly cow."

Tunçay shook his head. "She's resigned from her course? Are you sure?"

"Sure enough to advertise for a new room-mate. Hey, don't look like that. Not the end of the world. It's a shame for me, and for you too, I guess."

"Well, I ..."

"It's even a shame for the legal profession. She'd have made a great lawyer. But we should be happy for her. She's found her Mr Right. Her mother said they announced their engagement this weekend and they're getting married next summer. Wouldn't suit me, I want a career before I have kids, but her family's pretty traditional. And her fiancé is something impressive in the building trade, apparently. Good luck to her, I say."

"Of course. Good luck to her. I should go. I'm sorry to trouble you."

"No trouble. Hope to see you again sometime. Maybe we'll pop into your restaurant one of these days, just to say hello. I'm Rita. What's your name?"

"My name is Mehmet. Thanks very much. Goodbye."

He stood in the hallway of the *residencia*, his head resting against the wall and his feelings draining out all over the industrial-grade carpet. He told himself this was a good thing. It would make him lighter. He would go home with less baggage.

# Chapter 31

She told them everything. Almost. As soon as Jaime returned, pale-faced and sweaty, Salgado-the-slug joined them, with a brusque nod of acknowledgement towards Beatrice. He ignored Jaime completely. Beatrice gave a full account of what she knew and the source of her information. The only item she omitted was the current location of Matthew and Adrian. Without telling an outright lie, she inferred they were on their way back to the city, having visited a vineyard. She wasn't even sure why.

Salgado required frequent translations, eyeing Beatrice with great suspicion, as if she were using expressions such as 'trawl', 'scupper' and 'shaking like a leaf' deliberately to annoy him. After Milandro produced Ana's briefcase, she handed over all the documents. It felt like a second betrayal of her friend, but she had no choice. Salgado asked a question in Spanish. While they spoke in low, guttural tones, Beatrice got chance to talk to Jaime.

"I'm so glad you're here. I feel absolutely out of my depth. Are you feeling all right?"

Jaime shrugged. "I think I now understand the meaning of the phrase 'worried sick.'"

"Me too. I can't bear to think of those men ..."

"Beatrice, the one thing we must remember is that Ana is one of the most resourceful women I know. If anyone can find a way out of this, she will."

The senior officer shoved back his chair and with a dismissive nod in their direction, made for the door. Milandro stood, rasping the backs of his fingers against his chin.

"Detective Inspector Stubbs, I'll take you back to your hotel. Under the circumstances, I think you should stay there for the time being. I checked just now and your friends have not yet returned. Where are they?"

Beatrice didn't hesitate. "Sightseeing, probably. They'll be back for dinner, I'm sure."

Milandro's expression, blank as a snake's, still managed to convey disbelief. His black eyes bore into hers as if trying to force out the truth. Jaime broke the spell.

"I'll stay with her until her friends return, Detective. I hate to think of her being alone."

Milandro's eyes flicked away and back again, reminding her of a gecko, silent, patient and predatory.

"If you wish."

The drive to the hotel seemed interminable, as the streets were clogged with rush-hour traffic. Beatrice fidgeted in the back seat beside Jaime, who stared silently out of the window. She would bet he was wishing he'd never met Beatrice Stubbs. Milandro sat in the passenger seat, making occasional comments to the police driver. Beatrice tried to concentrate on how to proceed, but her mind replayed the expressions of the men she'd interrupted at Ana's apartment. Ugly, cruel and without compassion. She placed her hands to her temples and tried to massage away her imagination.

The hotel doorman was obviously intrigued by Beatrice's arrival in a police vehicle. He looked at them with a kind of amused respect until he saw her face.

Milandro got out. "I'll escort you upstairs, if you don't mind. I'd like to check your room." It was more of an imperative than a request. Beatrice didn't argue.

They crossed the marble floor towards the lifts, Jaime on one side, Milandro on the other, making her feel more like a convict than ever.

Once inside, she watched as the detective checked the room with methodical precision, trying window locks, testing the phone, searching the wardrobe, shining a torch under the bed. Jaime's phone rang, but he cut the chirpy tune dead. The atmosphere reminded Beatrice of the days when she had worked in witness protection. Long hours of tension, bored but alert, tuned to every irregularity. It wore her out. The sound of Milandro tearing back the shower curtain made her jump. Jaime reached across to squeeze her shoulder in a gesture of reassurance but unfortunately chose the left one, still tender from being wrenched by the seatbelt. Then someone knocked at the door.

Milandro emerged from the bathroom and Beatrice tensed as she saw him withdraw his gun. He jerked a thumb at her, indicating she should go into the bathroom. Despite her resentment at being bossed around, she knew how frustrating it could be when someone disobeyed orders. It was his investigation now and she was nothing more than a witness. She went into the bathroom but left the door ajar. She watched through the gap between hinges as Jaime retreated to stand with his back against the wall. Milandro checked the spyhole.

He holstered his gun and looked in Beatrice's direction with a half smile. "It seems we can call off the missing person search. She's here." He unlocked the door.

"Oh thank God!" Beatrice hurried across the room only to stop in her tracks. The dark-haired woman in the doorway with a suitcase and a basket of flowers wasn't Ana. It was Luz Aguirre.

Luz obviously had not expected Beatrice to have company. She looked from one to the other and her face showed more alarm than surprise. "I'm sorry. I didn't want to disturb you. But I have something for you." Her expression was hunted.

Beatrice made a decision. Whatever the reason for this

unexpected visit, she needed privacy.

"Hello Luz. You're not disturbing me. Just a case of mistaken identity, that's all. Detective, I've made the same error. This is an acquaintance of mine, and she certainly does look like Ana, I agree. However, the search is still on. Gentlemen, thank you both for your support. I'm tremendously grateful. But now I think I'd prefer to have some time to chat to my friend and have a restorative gin and tonic." She pointed towards the phone. "Can we agree to maintain mobile contact and update each other when we have news?"

Milandro moved to stand in front of her, his eyes like anthracite. "If you hear anything, I want to know. And I mean anything."

She nodded, forcing herself to maintain eye contact until he glanced at Luz.

Jaime reached forward to kiss her cheeks. "Call me. Anytime. I just need to know you're OK." He squeezed her upper arms as if to underline his sincerity and stared deeply into her eyes.

Beatrice tried to smile but instantly felt her lip crack and begin to bleed. She reached into her sleeve for a tissue. "I'll be in touch. And really, thank you both so much for your help. Detective, please find her. Remember what I said about *El Papagaio*. It must be worth a try."

Luz stood back and allowed them to pass. They watched the two men turn the corner of the corridor, Jaime's mobile audible once again. Poor man. The life of a newspaper editor was hectic enough without dropping everything to hold Beatrice's hand. She turned to her visitor.

"Please, come in."

"Thank you." Luz handed her the flowers. "These are for you. Did you have another accident?"

"Yes, this time with the wall of the police station. Seems I attract trouble."

Luz closed the door behind her. "No, I don't think you attract trouble. I think you go looking for it."

# Chapter 32

Take, take, take.

He only had himself to blame. Women were, always had been, his Achilles heel. They sucked him dry, took everything he had and came back for more. Aguirre stared out at the dense cloud, a black roiling fungal formation, a reflection of his emotional state. The private jet sank lower and Aguirre clipped his seatbelt before the attendant could advise him to do so. Even when it was in his own interests, Aguirre hated being told what to do.

Klaudyna made no move to return to her seat, still curled up on the buttermilk leather sofa, her back to him, sighing, sniffing and cuddling a sheepskin rug. Silly bitch. She'd dragged it out for almost half an hour now. Whining and griping all the way to the airport about their aborted evening, complaining and sniping for most of the flight about his family and then she'd crossed the line, suggesting Marisol had him by the *cojones*. His outburst sent both attendants into hiding and a fountain of tears flowed down that pretty Polish nose.

Enough.

The flight touched down at 17.20. Ten minutes late. The pilot blamed the weather. Like a gentleman, Aguirre gestured for Klaudyna to go down the aisle first. She threw a reproachful glance at him which evoked nothing more than repulsion. Puffy eyes, red nose and her messy make-up showed how far the mask had slipped. His decision was the right one and part of him already yearned for the next adventure.

They crossed the tarmac, where two vehicles waited. His Range Rover and a taxi. He motioned to his driver to collect his suitcase and signalled to the cabbie.

"Get that bag and take this lady where she wants to go. Charge it to my account."

"*Si, Señor Aguirre.*"

Klaudyna's eyes blazed. "You're putting me in a taxi? I don't believe it. Arturo, for God's sake, what is the matter with you!"

"It is finished between us, Klaudyna. I wish I could say I'm sorry, but in fact, that would be a lie. You are greedy and demanding and have no sense of your place. It's my own fault for indulging you. This is where it stops. Goodbye, Klaudyna, and good luck."

He got into the passenger seat of the Range Rover and closed the door, shutting out the infernal noise. For a foreigner, she knew some shocking words.

On the approach to the Castelo, Aguirre's phone rang for the seventh time. He checked the display and once again rejected the call. He switched the phone to silent and looked up at the house. Marisol waited in the doorway.

"Arturo, you mustn't blame Carmina. She's terrified and already had a panic attack this afternoon. It's not her fault and after all she's a housekeeper, not a security guard. Luz went out via the library and must have hitched a lift with the caterers. Carmina thought she was in her room. She had no idea she was missing until she took her lunch upstairs. Inez is on her way to Burgos and Paz is calling all her friends in Vitoria. I've been thinking. When we find her, we must send her away for a while. Maybe abroad."

Aguirre swept past her and strode up the stairs. "Arturo de Aguirre is well known for his refusal to tolerate incompetence. We never use those caterers again and ensure no one else in our acquaintance does. Carmina is due for early retirement and I will choose the next housekeeper. I think we'll have a man this time, someone discreet. More like a butler. As for your daughter, I'll decide how to handle this."

Marisol made to follow him but he held up a hand.

"If you don't mind, I'd like to see for myself."

He knew as soon as he opened the office door. The chair was halfway across the room, as if its last occupant had rushed out in a hurry. Aguirre would never leave the room that way. This place was his haven, his War Office, his operational HQ and each time he left, he prepared it with great respect for the next visitor – himself.

Years ago, he'd allowed the girls to join him for short periods. Pie charts, bar graphs and colourful graphics demonstrated their father's power and reach. Yet their tiny attention spans and irritating prattle had disappointed and bored him. Now, no one, not even Marisol, came in here. When the time was right, he would introduce Basajaun to his domain. When the time was right.

The machines booted up and he examined his work station. The mouse lay to the right of the mat. All the loose change in the drawer had gone. Two greasy smudges marred the screen. His browser history showed no activity, but recent items viewed included payrolls from the last two years, personnel data, private profit and loss accounts, and carefully worded letters to significant influential people in the wine trade.

He pressed his fingers to his temples.

Power.

His daughters were not beautiful or particularly intelligent, but they took after their father in one way. They understood power. Find it, ally with it, marry it, use it and hang onto it at all costs. Luz was powerless in the face of her father's strength and influence. So she had stolen herself some bargaining chips. She found a way into his private affairs and armed herself for battle. In a way, he admired her gall. He would win, of that there was no doubt, but Luz could be proud of herself. She put up a fight.

The battle would be one-sided, however. And the sooner it were over, the better for everyone. He reached for his phone and cursed when he saw fifteen missed calls. Eleven from Klaudyna, two from Tomas, one from Paz and the one he'd been waiting for.

He pressed voicemail and allowed his eyes to rest on a photograph. The three girls, apparent angels in soft-focus, surrounded their mother, who held a week-old Basajaun in a crocheted blanket. In the background, the Castelo de Aguirre vineyards. A family, finally complete. He would protect them with his life.

In his ear, laconic growls and adenoidal shrills told him Tomas and Paz had nothing to report. Luz was still AWOL. The final message, timed at 18.08, began to play.

*"Arturo? Call me back. We have a problem. Might be nothing, but if it's something, it's potentially ruinous. Your daughter, Luz, just turned up at Hotel Valencia. She came to see Stubbs, the British detective. Said she wanted to give her something. Call me as soon as you get this and please, for the love of God, tell me Luz knows nothing."*

# Chapter 33

The sun streamed through the open windows as Luz parked her suitcase beside a chair.

"Don't worry. I haven't come to stay. I'm going back to university this evening. But I wanted to talk to you before I go."

"Have you been waiting long?"

"Not really. About four hours."

Something about Luz made Beatrice uneasy. The girl seemed composed, determined and almost confrontational. Better to let her do the talking.

"I see. So it must be important."

"The two men that just left. Police and newspapers, right?"

Beatrice met her eyes. "Right. Do you know them?"

"Not really. I know who they are, but they don't know me. Unlike my sisters, I don't take every opportunity to get photographed with influential people."

An uncomfortable pause followed that non-sequitur.

"Luz ..."

"You're investigating my father, aren't you? On behalf of the British Police."

"Not exactly. I am a British detective inspector, yes. But I really am on holiday. Someone asked me for advice ..." She broke off as her stomach seemed to drop. How many hours since Ana had disappeared?

Luz nodded impatiently. "And?"

"This afternoon, she went missing."

"Not another one," Luz muttered. She clasped her hands together. "This is something else, something so much worse. He can't just dispose of people who cross him."

"What do you mean by that? Who? Are you talking about Alava Exports?"

Luz exhaled through her nose, a laugh devoid of amusement. "Angel? He wouldn't get his hands dirty. No, the people who killed Miguel Saez and Tiago Vínculo are sadistic, unpleasant bastards who are paid, by my father, to intimidate, wound and kill. They enjoy their work."

Beatrice pressed her tissue to her mouth. "Oh God. And they've got Ana."

"Is she a friend of yours?"

"Yes, she is. If they hurt her, I'll hound them all the way to hell if I have to."

Luz's expression of pity made Beatrice's throat contract.

"I understand. Just don't do it alone."

"Luz, if you have any idea where Ana might be, I need to know that first."

She shook her head. "I don't. I really don't. Who knows where these thugs do their thing. You've reported her missing to the police and that's the best you can do. How long has she been gone?"

"I lost her after lunch," said Beatrice, distracted. She mentally scanned every detail of Ana's life, or what little she knew of it. Her friends at the paper, that man at the mortuary, Enrique at *El Papagaio*. Could she trust any of them to help?

"So there's nothing else you can do. Why don't you sit down and I'll make you a drink. Gin and tonic, wasn't it? Mind if I join you?"

Beatrice sank into an armchair with a heavy sigh and watched Luz rummage around in the mini-bar. "Thank you. So if you didn't come here to tell me about Ana, why did you want to see me?"

"To help you. The fact is, my father is a criminal. He and his collective of white Rioja producers are growing wealthier and more powerful by committing fraud on an industrial scale. Quite literally."

Beatrice brought her mind back on track. "He's selling substandard product for export, isn't he?"

Luz raised her eyebrows. "Yes. You've got further than I thought. It's mainly to Britain, but there are other markets which are paying four times the market rate for something which contains less than two percent of the Viura grape. Here's your drink. Cheers!"

"Cheers." Beatrice took a careful sip, sensitive to her swollen mouth. Her eyes watered, not with pain but at the amount of gin. She glanced at the empty bottles on top of the fridge. Luz had used all four little Bombay Sapphires but only one bottle of tonic between them. No ice, no lemon. No-nonsense. Serious G&Ts. Beatrice approved.

"But from what I understand, the controls make it impossible to substitute poor quality wine at the vineyard. So it must be at Alava Exports."

"Not impossible, but far more difficult. Alava Exports, on the other hand, can not only reproduce labels, but buy bulk loads of industrially produced white and market it as Rioja. Not in Spain. But my father takes great delight in conning 'the country with no taste', as he puts it. I am proud of my country, and even prouder of my region. We have a brilliant reputation for food and wine, deservedly so. I used to be proud of my family, too. Now, my father has bribed or blackmailed more and more vineyards into participating, coerced my sisters and their husbands into collaboration, paid officials at every level to ease his path through bureaucracy and built himself a persona based on bullshit. He has the wine industry by the balls. White Rioja, with the right blend of grapes from carefully tended vines and made with care and respect, is a wonderful wine. What my father and his cronies are doing is pissing all over its reputation.

And I want you to stop them. I'm sorry for my bad language."

The sound of a text message dragged Beatrice's attention from the impassioned face in front of her. She grabbed the phone, deflating as she saw Adrian's name.

*Zilch happening. We're bored.*
*How much longer should we wait?*

Beatrice sent a rapid reply.

*A bit longer. I'll get a taxi and come fetch you.*

She returned her attention to Luz. "Sorry about that. I hoped it might be news of Ana, but unfortunately not. And as a matter of fact, I think your language is entirely appropriate. So how do we proceed?"

Luz took a long draught of her drink and gazed at Beatrice, before pulling a document file from her bag and handing it over.

"I'm not proceeding. You are. You need proof and I can give it to you. The one thing I ask is that you do this through the proper channels. You must work with the police because this is far too dangerous to tackle alone. This trail goes all the way to the top and some very powerful people would do anything to stop this information becoming public."

Beatrice frowned as she flicked through the printouts of emails, spreadsheets and bank statements. Two memory sticks dropped onto the floor. "How did you get hold of all this?"

"My father underestimates me." She reached over and withdrew two pages of despatch schedules. "Call the police and get them to intercept any one of these deliveries. Tell them that according to your enquiries, you suspect the Aguirre brand of being a fake. They'll get it tested and expose it for what it is. But you and I must be well out of the way. Please don't think I'm being melodramatic. You must not put yourself at risk. You have no idea how far they'll go."

Beatrice opened her mouth and closed it again. The police. If Aguirre, according to his daughter, had 'paid officials at every level', why should the police be exempt? Milandro had been deliberately obstructive and unhelpful, his supervising officer had made no secret of his dislike and despite two dead bodies and a missing person, no formal investigation had been launched to explore connections. Beatrice made up her mind to trust her instincts. She wouldn't go it alone. But neither would she involve the Vitoria police. She looked at Luz.

"OK. I'll play it safe. But I have a question. Loyalty to the region and passion for wine is one thing, but to blow the whistle on your own father? Your own family? Is there more to this story?" Beatrice placed her drink on the table. The potent effects of the alcohol were more than she could take at the moment.

Luz glanced at her watch and threw back the remainder of her gin. "Yes, there is. But it's complicated and I need to catch my train. Here's my card, but you can only call me if it's really urgent. Remember, the trail cannot lead to me. He has no idea I can hack into his computer and if he suspected, he'd kill me. And that is not immature hyperbole. He would have me killed."

The cramping acidity in Beatrice's stomach increased. "How do you know he didn't follow you here?"

"He's not back till tomorrow. My mother has probably raised the alarm by now, but he won't give up the chance of being on television to search for his daughter. He's doing a live TV broadcast from Madrid this evening." She gave Beatrice a sly smile. "Half past eight. You should watch it. He's quite an entertainer. Listen, I have to go."

"I'll come with you. I'll walk you to the station. You don't have to tell me the whole story; we could talk about the weather instead."

An oppressive fug hung over the streets. The blue sky and

sunshine of the afternoon was replaced by thick cloud cover, trapping heat rising from concrete, a lid on a boiling pan. Almost as soon as they reached the last of the hotel steps and hit the street, Beatrice started to sweat. An ashen bank of thunderhead built over the edge of the city, a mushroom cloud before the explosion. Beatrice sensed the city's inertia, leaden and in limbo, as it waited for the rain.

They passed the Parque de la Florida and followed Calle Ramón y Cajal towards the station. Exhaustion caused by heat, tension and alcohol frayed Beatrice's nerves. Every passer-by appeared suspect while Luz appeared intent on speed-walking, manoeuvring her suitcase and talking at the same time.

"My father is a traditionalist. He is of another world. He's a snob, a bigot and a bully. As far as he's concerned, his daughters are only useful for making good marriages. My brother, Basajaun, will be the heir. My father tried to block me going to university, but my mother battled him on my behalf. She was very sick at that time and he gave in, to keep her happy. She's pleased I'm getting an education, but even she knows I have no hope outside the Castelo de Aguirre network. When I finish my studies, I must get married. My parents have already chosen the shortlist. And every single one of them disgusts me. You know what, that gin's gone right to my head."

Panting, Beatrice stopped. Speech was impossible at such a pace. "That's barbaric. Nineteenth century sort of thing."

"I know, but it's true. Come on. I can get the 19.35 if I'm lucky. What makes it worse is that I've met the man I want to spend my life with. But it's a lost cause."

A flash caused them both to look up. The sky loomed lower and darker than before, the colour of dirty sheep, and a distant boom of thunder reached them.

"Why?" asked Beatrice, scurrying to keep up.

"My family ... let's be diplomatic and call them xenophobes. Marrying anyone who is not Spanish and not Catholic is unthinkable. All the shortlisted candidates check both boxes, they're mostly Basque, all rich and definitely influential. Tunçay is a Turkish Muslim whose family would be equally appalled by me. It's hopeless."

"But surely ..."

"We have another four years, until my degree ends. Then we must separate. We understand that, which is why we're making the most of every day. I can never be free to marry him, I know it. But I can be free of my father's choices. *Mierda*, it's raining. You should turn back."

Beatrice lifted her face to the sky, allowing fat dollops of rain to fall on her flushed face. "No, I'll see you onto the train. I want to know you're safe. Anyway, we're almost there."

Rain fell harder and faster, bouncing off the steaming tarmac, darkening Luz's shirt and soaking Beatrice's hair. They rushed across the street, splashing and gasping as they reached the station building. Beatrice wiped her forehead with a wet hand and shook herself. Luz pulled out some tissues and handed one to Beatrice. Her eye make-up had run, so black teardrops stained her cheeks.

"Just made it. Do you have a ticket?" Beatrice asked, mopping her eyebrows.

Luz patted her handbag. "I'm all prepared. Thank you for listening to me. I wish you luck with exposing all this corruption. Please be careful and don't tell anyone about me. I'm trusting you." She bent to kiss Beatrice on both cheeks. "And I hope your friend will be fine."

"So do I. Take care, Luz. I'll do everything in my power to bring this to light. Don't worry, I always protect my sources. I appreciate your trust."

Luz smiled, which did nothing to change her sad, stoic air, and made her own way onto the platform. She stamped her ticket at the machine, gave one last wave and heaved her case onto the train. With a sigh, Beatrice turned to look out at the weather. Glittering curtains of rain blurred the hectic scene of taxis and rushing commuters, thunder cracked away to her right and the smell of drenched streets and soggy people surrounded her. Regardless of how wet she got, she had to get back to the hotel. She took a deep breath, wrinkling her nose at the stench of pungent tobacco and launched herself into the deluge.

# Chapter 34

"This is getting ridiculous."

Matthew pressed himself further against the tree trunk and looked up at the drips falling between the leaf cover. "How much longer does she expect us to stand out here in the rain? We don't even know what we're supposed to be looking for."

Adrian sighed. "This is the reality of detective work, Matthew. Long, dull hours of surveillance. It can't be all car chases and shoot-outs, you know."

Matthew shot him a dour look. "I yearn for neither vehicular action nor gun-play. A cup of tea and a warm towel, however, would be most welcome. The point is, we offered our services as consultant oenologists. Why then, are we squashed against some Spanish foliage spying on a deserted warehouse? She's taking advantage."

Thunder rumbled like barrels across a wooden floor. Water trickled down Adrian's neck and he began to have some sympathy for Matthew's perspective.

"Look, it's almost half past eight now. What with the thunderstorm, we can't see much, so by nine o'clock, we may as well pack up and go back to the hotel. I admit to feeling in need of some creature comforts as well. Thirty minutes more, and if she hasn't arrived by then, you can call us a taxi."

Matthew inhaled and released a theatrical sigh-groan. "There has to be a reason you are so unwaveringly loyal. Fair enough, I hitched my wagon to her cattle train many moons past. But why does an urbane, gay sophisticate with a taste for Rodgers and Hammerstein carry such allegiance to a woman who with the best will in the world could be called difficult?"

A brilliant flash lit the sky, allowing a glimpse of sooty plum-coloured clouds, starkly exposed trees and the bald expanse of nothing in the car park of Alava Exports.

Adrian considered. "I can't say I've ever thought about that. If I had to define it, I'd say I can see qualities in her I wish I had. But she's also very much like me in other elements. We both have gluttonous, lustful appetites and indulge them without apology. Maybe we just see enough similarities to attract and enough differences to respect. Put it this way, I've never wanted to unfriend her."

Matthew looked at him. "An eloquent explanation, with the exception of that bastardisation of the English language in those final words. It does go some way to explaining your companionship, but why do you literally endanger yourself on her behalf? You could be at home right now, watching ... I don't know ... *The King and I* while sampling something delicious from the wine rack. Why are you standing in the damp gloom of a Spanish thunderstorm watching an empty car park ... oh, hello. What's that?"

Adrian followed Matthew's sightline, as a discreet sedan eased into the yard below them, pulling up beside the raised delivery bays. Still and silent, they watched as a tall, dark-haired man exited the car and climbed the steps to the huge doors. He seemed unaware of the rain, moving at an unhurried pace. He bent for a few seconds and a normal-sized door shape appeared in the corner of the massive shutter. Adrian hadn't even noticed it before.

The figure turned and scanned the area from the shelter of the eaves. Adrian held his breath and sensed Matthew doing the same. From such a distance, it was impossible to be sure exactly where he was looking, but both exhaled as he loped back down the steps and opened the back door of the car. Another man stepped out, who could have been the first's twin from this distance; same height, build and colouring. However, number two seemed more perturbed by the weather, holding his hand up to shield his eyes as he too spent several seconds checking the empty landscape. Adrian prayed the lightning would hold off.

Satisfied, the second man ducked back into the car. He heard Matthew's sharp inhalation as he dragged a young woman with long dark hair from the interior. One man either side of her, she was bundled up the steps, through the black opening and into the warehouse. As the door closed, Adrian struggled to contain his panic and motioned to Matthew with his eyes. Retreat.

He slipped backwards behind the tree, moving as gradually and subtly as he could manage. Once hidden in deeper foliage, he spoke.

"That was Ana. And she was not a willing guest."

Matthew's face sagged. "That's what I thought. So we've found Ana, but where's Beatrice?"

Adrian hit redial before Matthew had finished. The phone rang and rang. And went to voicemail. A flare of anger superseded his nerves.

"Where the hell are you? We've just seen two men take Ana into the warehouse. I hope you're already in a taxi, Beatrice Stubbs, that's all I can say."

He rang off and stared at Matthew. "Listen, I know what we promised, but I am not going to stand here and wait for instructions while those gorillas do what they want with that girl. We have no choice but to help."

"I agree."

Busy building up a head of righteous steam, Adrian was wrong-footed by Matthew's acquiescence.

"Oh. Good. So?"

"Call the police. Adrian, we are horribly under-prepared for any kind of encounter with the criminal element. We may well put Ana in worse danger than she already is. I know Beatrice mistrusts that one particular detective, but she's not available to advise us. In the circumstances, we have to call for professional help. We saw a woman forced into a building against her will by two men. Regardless of Beatrice's investigation, that is cause for alarm."

Adrian could see the logic. He desperately wanted to burst into that warehouse and stop them, but Matthew was right. Ana's safety came first.

"We must dial 999 immediately. Or whatever number they use here."

"112. The European Union countries all use the same. Apart from Britain, of course."

Adrian hesitated and dialled Beatrice one last time.

This time, she picked up. *"Hello Adrian, I ..."*

"Where are you?"

*"Just got out of the shower. I got soaked on the way back from the train station. I'm just getting dressed and then I'll call a cab. Be with you in a short while. Are you terribly wet?"*

"Beatrice, did you listen to my message?"

*"No, not yet. It's like Piccadilly Circus here. I have five missed calls and now the bloody doorbell's ringing. What was your message?"*

"They've got Ana. Matthew and I saw two men take her into the Alava Exports warehouse. We have to do something! Matthew and I think we should call the police. Immediately."

He waited for a reply.

"Beatrice! Beatrice?"

Matthew's eyes bore into him and he pressed the headset so hard to his ear that it hurt.

"Bea ..."

*"Sorry, Adrian, I had to open the door. Could you repeat what you just said?"*

"Two men, lookalike Sopranos rejects, took Ana into Alava Exports through the delivery bay. She is in there now. With them. On her own. Beatrice ..."

"*That's not Ana.*"

Adrian took the handset from his ear to stare at it in disbelief.

"And how do you know ..."

"*Because she's standing right here.*"

# Chapter 35

Beatrice stared at the girl in the doorway, transfixed. A lift pinged along the corridor and broke the spell. She pulled Ana into the room, locked the door and attached the chain. Then she grabbed her in a tight hug and felt Ana squeeze back. Somehow, the pain of squashed bruises seemed insignificant. She released her with a smile and lifted the phone to her ear.

"Ana's right here. How long ago did you see them take that woman inside the building?"

Ana stared at her, listening intently. She mouthed 'Who is it?'

Beatrice mouthed back. 'Adrian.'

Adrian sounded indignant. "*Just now! Two, maybe three minutes ago.*"

"Then it couldn't have been Ana."

"*Well, it was someone who looked exactly like her.*"

All the blood seemed to drain from Beatrice's body. Her hand felt weak and cold as if the effort of holding a tiny Nokia was too much.

"*Thing is, Beatrice, whoever it was, she was forced to go in there, so we have to call the police,*" Adrian hissed through clenched teeth.

Beatrice shook her head. "No. If I'm right, it was the police who tipped them off. I think the woman they've got is Luz, Aguirre's daughter. She came to see me today and Milandro was here when she arrived. He must have called Aguirre's thugs as soon as he left the hotel. But I put her on the train myself!"

"His daughter?" Ana's eyes were incredulous. "He'd never set those bastards on his own daughter, surely to God?"

Beatrice paced the room, searching for her shoes and talking to Ana and Adrian at the same time. "He would. She told me so herself. But he can't do anything yet, he's still in Madrid. Ana, put the telly on. Listen, Adrian, we can't call the police. They're in this up to their necks. But we absolutely have to get Luz out of there before Aguirre gets back. I'll call Jaime and see if he can't find us some reinforcements. And then I'm taking this to Interpol, to expose this bloody nasty little boys' club for the greedy, murderous cabal that it is. I'm on my way, but please don't do a thing till I get there. I'm serious. It's too dangerous."

Adrian didn't answer immediately and she heard him have a muffled conversation with Matthew.

*"OK. But do hurry. How's Ana?"*

Beatrice held the phone away from her head. "How are you?"

Ana shrugged. "Better than you by the looks of things. Where's the remote?"

Beatrice waved vaguely in the direction of the desk. "She's fine. We'll call a cab and see you in twenty minutes."

Ana flicked through the channels until she came across a panel discussion. The camera panned the table and Beatrice spotted a familiar face. Arturo de Aguirre, dressed in a deep blue suit, gesturing and posturing with typical éclat. She couldn't understand a word. Ana stood beside Beatrice and they watched Aguirre's confident, relaxed performance for several seconds.

Bored of guessing what the conversation was about, Beatrice turned to Ana. The familiar dark hair, sardonic eyebrows and suspicious frown at the television set induced a burst of affection and a genuine smile. Which restarted the bleeding.

"I'm so happy to see you. I imagined all sorts," she said, her voice muffled through bloodied tissue.

"I'm fine. Not a bother on me. But what the hell happened to you?" Ana winced in sympathy.

"To be honest, I am sick to the back feet of telling the story. Where did you go? I thought they'd got you. How did you get away?"

Ana shook her head with a laugh. "Saved by the smell. On the way back from the loo, I stopped off at the shop. As I went in, I caught the strongest stink of black tobacco. And that set off the most almighty alarm. I'd smelt it before. One of those goons who turned up at my flat was smoking that. It's rank."

"Did you see him?"

"Not at first. I ducked behind the CD racks and watched. I saw one of them come out of the restaurant. His mate joined him from the coffee shop and then they both went into the ladies' loo."

"The ladies' loo? And no one objected?"

"Sure, but they don't give a toss. They were looking for me. No doubt about it. So I was about to take my chance and run for the exit when I copped myself on. If two of them were inside, looking for me, the other two were outside, looking for you. So I sent you a message and got myself arrested."

Beatrice gawped.

"When trying to escape from men with guns, the best place to hide is behind other men with guns. I ditched the phone in case they could trace it, snatched a handful of CDs and walked out without paying. The alarm went off and the security guards marched me up to the office. I was arrested and charged and taken back to San Sebastian police station. Arsewit and Dickhead must have thought I'd disappeared down the plughole."

"Arrested!"

"Petty crime. They flexed a few muscles, lectured me a bit and told me to piss off. So I got on a bus and came back. Picked up my Vespa and rode over here. Then I watched the hotel from the café over the road, just in case. You know the police are outside?"

"Milandro?"

"Nope. But there's a plain-clothes guy outside I'd swear is a cop. Now tell me what the hell happened to you and your face. How did you get back to Vitoria?"

"I drove."

"No way! You told me you were useless behind the wheel."

"I am. Hence my face. I wrote off Jaime's car. Which reminds me, I need to call him. And I'd better let Milandro know you're here. And would you call us a cab?"

"Sure. But can I use your bathroom first?"

"Be quick. We need a plan."

Milandro actually sounded relieved to hear Ana had turned up unharmed. He made an appointment for them both to come to the station in the morning for a formal statement. He didn't exactly order her to stay in the hotel, but strongly suggested they stay in and enjoy room service. Beatrice agreed that would be best, all the while lacing up her trainers in preparation for their departure. After finishing the call, Beatrice took several deep breaths, ignoring the twinges all over her torso. Her mind attempted a logical analysis of a situation which frightened her witless.

Aguirre was cornered. His malpractice was on the verge of being exposed and the only question now was how far the corruption went. Killing off everyone who knew the details would be impossible. Jaime could run the story as soon as the day after tomorrow, tugging at the thread which would unravel the whole affair. But how to protect Luz? Beatrice had no back-up, no authority and no plan.

It would not do. Whatever was going on at the warehouse put them all at risk and Beatrice needed an insurance policy. She scrolled through her phone until she found the number of Conceição Pereira da Silva. An Interpol agent and ex-colleague, Conceição would be the perfect person; guaranteed to understand and ask no stupid questions.

As she pressed dial, she relaxed in anticipation of hearing Conceição's magnetic voice, recalling those bright eyes, her huge smile and constant air of amusement. But there was no reply. Beatrice left a brief message explaining where she was and why and asking Conceição to sound the alarm if Beatrice had not called back in twenty-four hours. Then she called Jaime, informed him of Ana's safe return and explained the situation.

"As far as we know, there are two men holding a young woman in that warehouse. My suspicion is they have Luz Aguirre, that girl who turned up here this afternoon. They're probably waiting for instructions from her father. If you can join us, that's five against two, even if we are unarmed. That should give us the edge."

"Of course. I can be there in around half an hour." Bless Jaime, the man who never said no. "So, let me understand. Matthew and Adrian are already there? Inside the warehouse?"

"No, they're watching it from the forest behind. They have a clear view of the delivery bay, which is where the girl was taken."

"I see. Have you called that detective?"

Beatrice hesitated. This was no time for double-dealing. She chose to put her cards on the table.

"Jaime, I'm afraid Milandro may well be a part of this. My priority now is to get Luz to safety and then I'm taking this investigation to Interpol. I think the police are probably on Aguirre's payroll."

"Really? My God! Are Interpol already involved?"

"I've got to assemble a case first. I believe Luz has given me everything I need. I'm just afraid Aguirre has found out what she's done. If he has, she's in trouble. We must get her out, Jaime."

"You don't really think he'd hurt her? This is his daughter we're talking about."

"I know. But I have a nasty feeling that makes the betrayal so much worse. When he gets back from Madrid, I want Luz somewhere safe and an airtight case prepared for his arrest."

"OK, Beatrice. I'll make some calls and join you as soon as I can."

"Thank you, Jaime. I'd be lost without your constant support. You've been right with me, every step of the way."

"No problem. Please look after yourself. And give Ana a kiss from me."

Beatrice smiled and rang off. She picked up her gin and tonic, took a slug and pulled a face. Lukewarm.

Then she froze, gazing into the middle distance.

*Every step of the way.*

Milandro wasn't the only person to see Luz this afternoon. And Jaime had shown no surprise on hearing the name of Luz Aguirre. When Beatrice was supposed to be in Jaime's flat, the gang had shown up. How had they known she was there alone? It could have been coincidence. And today, Jaime had loaned them his distinctive powder-blue BMW. Their fears about being followed on the way to San Sebastian were groundless. Of course. Aguirre's crew already knew where they were going. The hoods would have had no difficulty tailing them on the way back. She'd kept Jaime informed of every last movement. And he knew perfectly well who Luz was because he was working for her father.

She shook her head. Paranoia. She'd be suspecting Ana next. But if Jaime *was* a snitch, she'd just dropped Matthew and Adrian right in it. And possibly jeopardised herself and Ana. It wouldn't be difficult to arrange a "taxi" for them, driven by God knows whom.

Raging paranoia. But if she couldn't trust the police, Jaime or even the hotel staff, where the hell was she to get back-up?

By the time Ana came out of the bathroom, Beatrice had convinced herself. She stood in front of Ana with her hands on her hips.

"How long have you known Jaime?"

"About eighteen months or so, why? Ah, Beatrice. Tell me

you're not suspecting him."

"Think about it. We've told him everything. If he's passing on information to Aguirre, we've been undercover investigating in broad daylight."

"No, he wouldn't. This is a false alarm. He was the one who put Tiago onto the Saez case." She checked her watch.

"Which was supposed to lead nowhere. Only Tiago found out rather more than expected. No one else, apart from you and Jaime, knew how much. So how come Aguirre's mob disposed of him?"

Ana hunched her shoulders. Several seconds passed.

"Jesus. That makes a twisted kind of sense. And Jaime knew enough about Tiago to use me as a lure."

Beatrice stated the obvious. "Tiago was in love with you, wasn't he?"

Ana paused. "I suppose so, yeah. I'd picked up a fair few hints. Jaime could have sent him an invitation from my work computer, knowing damn well he'd not be able to resist."

"On Saturday morning. And of course he wasn't surprised when Tiago didn't turn up on Monday. The mutilation of Tiago's face was a warning to you."

Beatrice watched Ana's expression change from horror to incomprehension to anger. In a couple of seconds, her whole demeanour changed and she began pacing the room, gesticulating in every direction.

"I can't believe this. What a piece of shit! And he went to the funeral! He stood there, expressing the most sincere sympathies for Tiago's parents, when the whole time he'd set the poor bastard up. I believed he was one of the few people I could trust. What a stupid cow! And I prided myself on not falling for his bullshit charm."

Beatrice flushed, recalling her own susceptibility. "It's quite effective, I admit."

"Thing is, if it was Jaime who gave Aguirre all he needed, does that mean we can trust the police? Should we call Milandro?"

"No. We trust no one. Where's your Vespa?" She scrabbled in her bag for her phone and began dialling.

"Round the corner. I thought we were getting a cab."

"Change of plan. And I'd like to leave the hotel via another route than the front door. Ideally, we should get out without being seen. There must be a staff exit or ... Oh hello. Is that Kev? It's Beatrice here. How's the trip going? Are you still in Vitoria? Oh good. Listen, Kev, I have a bit of a problem and wondered if you might be able to help."

"Beatrice ..." Ana had changed channels to a football match.

"Just a sec." She covered the mouthpiece. "Ana, I'm on the phone."

"Yes, but ..."

Beatrice scowled and shook her head, returning to the call. "Kev? Sorry about that. The thing is that a friend of mine is in trouble and ..."

"Beatrice!"

The intensity in Ana's voice made Beatrice turn. Ana wasn't looking at her, but at the television. She'd switched back from the match to the bunch of suits talking. Beatrice could see nothing of significance. Ana flicked to the football again and back to the panel.

"Kev, bear with me a moment, I'm sorry about this." She pressed her thumb over the microphone and turned to Ana. "What's the matter now?"

Ana prodded her finger against the screen, indicating a ponytailed man with stubble and an earring. "That is Julio Villa, Real Madrid's star striker."

"And?"

"And, as you can see," she flicked to the football, where the crowd were leaping up and down and roaring, "he's just scored a goal against Atlético Madrid."

"The football's live?"

"Mm-hmm. People tend to prefer it that way. Which means this ..." she pressed the button to bring back the studio discussion,

"... was pre-recorded. As for the current location of Arturo de Aguirre, we haven't got a bloody clue."

# Chapter 36

Dusk settled over the landscape, light evaporating below the western horizon. A Hunter's moon offered an eerie monochrome illumination, when not obscured by fast-moving clouds, the last remnants of the afternoon's storm. Ana scrambled back onto the road and Beatrice gave her the thumbs-up. The scrubby bushes completely concealed the Vespa from view. In silence and with ears alert for the sound of vehicles, they set off into the forest, keeping a parallel course to the driveway to Alava Exports.

The warehouse, a grey malevolent monolith gave no indication of being occupied.

Several kilometres from the nearest village and set back from the main road, with nothing but forest around, it was the perfect place to hide something. If you had something to hide. As they approached, Beatrice could make out the white markings of visitors' parking spots and the glass windows of reception. A Range Rover and another smaller car occupied the spaces nearest to the door. The drive continued to the right with a sign indicating the lorry route. Beatrice frowned. The delivery bay must be round the back. So how could Adrian and Matthew have seen the girl taken from the car?

Ana stopped frequently to listen and check if they were being followed. Beatrice kept her eyes on the trees ahead, peering for any sign of Adrian and Matthew. She couldn't decide if the wind were help or hindrance. Trees cracked and whipped, leaves danced in Van Gogh swirls and the absolute lack of human movement both impressed and alarmed her. Of Adrian and Matthew, there was not the smallest indication. Either they were behaving as instructed, keeping quiet and concealed, or, far more likely for the two least restrained men in her acquaintance, they had already been discovered. She sped up, still scanning the forest and walked straight into Ana.

Ana jerked her head to the sedan in front of the vast shuttered bays.

"If that's the car that brought Luz here, where did those two round the front come from?"

"Just what I was thinking. I wonder if I should call Adrian. Or maybe send a text in case he hasn't switched his phone to silent."

"I'm not that stupid."

The voice made them both start and twist around. From behind a tree trunk, Adrian appeared, followed by Matthew.

Beatrice exhaled. "Thank God. Are you all right?"

"We just had a bit of a fright," said Adrian. "After I spoke to you, two cars came down the drive. No idea where they went, but a few minutes later, those goons came out of the back and headed straight for us. We retreated further into the forest, but they didn't come far. They spent a while searching around the edges then went back inside. It was as if they just wanted to scare us off. Beatrice, you look terrible. Are you OK, Ana?"

"I'm grand. How about you two?"

A rather damp and cold-looking Matthew moved towards them, his expression impossible to read.

"We're fine, although I am unconvinced by the argument for acting alone. A handful of half-baked incompetents versus who knows how many men, probably armed and in possession of a hostage, with no hope of professional back-up. Not only that, but we can't even speak the language with any degree of accuracy."

Ana stepped in front of Matthew. "I can. And I'm not incompetent. The thing is, Matthew, we must act quickly because we're pretty sure Aguirre is heading in this direction. We have to get to Luz before he does. Reinforcements are on the way."

Matthew's face, lined and shadowed by lunar light, seemed to contract into a deeper frown. "Reinforcements? You mean your editor, most likely accompanied by a photographer, just to guarantee an exclusive front-page splash?"

Beatrice chose economy of truth. "That's a good point. We don't really know how many people are in there, so it might be wiser to wait until the cavalry arrives. The reinforcements are trustworthy, Matthew, believe me. Let's approach this logically. When you did the tour today, did you see the whole building? What I mean is, how well do you know the layout?"

Adrian glanced at Matthew. "Correct me if I'm wrong, but the reception and offices are at the front. There's a middle section containing the bottling plant and packing areas." He pointed to the delivery area. "That section is divided into wine storage on the right and the warehouse section on the left. That's where they took the girl. It's stacked with boxes of wine ready for despatch in different sections. UK export was quite clearly marked."

Beatrice motioned for Adrian to drop his voice. His enthusiasm and conviction had raised his pitch. They stood in silence for several seconds, checking for any sounds or movements in the forest, from the lorry bays or in the building, before Adrian continued in a stage whisper.

"No detail is insignificant, you told me. So I watched Angel Rosado very carefully and decided he is extremely vain, seriously uninformed about his own operations and unquestionably a friend of Dorothy's."

"A what?" Ana hissed, her irritation visible. "What in the name of ..."

Again, Beatrice raised a hand for silence.

"In Adrian's opinion, Angel Rosado is a homosexual," she said.

Ana snorted. "Bollocks! Would you ever cop yourself on? The man's married to Aguirre's daughter. No disrespect, Adrian, but do you not think you maybe got the wrong signals because you were staring at the poor f..."

A torch lit Ana's face and at the same time, the unmistakeable sound of safety catches being released announced the fact they had company. Another torch joined the first, moving over Adrian, Matthew and shining directly in Beatrice's eyes. She raised her open hands to shoulder height, blinking into the glare.

A voice, rasping and low, gave an incomprehensible order.

Ana translated. "Hands in the air, turn round and start walking. "

They made their way through the trees in silence, apart from the sound of a cigarette being lit behind them. Ahead, the huge shutters rolled upward and Beatrice could see the figures of three men silhouetted against walls of white cardboard boxes. They walked out onto the platform to meet them.

As they crossed the car park, light from the plant spilt out and the torches went off. Beatrice took the opportunity to glance back and recognised their escorts. Tweedledum and Tweedledee in identical black suits and slicked-back hair carried matching accessories; handguns and torches. The grizzled older man was smoking some foul-smelling tobacco, while his gun dangled by his side. He saw her look and motioned she should turn around. He used his gun as a Japanese courtesan might use her fan, in a professional, yet unambiguous gesture.

She couldn't be sure of the weapons the Thompson twins were carrying but the ugly man's stainless steel piece was a SIG Sauer, probably a P226. A favourite with police forces everywhere.

Beatrice looked past the three men waiting on the platform and squinted into the space behind them. A forklift truck, a stack of pallets and blocks of cardboard boxes filled the space, but no dark-haired girl to be seen. They stopped at the base of the steps and Beatrice lifted her head.

Aguirre stared down at her, his face resembling that of a gargoyle, his hooked nose carved from grey stone. His eyes bored into her as if she were the only person there. The second man, also dressed in a suit, seemed ill-at-ease, his eyes not resting anywhere for more than a second. Angel Rosado, undoubtedly. The final individual had a face like Samuel Beckett and he beckoned them forward with a repulsive smile. But rather than using his index finger, he used his whole hand. A classic police gesture. Palm upwards and four fingers waving inwards. Or in his case, only three.

# Chapter 37

Outnumbered. Six men, at least, all with visible guns. Beatrice's toes curled in frustration as she watched one of the younger hoods take his time over frisking Ana, purposely groping her breast with a nauseating leer. Ana remained expressionless.

After fixing their captives' hands behind them with plastic ties and relieving them of mobile phones, the twins ushered them to sit on a small stack of pallets near the back wall. Beatrice sensed an uncertainty in their behaviour. Apart from taking liberties with Ana, the treatment of them was restrained, almost polite. No shoving, no casual violence. One of the identical macho men raised a finger and drew it across his lips, meeting each pair of eyes in turn. Then he and his fellow thug moved away to join the others. Grizzly, Rosado and Three-Fingers stood inside the closed shutter doors having a hushed conversation. Aguirre had disappeared through an internal door. Grizzly occasionally pointed his gun in their direction, less as a threat and more of a conversational gesture.

Beatrice leant forward to look past Ana at Matthew. He was disturbingly pale, an odd blue tinge to his lips. He shouldn't even be here. None of them should. The cold of the warehouse seeped into her clothes, while a hot surge of guilt flushed over her. She had to do something.

"What are they saying, Ana?" she whispered.

She felt Ana's shoulders shift against hers as she shrugged.

"I'm not sure. They're speaking Basque, so I can't understand much at all. They keep saying they're shocked, that they can't believe it. But I don't think they're talking about us. And I get the impression they're debating a decision."

Adrian spoke from her other side. "Have they said anything about the girl?"

Beatrice dropped her voice still lower. "It's vital that he thinks we're just snooping, investigating the wine issue. We know nothing about any girl. Don't even mention her name."

"What do I say about Tiago?" asked Ana.

"Nothing. You're taking over his story. As far as you're concerned, he had an accident, and you are now chasing his leads. The fact that you know Tiago was murdered, probably by this lot, has to remain our secret. That's our most likely chance of getting out of here."

Matthew cleared his throat, but did not speak, as the group of men turned to look. After they'd returned to their conversation, Matthew spoke in a deliberate whisper.

"And the cavalry? Does *anyone* know we're here?"

"Yes. Firstly, I left a message with Interpol, explaining my intentions. So if anything happens to us, they know where to look."

"That's comforting," said Matthew.

"Secondly, ..."

Someone banged on the metal shutters, galvanising the men and shooting tension through the group on the pallets. One of the younger men opened the door, allowing Aguirre access.

Beatrice watched the body language of the group with curiosity. The men bowed their heads, in an oddly deferential gesture of respect. It reminded her of mourners at a funeral.

Rosado dabbed a handkerchief repeatedly to his mouth, staring at the ground with wide eyes, fidgeting and awkward, as if no comfortable position existed.

Aguirre spoke to the men in hoarse tones, indicating with his finger at every individual as he seemed to deliver instructions.

Each nodded, crossed the vast space and left through the internal door. Leaving one of the twins. The young gunman moved forward to train his weapon on the seated group.

"Oh my God," murmured Adrian.

"They won't shoot us," said Beatrice. She knew she was right. The hood held his weapon in a state of readiness, not with intent. And disposing of four executed bodies without trace would be a challenge for even Aguirre. Still, Beatrice could feel both Ana and Adrian tense against their ties.

Aguirre approached to stand in front of them. His expression, that of a wounded bull, bore equal measures of pain and rage.

"Ana Herrero. It was a simple enough instruction. Was 'Go back to Portugal' so hard to understand? Detective Inspector Beatrice Stubbs. I should have known. Bad luck to spill blood on my steps. An unfortunate day, for all of us."

Her body immobilised, Beatrice had access to only two elements of her arsenal. Her mind and her mouth. Both of which had previously proved unreliable.

"Señor Aguirre, I acknowledge the fact that we have been trespassing, but I must insist you let us go. Such treatment is absurd. Feel free to call the police and have us arrested, but you cannot truss us up like so many turkeys."

Aguirre shook his head, pressing his hand to his eyes. He swallowed twice and looked at Matthew.

"And you two? Bailey and Son, wine importers who conveniently forgot their business cards? I don't think so. You are friends, or possibly colleagues, of Detective Inspector Stubbs. Which is your misfortune."

"My name is Professor Matthew Bailey, oenology expert and my colleague is Adrian Harvey, wine importer. For your information, both of us have found our association with Beatrice Stubbs to be extremely fortunate." Matthew's tone was calm, measured and a little condescending.

Aguirre narrowed his eyes. The interior door reopened and Three-Fingers returned with a carafe of liquid. Aguirre nodded once, gesturing with his forehead towards Matthew.

"No!" Beatrice jerked forward, trying to get to her feet, but bounced back onto the bench. "If you plan to punish anyone with your brutal bully-boy techniques, you can bloody well pick on me. These people are not involved. Leave him alone."

"Leave him alone? The way you left me and my family alone? I'm afraid not. We told you to go away and mind your own business. But I've noticed that women rarely listen. They can talk, oh yes, but cannot listen."

Three-Fingers knelt beside Matthew. With a certain amount of weariness, he poured some liquid into a small glass, pointed at Matthew and mimed drinking it. He nodded and gave the thumbs-up. Then he mimed refusing the glass and averting his head. With a shrug, he pulled out a flick-knife and with a total absence of drama, demonstrated slashing a face. He opened his palm, as if to ask 'What'll it be?'

Before Beatrice could open her mouth, another voice rang out. Angel Rosado placed his hand on Aguirre's shoulder, his eyes fixed on Matthew.

*"No. Él no tiene la culpa. Deja-le!"*

"He's saying he's not guilty and let him go." Ana kept her eyes on the two men in front of them, but muttered, "You might have been right."

Aguirre did not acknowledge the plea, turning instead to the gunman. Rosado, who up until the last two minutes had seemed practically catatonic, shrugged off the gunman's guiding hand and pulled at Aguirre. The gunman didn't hesitate, bringing the butt of his weapon with full force against Rosado's head. The pallets wobbled as all four observers recoiled. Rosado collapsed onto the concrete floor, clutching his head as he was dragged to the other end of the room. Aguirre had maintained his intense focus on Beatrice, but now turned to the gunman and yelled. The man dropped Rosado and exited via the door in the delivery bay. Aguirre barked at Three-Fingers.

*"Vamos,* Tomas!"

Spell broken, the man offered the glass to Matthew, the knife poised in his other hand. Beatrice writhed against her restraints.

"Stop! Aguirre, make him stop! What is that stuff? If you poison him, I ..."

"Women. Always talking. Cannot keep their mouths shut." Aguirre shook his head and walked a few paces, like a general inspecting his troops. "It's *aguardiente*. Fire water. Hooch. That's all. He might enjoy it." He stopped to observe the show.

Matthew pressed back from the glass until he could stretch no further. The glass, and knife, kept coming. Finally, after a pat on the cheek with the flat of the blade, Matthew opened his mouth. Tomas poured a small sip into his mouth, dropped the knife to the floor and reached in his pocket for a blue-checked handkerchief. So he was ready for the inevitable spluttering and coughing. He wiped Matthew's eyes and mopped his nose, while patting him on the shoulder. He stopped short of a smile, but nodded and made the thumbs-up sign.

"Matthew, are you OK?" Beatrice asked, peering into his flushed features.

"Yes, it's like grappa. Just a bit stronger than I'm used to. Powerful stuff."

Tomas seemed pleased and raised the glass again. This time, he didn't bother with the knife, but readied the hanky.

Aguirre sniffed. "You see, he's enjoying himself. So he should. That's a top quality product. He needs to be drunk, and this is the fastest way to do it."

Beatrice understood. "You're going to put us in a car, Matthew behind the wheel and shove us off a cliff. Your men are preparing the car right now, just to make sure we go up in flames and all evidence is destroyed."

Aguirre watched the ritual once more, apparently ignoring her. A moan came from the end of the room, where Angel Rosado sat up and pressed a hand to his head. He seemed to be crying. Matthew swallowed once more, cheeks flushed, while

Tomas patted him and wiped his face, as if he were a wrestling coach between rounds with a prize fighter.

Ana glared at Aguirre, her eyes black and furious. "You have no conscience whatsoever, do you? When's it going to stop, Aguirre? Six deaths on your hands already and those are only the ones I know about."

Aguirre looked at Ana. "Why is it that smart girls don't know when to shut up? You know, I should just give you to Tomas. He knows the best way to keep a woman quiet, isn't that right? *Tomas sabe callar a una mujer*?"

Tomas showed his top teeth, rendering him uglier than before, caught hold of his own crotch and gave it a shake.

# Chapter 38

Four men shaking hands.
Three in suits.
Two carrying handguns.
One smoking.
Zero signs of target.
Cloud cover sporadic, night visibility variable.

Kev watched as the four men exchanged handshakes. The new arrival held something out to the older suit who took it and indicated over his shoulder. All four turned to look in Kev's direction. He dropped lower on his forearms, but they weren't looking as far as him. Their sightline was lower, towards the stream.

He tensed as he heard a sound behind him. Jase, returning from the recce. Kev squinted and frowned. They'd done their best with shoe polish but the white of his trainers still shone through the camouflage. Tyler, silent as a cat, approached from the other direction and crouched beside him.

"Nothing. She's not in this side of the forest." He looked up at Jase, who shook his head. "OK, so she must be inside. Lights are on in the depot but the rest is deserted. What's going on with this lot?" He jerked his chin at the group of men.

"The Rhinestone Cowboy down there turned up three minutes ago. In that Peugeot. Handshakes, a friendly chat and there's something interesting about that ditch."

Jase squatted next to Tyler. "Access from the front and delivery bay. Four fire doors, two either side, probably alarmed. Roof this end has windows. Too high for surprise entry but helpful for surveillance assessment via metal service ladder twenty-six metres to our right."

The three men breathed, waited and watched. A hum built in Kev. A hum born of training and experience. This situation was unknown and their role unclear. But when it came to scoping a location, identifying risks and minimising danger, he could rely on his team. Beatrice needed their expertise and anyway, he'd had enough of *tapas*.

The man in the leather jacket did the round of goodbye handshakes, but didn't get back in his car. Instead, he revved up the Corsa and drove back up the access road.

"Shit," spat Tyler. "Too dark to see the fooking number."

Kev grinned. "Already got it, mate. What are those bastards up to now?"

Each of the three men hauled something from the back of the Range Rover and strode towards the delivery bay.

Jase took a deep breath. "Petrol cans. They're gonna torch summat."

Employing his stealth training: heel-ball-toe walk, deep breathing and low crouch, Kev crept through the trees, stopping, listening, watching and waiting; Tyler and Jase moving with him like shadows. Once their sightline cleared the corner, they dropped onto their chests. Two men were opening all the doors of the black sedan, while the other removed the number plates. One picked up a can and unscrewed the top. The smoker flicked his glowing butt into the ditch and they began soaking the whole vehicle in petrol.

"Right, while they're busy, I'm having a look at what's going on indoors."

Kev checked out the route. Jase slipping through ten metres of trees, over the ditch and a sixteen-metre stretch of moonlit tarmac unseen in radioactive trainers? No way.

"Swap shoes. This is one hell of a sacrifice. Your feet have plagued me worse than any Afghani insurgent ever could. If you're not wearing Odor-Eaters, I'll kill ya."

Tyler took point, Kev followed. Neither checked Jase. His feet might be rank but he could be trusted to do a proper job. The situation was risky. No doubt the suits were busy round the back, but if one of them popped back to check the coast was clear, he and the lads were unarmed and as vulnerable as rabbits. Rabbits in white trainers.

As they reached the stream, Kev nudged Tyler and pointed to his feet. "I'll dip these in the ditch, see if a bit of mud will help."

Tyler's head scanned the area like an owl. He crouched into the scrub and Kev spotted a glint of metal in his hand. "Be quick, then. I got you."

Kev slid down the bank into the blackness below. His feet hit mud and instantly the cheap trainers absorbed water. Typical. Kev focused on dirtying his footwear, revolving his ankles to attract maximum muck. As he turned to yank himself out, his left foot caught on some weeds. He pulled again, trying to release himself and looked back at whatever was holding him. Dark fronds wrapped his ankle. He lifted his leg and the fronds came with him, dragging behind them a human head.

# Chapter 39

"Where are you from, Señor Aguirre?" Matthew's authoritative tone caused everyone to turn, even Tomas.

Aguirre's eyes hardened as he turned to face the tired, pale and bedraggled man who Beatrice loved more than anything in the world.

The jut of his jaw made Beatrice simultaneously swell with pride and cringe in dread. Matthew, powerless, vulnerable and faced with armed, violent men had chosen to pick a fight.

"I would have assumed you were Spanish, until now."

Aguirre's voice was quiet, but still carried the marks of an orator. "Spanish is a big word. Each Spaniard has a complex identity, based on his country, his region, his language, his community, his family. You should be able to understand that, Professor Bailey. Being British used to mean something. Being Spanish still does."

"True. The essence of Spain, I would suggest, is about honour, about pride. You have a sense of loyalty, despite the divisions and rivalries between the various regions, to the concept of Spain. Rather like The United States. Which is why I find you as an individual rather an anomaly."

In a second, Beatrice caught up. Matthew may not have carried a SIG Sauer or a flick-knife, but his intellect and comprehension of the enemy had already exceeded hers. He stepped into the role of *toreador*, with every intention of baiting the bull.

Something flickered in her peripheral vision. Both the high walls to her left and right had windows at the top, presumably to permit natural light. At that time of the evening, internal light and external darkness made it impossible to see anything outside. But high up above Tomas's head, there was a movement. Someone was out there. Her heart pumped faster and she tried not to stare.

Aguirre laughed. "That is because you are a snob. A typical British snob. You are offended by my business proposition, which is to give people what they want. Do you want to tell me the British are unhappy with my wines? That is ridiculous. They will drink anything, if it has the right label and reputation."

Ana leant into her, applying pressure to her shoulder. She looked up and right as if stretching her neck, then returned to her previous position. Beatrice waited a second before looking in the same direction and forced herself not to jump. A face, streaked with dark marks, looked down at them. At that distance, she couldn't recognise him, but whoever it was, that was army camouflage.

"I'm afraid I disagree, Señor Aguirre. If, as I believe to be true, you export a blend of various whites and call it Rioja, how are you furthering the image of Spanish wine? I wholeheartedly applaud your successes in your domestic market, but by selling an inferior product to your chief importers, you are an embarrassment. To your vineyard, to the Rioja region and to Spain. As for you personally, you should be ashamed."

Tomas looked up at Aguirre, evidently judging by the tone of Matthew's voice that a challenge had been issued. Aguirre caught his curious expression and glared, pointing an impatient finger at the bottle. Tomas filled the glass and lifted it to Matthew's lips once more, with a compassionate pat of the shoulder. Matthew swallowed, gagged and retched, but kept it down. His eyes were wet. Ana nudged Beatrice, using her eyes to indicate the doors. Beatrice frowned. She could hear nothing and see even less. Ana sighed, shifting in her seat and indicated once more with her eyes. Tomas's knife, beside Beatrice's foot.

The trouble with this generation was watching too much James Bond. If Ana thought there was any chance of retrieving and concealing the knife without raising suspicions, she was deluded. And in any case, Beatrice was far too concerned about Matthew sticking his head in the lion's maw.

Aguirre had not moved. His eyes, locked onto Matthew's, seemed oddly devoid of life. His voice creaked, as if an ancient gate had opened.

"You know nothing of shame."


Kev pressed back against the warehouse, feeling the tension in Tyler and Jase either side of him. Three heads twisted left, observing the preparations.

They watched as the older man walked away from the petrol-soaked vehicle towards an outdoor tap above a drain and gave an order. One of the sharp suits started slamming the car doors shut, while the other one picked up the empty cans and headed in their direction. Kev spotted the opportunity and whispered his instructions.

"OK, Tyler, while he's got his hands full. Go!"

Tyler, smooth and noiseless, timed his attack to perfection. He waited till the man had almost drawn level with their vantage point. Any second now, he'd see them. In two long strides, Tyler broke cover, grabbed the man by the chin from behind and pressed a knife to his throat. The petrol cans hit the ground. Kev acted fast. In his experience, a hostage was not always the best bargaining tool. He knew nothing about this bunch and their loyalties. All he knew for certain was that they were armed. Whether they'd give up quietly or sacrifice their mate – he decided not to take the risk.

He ran to Tyler's side, located the pistol tucked into the man's belt, threw off the safety, twisted and crouched. Jase remained in the shadows, their secret weapon.

They took their time. When they finally rounded the corner,

the older bloke's timing worked in their favour. He was lighting a fag, the stupid bastard. The young one's reactions were slow. He saw his mate, took in Tyler's knife, then made for his gun before he spotted Kev, who knelt, arm steady, aiming the SIG Sauer at his head.

"*Me cago en la puta!*" he swore as he raised his hands to head height.

So Kev was right. The bloke with the blade against his windpipe and the curser looked close enough to be brothers, but the latter had still reached for his weapon. Seems blood wasn't all that thick.

Jase slipped out from the recess and with practised skill, removed both their guns and a vicious-looking knife from the old fella's boot. The plastic ties he found in the younger bloke's suit pocket came in handy and in under ninety seconds, he'd tied all three men's hands behind them, attached them to each other and had them facing the wall.

"Nice work, Lance Corporal. And that was a bloody classy jump, Tyler. You've still got it."

"Still got it? Bollocks. I just keep getting better. What do we do with the Reservoir Dogs while we tackle the warehouse?"

"Leave 'em here. We've got to get in there as soon as poss because whatever they ..."

Jase hissed. "At the ready, Sergeant. Three, armed, incoming at one o'clock."

Kev saw them. Three figures in night gear, emerging from the trees with no attempt at stealth. Jase and Tyler aimed their weapons at the approaching men while Kev scanned all other directions.

"Two more at eleven o'clock, two more at twelve. All carrying," he reported. They were surrounded.

As Kev watched, the man leading the first group raised his hands. He still held his gun but the gesture was conciliatory. He kept walking until he was close enough to be heard.

"Police. Do you speak English?"

"Yes."

"Drop your weapons, please. What are you doing here?"

They each engaged the safety and allowed the guns to fall to the ground. Kev answered the question.

"A friend of ours asked us for help. She and three others are tied up and held at gunpoint inside that warehouse."

"A friend? Detective Stubbs, I assume. Are you also police?"

"No, we're British Army officers."

He came closer. "I thought there must be some kind of training involved. That," he nodded his head at the row of backs, "was a very impressive ambush. But I must ask you to stand down now. This is a police operation and we can take it from here."

He moved closer into the light and holstered his weapon. Something odd about his face made Kev uneasy. It wasn't till he stepped into the floodlights that he saw what it was. The Spanish copper only had one eyebrow.

Matthew groaned and coughed. Tomas jumped backwards, just in case. He showed the bottle to Aguirre. It was two-thirds empty. This seemed to satisfy Aguirre, who jerked his head towards the doors, turned and strode off towards the main building. Tomas shoved the bottle into his pocket and bent to retrieve his knife. Then several things happened at once.

Matthew threw up a violently colourful shower, just as the door in the delivery shutter opened. Two men, dressed in black, dashed in, aiming their weapons at Tomas. Aguirre had almost reached the far door leading to the main plant when it burst open, admitting two more dark-clothed men. In a second, Aguirre ducked behind the stacks of cardboard boxes and a shot was fired, making everyone on the makeshift bench, with the exception of Matthew, jerk backwards in alarm.

Beatrice looked for Tomas but he had disappeared. However, a box on the corner had sprung a leak and white wine trickled out, staining the cardboard. The whole room held its breath.

Milandro entered from the delivery bay and shouted

something. Beatrice only understood the word *Policia*, but understood the tone.

Ana muttered a translation. "Give yourselves up, no point in any further loss of life, the entire building's surrounded and your associates are already in custody."

"Further loss of life? Oh God. If Kev or the boys got hurt ..."

She sensed Ana and Adrian staring at her and assessed the situation. Four sitting ducks in the middle. A ruthless criminal, ready to go down firing, hiding in a stack of boxes to her right; his henchman, with nothing to lose, on her left. There was someone missing.

"Where's Rosado?" she asked.

Adrian was chewing his lip. "He went into the main building. His head was bleeding. Is this really the police, Beatrice, or should we be worried?"

Ana spoke. "God knows." She bunted Beatrice with her shoulder. "Get the bloody knife. I'm not sitting here while they shoot it out."

Tomas's knife lay in a pile of fresh vomit, which consisted of alcohol, fish and tomato skins. Matthew's head hung forward, a thin strand of drool hanging from his lips. He couldn't help, even if he wanted to. Beatrice shuffled closer and stretched her foot out over the pool of puke. Using her heel, she scraped the knife towards her, shoving it under the bench and behind them. Ana arched backwards, a Tchaikovsky swan, and scooped it up. She twisted sideways towards Beatrice's bound hands.

A loud rumbling began and the first shutter began to rise. Beatrice watched as the tarmac came into view and was surprised to see no flashing lights, no police vehicles, no Kev. But at least ten crouching figures, all in night combat gear. Another shot startled them all, including Ana, who accidentally stabbed Beatrice's thumb.

The shot came from behind the opposite wall of boxes. Aguirre had taken aim at the men outside. A gun battle was more than likely to erupt, with the four of them sitting like fairground targets. Beatrice breathed deeply, imposing an artificial calm on herself. Shaking hands would make Ana's task all the harder.

The sound of shattering glass and hoarse male shouts resonated from the main building. Bullets rained through the delivery bay, horrifically loud, punching into the metal doors. Aguirre was not going to run, but fight like a cornered beast. Beatrice could only hope he'd forgotten his hostages. Ana manipulated the slimy knife between Beatrice's wrists, adding the pain of nicked fingers, hands and forearm to the increasing stiffness in her shoulders. Eventually, she found purchase on the plastic tie, slicing through it in a second. Relief spread across Beatrice's upper body as she took the knife and returned the favour.

Shots could be heard from the other side of the building as she cut Ana loose and handed her the knife to free Adrian. She turned to the wretched creature on her right.

"Can you stand, Matthew? We really must get out of the firing line. Can you hear me? Matthew?"

He turned his head but did not lift it. His eyes remained closed. He looked like a blinded war horse, responding to a familiar voice. A burst of agonising empathy suffused Beatrice.

"Ana, give me the knife! And you two take cover. We'll be right there."

"Here."

She clasped the sticky handle and turned to Matthew's wrists.

Then the lights went out and everything stopped.

She felt her way carefully down Matthew's arms, trying not to tremble. She heard the stealthy movements of Adrian and Ana retreating into one the many cardboard corridors behind them.

"Beatrice, this way! Run!" Ana's hoarse whisper carried urgency. Beatrice caught hold of Matthew's jacket and attempted to haul him to his feet. A dead weight. He keeled to one side and Beatrice knew they would be running precisely nowhere. Instead, she rolled him onto his back. He didn't protest. A stack of wooden pallets could hide a comatose Classics professor until the action was over. Feeling her way, she half-rolled, half-dragged him to the back edge of their makeshift bench and clenched hold of his clothing. As she shoved him over the edge, she broke his fall by holding on as hard as she could. He'd be bruised, but that couldn't be helped.

Ana's angry voice came again. "Beatrice! Get out of sight!"

"Nearly there ..." She spent several more seconds placing Matthew in the recovery position, then hurried to join Ana.

"Where's Matthew?" Adrian whispered.

"He couldn't move. I've left him behind the pallets. He'll be safe enough there." She wasn't even convincing herself.

They hid behind the first section of boxes. Like a corridor, the path between the stacked wines cases stretched almost the length of the room. As far as she could tell, Aguirre had darted behind the stacks along the right-hand side, but by now, he could easily be at the other end of their bolthole. It was impossible to see in the blackness. Tomas must be somewhere in the left-hand stacks. There was a sizeable gap between their stacks and his, so he'd be unlikely to break cover. Ana and Adrian pressed their backs against the far wall, Beatrice as close as she dared to their left. That way, she could just see the spot where she'd left Matthew. The three of them stood in the darkness, listening.

More shutters clattered upwards, exposing the warehouse and its contents. A cry of pain pierced the air, Beatrice couldn't tell from which direction, followed by more gunshots. A silhouette dashed through the nearest doorway and disappeared into the shadows.

"Beatrice Stubbs!" She recognised Milandro's voice. "You and your friends, stay where you are. Don't move."

Ana whispered. "Do we trust him?"

"We don't have a choice," said Beatrice.

Police vehicles rumbled into the car park, turning to train their headlights into the warehouse. Visibility improved but the horizontal angle threw deep shadows across the concrete floor.

However, Beatrice could see well enough to be sure that no one else was lurking in their corridor.

A megaphone screeched into life and a male voice addressed Aguirre. Even without the distortion, it was impossible for Beatrice to understand.

Ana began translating. "There is no way out apart from surrender. They're telling him to throw his weapon into view and ... what the hell is that?"

A small light had appeared halfway along the corridor, bobbing along the floor towards them. A torch. The light swung upwards and illuminated a face. Angel Rosado. He held the torch at arm's length to show he was unarmed then shone it back at the floor to illuminate his path. They froze and watched as he came closer. He waved the torch briefly over them, then stopped, shining it up at his own face. The blood on his temple and the ghoulish uplighting did him no favours.

"I don't want to hurt you. I can help, I can get you out. There is a gap halfway along here and we can get into the bottling plant. Follow me."

Beatrice stared. "Why should we trust you? The police told us to stay put."

"The police don't want you to move in case my father-in-law shoots you. But if you come with me, he won't even know you've left the warehouse. Please. I want to help. This has gone too far."

"It's almost over. They're telling him to surrender," said Adrian.

"He'd never do that. It goes against all his principles of honour. He'll stick this out to the end. I know him."

Ana spoke. "Have you got a gun?"

Angel hesitated. "Yes. Hold this." He handed Ana the torch and reached behind him to bring out a stubby pistol, which looked like a Beretta Tomcat. He offered it to them.

"Fair enough." Ana took it. "We keep the torch and the gun and we'll follow you."

"Not me," Beatrice said. "I have to stay with Matthew. But I think you two should go. Just be very careful."

The megaphone stopped and silence filled the void.

Adrian dropped his voice to a whisper. "There's no point in staying with him. He's out of it. The best thing is to leave him where he is. We can escape with Angel, get round the back and show the police we're out, then they can take the scene by force. It's the best way."

"You go. Tell them exactly where I am and where Matthew is and where we think Aguirre and Tomas are hiding. But I'm staying here. I have to keep an eye on him. Now go, and be incredibly careful."

Ana shone the torch at Beatrice's face. "Are you sure?"

"Absolutely. Do stop wasting time and get out of here."

Adrian's arms enfolded her and she noted that even after an evening hiding in the forest and tied up in a warehouse, she could still smell his lemony aftershave.

"See you on the other side," he whispered.

Beatrice watched as they crept back along the corridor and abruptly disappeared to the right. Somehow, she trusted Angel to keep his word. Now all she had to do was wait. With the intelligence the three of them could provide, the police would be able to employ much stronger tactics. This could be over within the next fifteen minutes.

A grunt snapped her attention back to the gap. She pressed herself against the very edge of the boxes and looked out at the sliver of warehouse she could see. The sight horrified her. Matthew, lit up like a Roman monument, was staggering to his feet.

The police had no idea who he was. Ana and Adrian hadn't got out yet; mere seconds had passed since they'd gone. So a marksman could easily shoot him, if Aguirre didn't get there first. Matthew fumbled with his fly and looked sleepily around for a suitable spot.

The megaphone came again, probably instructing him to put his hands up. Even if it had been in English, Beatrice doubted he would have understood. She had to help him. She dashed out into the warehouse and heard an order yelled from the car park. She caught Matthew's jacket and dragged him towards her hiding-place. A shot punched into the boxes behind her.

A silhouette appeared at the side of the shutters. "Beatrice Stubbs! Get down! Now!"

She threw herself backwards, yanking Matthew with her. They stumbled to the ground, Beatrice's elbows taking the impact and Matthew crumpled like a bag of compost. She turned in the direction of the voice. More shots rang out and Detective Milandro hit the ground.

# Chapter 40

Angel loped silently between the lines of boxes, while Ana kept the torch trained just ahead of his feet. Adrian could hear nothing but their breathing and the distant sounds of police radios. Suddenly Angel disappeared into a gap on their right. Ana ducked after him and Adrian followed. This corridor of cardboard boxes was much shorter and lighter, thanks to a glass door at the end. Beyond, fluorescent lights illuminated a mechanised production line, which snaked and looped around the room like a Scalectrix track.

Angel held the door open for them and Adrian was just about to step through when he heard the megaphone. The amplified voice held a new sense of urgency. Ana stopped and opened her mouth to say something when a shot made them all jump. Another voice shouted an indistinct order and more shots filled the air. Angel pulled at Ana's jacket.

"Please, we must get out. It is the only way to help."

Ana's face reflected her fear. Adrian put his hand to her shoulder both to reassure and guide her forward. His hand shook.

"This way. Come!"

They ran diagonally across the huge room, weaving between the lines of bottles, under pulleys and tubes and past pallet trucks, their feet echoing off the tiles. Angel led the way towards a door under some steel steps and they found themselves once more in darkness.

Ana flicked on the torch, enabling Angel to locate the light switch. The sunken spots glowed into life and Adrian recognised the foyer where he'd met Angel only that morning. The marble reception desk, the annual reports on the table, the state-of-the-art coffee machine all looked the same. But rather than being greeted by a young woman with a pleasant smile, this time they faced three police officers, pointing guns.

Adrian felt frustrated and impatient. Once identities had been established, it seemed everyone except him could be useful. Angel guided the three officers back through the bottling plant. Ana accompanied a detective to the despatch bay to indicate the precise location of Beatrice Stubbs. Adrian was to wait around the corner, behind the vehicles and out of harm's way. It seemed terribly unfair, but he did as he was told. Two other men stood in the shadows, and nodded to him as he joined them. Although Adrian couldn't see what was happening in the delivery bay, he had a clear view of the driveway, and watched as blue lights from three ambulances flashed towards them. The night air penetrated his linen jacket.

One of the men murmured to the other. "Don't like the look of that. Unless the other two are a precaution."

Adrian had never been happier to hear a northern accent. "You're English! Thank God for that. Do you know what's going on?"

"Not really. We're here to help a friend out. But as far as we know, she's still in there."

"Oh, you must be Beatrice's cavalry! Yes, she's still in there. We managed to escape through the building, but she wouldn't leave Matthew. They got him drunk, you see."

"Yeah, that's what Jase said. Another mate of ours. He's up on the roof with the police now. He was watching you through the window."

"Beatrice thought they were going to put us in a car and push it over a cliff with Matthew in the driver's seat."

The two men exchanged a look and the tall one spoke. "She weren't wrong, mate. There's a Seat Toledo round the back doused in petrol. You'd not stand a chance."

Adrian's stomach plummeted and his skin cooled still further. Trapped in a car, burning to death.

Police officers directed one ambulance to the forecourt and the other two past them to park just out of sight of the delivery bay. Medical staff jumped out and wheeled out stretchers. Adrian turned to check the other vehicle. The crew remained in the cab.

The first man followed Adrian's sightline. "My name's Kev. This is Tyler. And as I said, our mate Jase is on the roof." He held out his hand.

"Adrian." He shook both hands, distractedly. "You said just now you didn't like the look of two ambulances. Has someone already been hurt?"

Tyler looked away, but Kev answered. "Judging by the shouting, someone's down in the warehouse. But that," he pointed to the inactive ambulance, "is to collect the body. They're just waiting for the coroner to finish. Look, mate, I'm sorry, I'm not sure if it's someone you know, but there's a woman in the ditch over there. She's been shot."

A sudden barrage of yells went up from the delivery bay and the ambulance crew dashed around the corner. Adrian forgot his instructions and ran towards the action, unable to comprehend what Kev had just said. A single phrase ricocheted around his mind – 'someone's down in the warehouse'.

Kev and Tyler were right behind him as he took the corner. He scanned the scene. Tomas, cuffed, being led down the steps. Police everywhere. Two clusters of paramedics bending over prone bodies. And Ana, standing with her arms wrapped tightly around Beatrice Stubbs.

# Chapter 41

One ambulance raced away, bearing the stricken detective and an injured officer. The second crew loaded a comatose Matthew onto a stretcher. Beatrice kept her concentration on him, even as the two police cars drove past. She had no desire to see Tomas's repulsive sneer or the face of Arturo de Aguirre.

"*Señora?*" The paramedic came to the door of the ambulance.

Beatrice called across to where Ana was talking to a tall blond chap in a long coat. "Ana, sorry to disturb, but can you translate?"

Adrian, Kev, Jase and Tyler all gathered around her, each face full of concern, as Ana listened.

"He's going to be fine. She says it looks like alcohol poisoning and they want to take him in for observation, but she reckons that with decent hydration and rest, he'll easily be on his feet tomorrow. Do you want to go with them, Beatrice?"

"No. I'm sure they will take good care of him. I'll go in later but first I need to talk to the police. Check which hospital, though."

"I meant for a check-up yourself. You had a nasty fall."

"Bloodied elbows, that's all. To add to my collection. Just ask where he's going, because we need to get on."

Ana took out her notebook and turned to the paramedic.

Adrian placed a hand on Beatrice's arm. "It's fine. We don't have to talk to the police tonight. They agree we should go back to the hotel, get some rest and go into the station in the morning to provide statements."

"It's not about statements. I need to know what's happened to Luz."

The ambulance doors closed and Beatrice watched it roll away. Look after him, she thought, he's very special. Only then did she notice all five of her companions wore the same sorrowful expression.

Ice spread from her scalp and for the first time that day, she sensed the onset of tears.

"She's dead, isn't she?" she said.

Kev nodded. "I'm sorry, Beatrice. We found her, by accident. They took the body away before we even got you out of the building. She was in that ditch." He indicated the stream behind them, black, cold and shallow.

She couldn't bear to know but she had to ask. "What did they do to her?"

Kev took a deep breath but Ana answered first.

"I don't think 'they' did anything. From what we've worked out, Aguirre did it himself. Looks like the forest sweep for Matthew and Adrian was a distraction. Seems Aguirre's guys knew they were there. So they made a half-arsed search, checked there were no observers, and Luz was taken out front and left in the car. Then Aguirre's mob did a wider circle and prepared a trap. All they needed to do was wait for you and I to arrive. They were very well informed."

Jaime.

A rage boiled up which Beatrice controlled by clenching her jaw and fists. "I asked you what happened to her."

Ana continued. "With us tied up in the warehouse, Aguirre went out – remember – and disposed of his daughter."

"Disposed? Don't pussycat round me, Ana. How did she die?"

"He shot her in the mouth."

Adrian, Kev, Jase and Tyler all dropped their heads.

Beatrice fanned her fury. Fury was good, active and articulate. Grief was debilitating and blocked her throat. "In cold blood, he took his own daughter to a mean, lonely ditch and shot her, just to protect his business interests. The man is evil. How the hell did he expect to get away with that?"

"We reckon he planned to fake her suicide," said Jase. "The gun was in her hand when they pulled the body out. Wouldn't surprise me if there's a typed 'I have to end it all' note at home in her bedroom."

"Nor me," agreed Ana. "But that's not all. I just had a chat with the coroner's assistant. He checked out the surroundings: pockets, handbag and so on. She had a pregnancy test in her bag. Positive."

Beatrice's head reeled as she went through the options. If Luz was pregnant, it would certainly be complicated. According to her, the boyfriend would never meet with parental approval. Allowing grief the upper hand, Beatrice pictured her. Dark hair, kind eyes and her prominent nose as she dipped into her gin and tonic.

Gin and tonic. A newly pregnant woman, slugging back a G&T? Something smelt off. But if Aguirre wanted to add a reason for her to take her own life, a positive pregnancy test would convince most coroners. Despite advances in understanding, for many single mothers a sense of shame remained. Was it possible to fix a pregnancy test and plant it on someone? If so, the man was a truly twisted individual.

"But how did he work the logistics? How was Luz supposed to have got here?"

Kev nodded. "That's what I thought. Then I remembered what we saw when we first arrived. The Reservoir Dogs bunch was out front when some bloke arrived in a Peugeot. I thought it were weird. He stopped for a quick chat with his mates and left in the Corsa. My money's on the Peugeot belonging to the dead woman."

"Luz," Beatrice insisted. "Her name's Luz. What did this bloke look like?"

"Mid-thirties, dark hair, leather jacket and cowboy boots. Kind of fancied himself, I thought."

Jaime. Lying, duplicitous, venomous rattlesnake. Beatrice looked at the ditch where Luz had died at the hands of her own father.

"Right, so let's wait for the forensic pathology report and give full statements to the police tomorrow. In the meantime, there's someone I want to talk to. Where's your car, Kev? I'd like to visit Jaime."

# Chapter 42

She came empty-handed. He couldn't eat grapes, and flowers were banned in his room. In any case, she wasn't even sure if they'd let her in. Generally, hospital staff took their lunch immediately after the patients, so Beatrice grabbed the opportunity and ascended three floors to Intensive Care.

The nurse held up a splayed hand. "Five minutes, OK? Is very tired."

"Of course. No problem." The trembling began again as she walked down the corridor to Room 223. A deep-seated shudder which spasmed though her whole body at random intervals. Delayed shock reaction, that's all, nothing to worry about, she told herself. All the same, she might just share it with James when she got back.

She knocked lightly and pushed open the door. A low hum from the various machines was the only response. The curtains were half-drawn, creating shadows in the corners while dust motes seemed suspended in the sunlight across his feet. She approached the bed, taking in the neatly folded sheets, the tubes piercing his bruised flesh and the bandages around his shoulder. His face, despite the intrusion of stitches and tape securing his oxygen tube, seemed peaceful and calm, a different picture from the rictus of pain he'd worn last time she'd seen him. His dark eyes opened and focused on her, sending a jolt of surprise along with the shakes.

"Good morning, Detective ..." she ran out of words.

Milandro blinked and unfolded his hand. She grasped his fingers in a simulation of a handshake.

"I know you can't speak yet. But I had to come. I want to, well, first of all ... how are you feeling, on a scale of one to ten?"

Milandro dropped his eyes to his hands, limp on the white sheets. He uncurled his right hand to display four fingers, considered a moment and added two more from his left.

Beatrice smiled with relief. "That's wonderful. We were all so worried about you. Detective, my main reason for coming is to apologise. I mistrusted you, suspected the police of corruption and thereby endangered ..."

He lifted his hand, took a moment and opened his mouth. "You were right." His voice sounded painful.

"Don't talk. Firstly because it sounds like it hurts. And secondly because I haven't finished yet."

He ignored her. "The police *were* corrupt. My superior officer was on Aguirre's ..." He coughed once, winced with pain and squeezed his eyes shut.

"Please, Detective, you must rest. I won't be the cause of you tearing your stitches or rupturing something else. I do have a few questions, because the police officers at the station will tell me absolutely nothing. It's a closed shop. But all I need at this stage is a yes or a no. Can we agree to that?"

Milandro opened his eyes, blinked and indicated the water jug. Beatrice poured a small amount into a glass and twisted the straw to the right angle. She placed it between his lips and watched as he swallowed two tiny mouthfuls. His face was grazed along the cheekbone and dark stubble with flecks of grey covered his chin. Even with the striking scar tissue, he was a good-looking man. As if he could hear her, he looked up with amusement in his eyes.

Beatrice fussed over returning the glass to cover her awkwardness.

"Finished? OK, I'll put this here in case you want some more later. Now, as I said, there are just a couple of things I'd like to know. You said Aguirre had nobbled your superior officer?"

Milandro dipped his chin slightly to indicate the affirmative.

"So it must have been Salgado who called Scotland Yard. I thought it was you. Within an hour of our first meeting, my boss phoned me and told me to mind my own business. Said I was a bloody nuisance."

Milandro nodded again.

"Are you saying yes to the fact it was Salgado or agreeing that I'm a bloody nuisance?"

Milandro twitched his eyebrow and smiled. Beatrice pressed on.

"I realise it was stupid to tackle Aguirre's people alone, but you understand I had no faith in ... well, in the force. Can I ask how you knew how to find us at Alava Exports?"

He pointed an index finger to his right eye, pulling down the lower lid.

"You watched the hotel. You didn't trust me. I suppose I should be glad, because you were absolutely right. Seems I placed too much faith in certain people. I presume you know Jaime Rodriguez has disappeared."

Milandro fixed her with a furious glare.

"I know. I feel more stupid than I can express. No wonder Aguirre was always one step ahead. Jaime and all his worldly goods have vanished, including the contents of his office."

The indignity of being played for a fool rose up in Beatrice like bile. She walked to the window, paced back to the door and back to the window, unable to keep still.

"That sly, evil, devious, two-faced, foul, ingratiating little weasel! How could anyone behave like that? So sincere, so caring! Good God, we were totally taken in! He definitely set Tiago up, you know, and would have thrown Ana to those wolves. The dirty little sleazebag! And he must have told Aguirre about Luz visiting me."

"Luz?"

Of their own volition, Beatrice's hands assumed a prayer-like pose over her nose. She stared at Milandro and spoke with a steady voice.

"The woman who came to my hotel room on Friday was Aguirre's youngest daughter. She gave me all the necessary documentation to expose him and his operation. He found out and he shot her. In the head. That bastard intended to fake her suicide, with a note and everything. He'd even planted a pregnancy test in her handbag, as if that would provide just cause. What kind of man is he?"

Milandro's mouth twisted in an expression of sympathy or disgust. He shook his head and went to speak. The door opened and the nurse bustled in with a trolley bearing pills, dressings and the suchlike.

"*Señora*, you go now. Is time. Bye, bye."

"Yes, of course." Beatrice gathered her bag and got out of the way. "Thank you for your time, Detective. I wish you all the best and a speedy recovery. And I really am sorry."

He smiled and raised a hand a couple of centimetres from the bed.

An impulse swelled in Beatrice and she knew this was her chance.

"Detective? Would you give me permission to see him? They'll never let me in without your say-so."

Milandro's eyes hardened, as if he were trying to read her mind.

His voice scratched out, provoking a frown from the nurse. "Why?"

"It's just something I need to do."

His gaze lingered a second longer and his chin dipped once more.

"Thank you."

# Chapter 43

After reading two articles on Hellenic politics and British artefacts in *The Times*, Matthew dozed off. She waited several minutes before tiptoeing into the bathroom to call Ana.

"Hi Beatrice. You got my text?"

"Hello. Yes, I did. Still no trace of Jaime?"

"Nope. The man has gone up in a puff of smoke. But I have got the autopsy results on Luz. She wasn't pregnant."

"So why was a pregnancy test in her bag?"

"I think I can answer that. I went to the Aguirre estate this morning. Closed shop. Marisol's still sedated and the sisters set security on me. But I had a nice chat with the housekeeper. Firstly, Inez is up the duff and receiving medical treatment. The shock of her sister's death, father's arrest and husband's departure is seen as extremely dangerous for 'her condition'. There's your pregnancy test. I reckon she was in on this. The housekeeper also said Aguirre and Luz had an almighty row at breakfast on Friday. She thinks he wanted Luz to drop out of university and come home. And get this. Our junior reporter just got back from Burgos. According to Luz's roommate, Marisol Aguirre had already cleared out Luz's university room on Friday morning."

"So the whole family conspired to get rid of her?"

"Dunno. Nothing concrete yet, but it stinks to high heaven."

Beatrice stared at herself in the mirror and made her decision.

"Are you still at the paper, Ana?"

"Is the Pope Catholic? Got in at six this morning and been flat out ever since. But I'll make it to the restaurant tonight, don't worry. How's Matthew?"

"Asleep at the moment, but improving all the time. I think we're all going to fly home tomorrow."

"All of you? I thought you had a grand tour of Spain planned."

"I had. Still have. But I may just do it in small doses. Right, I'm going to get my head down for an hour. See you at *La Cepa* at eight."

Lying was like any other activity. The more you did it, the easier it became. Beatrice splashed some water on her face and thought of Shakespeare. *If it were done when 'tis done then 'twere well it were done quickly*. Quickly. It had to be now. Ana was at the office, Matthew asleep, Adrian distracted and Vitoria on a Sunday timetable. She packed her handbag, including Milandro's letter of permission, and wrote a breezy note for Matthew. She propped it against his litre-bottle of mineral water and blew him a silent kiss, before hurrying along the corridor to Adrian's room. He opened the door, barefoot and smiling.

"Hello. I was just about to pop along and check how he is. Did our lunch excursion wear him out?"

"It seems that way. He's got his feet up on the sofa and he's napping. A post-prandial snooze always does him good, even without the upsets of the last two days. I need to toddle along to the police station for a short while. Might you be good enough to look in on him occasionally?"

"I'd be delighted. Why do you have to see the police again? We gave them the whole story at least five times yesterday. I even dreamt about it last night. Do you need my moral support?" He assumed a concerned frown.

Beatrice waved a hand in a vague gesture. "That's very kind of you but this is boring paperwork, more line-of-reporting stuff. I'd be happier knowing you were keeping an eye on Matthew."

Adrian's face relaxed. "Rather you than me. So if he's feeling fit enough to travel, shall I see if I can find us some flights for tomorrow?"

"Yes, please do. Morning if you can manage it. Right, I'd better make a move. Back by six at the latest."

Adrian glanced at his watch. "Six? A bit more than 'a short while', then. Just remember, I'll need at least an hour to get ready for tonight."

"Is that all? Don't worry, I'll be back in plenty of time. In fact, I'm heading to the police station on foot, with the sole purpose of walking up an appetite."

And to make sure that no one knew where she was going. In quite the opposite direction to the recently damaged police station, Beatrice headed towards the medium-security custody centre at the Alava Psychiatric Hospital. To interview Arturo de Aguirre.

While receptionists, medics and nurses studied the paperwork behind a glass door, Beatrice concentrated on looking relaxed. There could be no doubt about the authorisation, so it was a matter of patience. She breathed slowly and deeply, assuming her role. In order to convince him, she had to believe it herself. She repeated certain phrases, rehearsed certain emotions and visualised her own body language. Every minute or so, a small voice would ask, *Is this the right thing to do*? A blazing roar answered in the affirmative.

"Detective Stubbs. Sorry to keep you waiting. It was necessary to check your permission and as you are not on official police business, we have to ask the patient if he is willing to talk."

Beatrice stared at the earnest young chap in a yarmulke and white coat. She hadn't even considered Aguirre might have the opportunity to refuse.

"I see. And?"

"Everything is fine. The authorisation is confirmed and Señor Aguirre seems keen to speak to you. Please follow me."

He led the way past the glass doors and along the grey, muted corridor. Beatrice grabbed her things and followed, as he was still talking.

"It's such a shame our senior clinician isn't here today. He would love to have heard about this project of Scotland Yard's. Research on empathy is his own personal area of expertise. Would you have any time to come back again tomorrow? I know he'll be disappointed if he misses such an opportunity to discuss your work."

Beatrice pulled a pained expression. "Unfortunately not. I have an early flight back to London in the morning. But look, here's my card. He can email me at any time. I'd be delighted to discuss our project with such an expert."

And she'd cross that bridge when she came to it.

His trainers squeaked as he stopped and he took the card. "A Detective Inspector? How fascinating." He tucked the card into his breast pocket with a smile. "Thank you. He'll be so pleased. Here we are. I'm afraid you will need to leave your bag and coat outside. Also, a supervising orderly will attend your interview."

"That's not a problem. If I get into any language difficulties, he or she can help."

The young doctor shook his head as he peered through the window. "Oh no. No, orderlies are there to guarantee safety of both interviewers and patients. Juan is simply your insurance policy and in any case, he doesn't speak English."

Just for a second, Beatrice closed her eyes and beamed. Then she followed the verbose young man into the room, forcing her features into an expression of contrition and sorrow.


Jeans and casual shirt notwithstanding, Arturo de Aguirre retained every inch of his dignity, rising from his chair as they entered in a gallant gesture, as if he were receiving her in his office. He exchanged a few words in Spanish with the doctor, who gestured to a tall orderly in white overalls, before turning to Beatrice.

"Nice to meet you, Detective Inspector. Good luck with your project. Juan will see you out after your interview. Have a nice Sunday."

"Thank you, you've been most kind."

The doctor left, eventually. Beatrice faced Aguirre, who gestured to a chair. His expression was mild, with a hint of a smile.

"Thank you for seeing me, Señor Aguirre. Rejecting my request for a meeting would have been perfectly understandable, under the circumstances."

Aguirre sat and faced her, his eyes hard. "My understanding is that our conversation is to be informal. This interview is not being recorded and is therefore legally inadmissible in court. There are no witnesses who understand the lingua franca and your permission explicitly states that this conversation is not part of the current criminal enquiry. You have presented a letter of permission from the judicial Spanish police entitling you to discuss the subject of empathy with me. Under such circumstances, I find myself agreeable to a debate on the subject. I will not discuss the charges against me but can offer some insights of value regarding human motivation."

Beatrice blinked. His grandstanding had lessened not a jot since being incarcerated. She took a moment to retrieve her notebook and pen from her bag.

"I hope you can. I only have a few questions, which should take no more than fifteen minutes. Before we begin, and this is not an attempt to draw any incriminating statements, I'd like to say how sorry I am for the loss of your youngest daughter. I only met her twice but I liked her enormously."

Aguirre dropped his eyes and inclined his head but did not reply.

"My first question is about something you said on Friday evening. In response to an accusation, you told Professor Bailey he knew nothing of shame. Could you explain what you meant by that remark?"

He clasped his hands together as if about to pray. "I think that is obvious. The man attempted to berate me by invoking my sense of national pride. It was a crude effort, much like the losing poker player accusing the winner of having a better poker face. In order to feel shame, you need to have self-respect. That is what shame is, the direct opposite of pride. My point was simply that the British, in many ways, but let's stick to wine, have no self-respect, no taste and no pride. Therefore, they cannot feel the opposite. They are not ashamed of themselves."

In a moment of absolute clarity, Beatrice realised he was lying. And further, he was trying to provoke a reaction. She played it as coolly as possible, continued making gibberish notes and forming her own poker face.

"Thank you. An interesting theory. Perhaps we can pursue that point a little further. You have confessed to the fraudulent export racket ..."

"Confessed? That makes it sound as if I am ashamed, which is not the case. I regard the boom of the Viura grape and the change in the reputation of white Rioja a huge success. Not only that, but selling substandard product to the British for full price has been one of my greatest triumphs."

Beatrice smiled, observing a man in thrall to his ego. "You have pre-empted my question. I was going to ask if you felt any remorse at having devalued the image of the Spanish wine-making industry, but I can see you do not."

He snorted. "The expressions of outrage and apologetic hand-wringing you see on television are a diplomatic mask. The wine-making industry, if not the entire gastronomic world of Spain is secretly laughing behind your backs."

"Really? Well, I'm sure you're right. Although I can't say I've encountered anyone of that opinion. The word most people are using to describe Castelo de Aguirre is 'disgrace'. But you're bound to know best, as they're unlikely to tell me the truth. Now I have one last question. International wine fraud is one thing, but premeditated murder is another."

"Correct. While I excel at the first, I deny all charges relating to those men's unfortunate accidents."

"I will not ask you any questions regarding Tiago Vínculo or Miguel Saez, as these are charges yet to be tried in court. However, you claim your daughter's death was by her own hand. Not yours."

His eyes seemed to soften, his mouth pinched and his shoulders sagged. The impression was of deepest sorrow. He was quite a player.

"That is the truth. A tragic truth, most certainly. A parent should never suffer the suicide of a child."

"Why do you think she took her own life?"

He looked up at the ceiling for several seconds before training his eyes on her. "I think you are probably more aware of her reasons than I am. After all, you were the last person to see her before she died."

Beatrice's cue. She was ready. She dropped her head and generated a blush. For this performance, every single word must be chosen with precision.

"Yes. I admit to feeling some considerable discomfort at my own role in this sad event. But although I refused to help her, the young woman I walked to the train seemed anything but defeated. This is what I cannot understand. She intended to catch the train back to Burgos and continue with her studies, but she had no intention of giving up her battle."

Like a cat, aware of the danger but fatally curious, he watched her: suspicious, alert but unable to resist.

"I'm not sure what you mean by 'her battle'. Why on earth would she need *your* help?"

The balance had shifted and he knew it. The contemptuous emphasis sealed her conviction that he was still attempting to crack her composure with increasingly feeble blows. Beatrice gazed wistfully into the distance and brought out the big guns.

"I don't have children, Señor Aguirre. Something I don't regret. But hearing Luz use every ounce of passion she possessed to persuade me to drop my investigation into Castelo de Aguirre ... well, I realised I would never know such filial loyalty. Such fierce love. I couldn't agree to her request, of course I couldn't. But I said goodbye with nothing but admiration for her efforts. I was deeply touched by her love for you."

She shook herself and sought his eyes. "As I said, I only met her twice but I won't forget her. A true lion heart. But at that stage, we had all the information we needed and arrests were imminent. Our informant had delivered all the proof we needed to go to Interpol. We'd realised by then that Salgado was corrupt and chose to effect our operation ..."

"Stop." His body seemed frozen, all his energy concentrated in his eyes. "Luz wanted you to leave me alone?"

Beatrice feigned puzzlement. "Of course. She's not, sorry, she wasn't stupid. When she drove me back from the Castelo the first time, she asked some very searching questions. She knew who I was. The day she went back to university, she came to the hotel specifically to ask me to leave Vitoria and forget the story. In fact, she was so determined, I almost had her in the frame for the witness murders. But our contact had already identified Tomas and friends."

"Your contact?"

Beatrice gave him a reproving look. "You know I can't divulge that information. A good police officer should always protect her sources."

"But you're on sabbatical. Officially, you aren't a police officer at the moment."

*And all that is left is to reel him in.*

Beatrice looked at her watch. "I must go. You've been most kind and very informative. I will see you again, when the case comes to trial, naturally."

She placed her notebook and pen back in her handbag and lifted the card.

Aguirre leant forward, his arms on the table. "If not for me, for my daughter. Tell me the name of the mole."

"I'm sorry, I can't do that." Beatrice stood. "But I will say congratulations. I understand your daughter Inez is expecting her first. That must be some consolation under the circumstances. Goodbye, Señor Aguirre. Thank you for your time."

She held out her hand. He got to his feet. His eyes bored into her and she had no idea if he would spit, shout or accept the gesture. If he didn't, she'd have to find another way. Eventually he reached out and shook her hand. To his credit, he betrayed no surprise. The orderly opened the door and Beatrice exited the room.

She walked in a straight line, following the white shoes, concentrating on her breath, her steps and the image in her head. Aguirre alone, sitting at that table, looking at the business card she'd slipped into his hand.

Jaime Rodriguez, Editor of *El Periódico*.

# Chapter 44

"Sorry, sorry, sorry." Ana flopped into her seat, shrugged off her jacket and brushed her hair out of her eyes. Her face was free of make-up and evidently tired, yet she looked lit from within.

"Left at ten to eight but I couldn't get a cab for love nor money so had to go back for the Vespa. I'm so shagged I can't tell you. How're you doing, Matthew? How's the head?"

Matthew raised his glass of sparkling water. "I've sufficiently recovered to try another local brew. I'm very glad you made it. I know it must be enormously stressful at the paper today."

"Stressful? I've never known a day like it. Manic from morning to night. Where's the waiter? I have a desperate thirst. What's the story with the flights, Adrian? Good God, you're looking sharp enough to cut yourself."

Adrian smiled the smile of a compliment well-earned. "Thank you. And I must say, after fourteen hours in the office, you don't look anywhere near as wrecked as I'd expect. That's the joy of fine bones, you see. We're flying out at quarter to ten in the morning. So tonight is both a celebration and a farewell."

"You have a way with words, my man. Can I have a swig of your water?"

Beatrice hailed the waiter and ordered two bottles of cava and more water. A beeping came from Ana's jacket and she snatched up her phone. Her face softened into a smile. She turned the screen to Beatrice, and then to Matthew and Adrian.

The image showed three laughing lads holding beer bottles – Kev, Jase and Tyler. And the sender and text beneath hadn't escaped Beatrice's notice.

"Looks like the stag weekend has begun in earnest," she said.

Ana looked at the picture once more. "I'd say it has. Lock up your daughters, Bilbao."

"And apparently you're joining them tomorrow?" Beatrice kept her enquiry light and innocent, as she continued to butter her roll.

Ana snorted with laughter and shook her head. "I should have known you'd spot that. You don't miss a trick, do you? Yes, all right, I'm joining them for lunch. Kev invited me. He seems like a decent bloke."

"Definitely," Adrian agreed. "Not to mention totally ripped."

The waiter brought an ice bucket and the first bottle of cava.

"Ana, you must be exhausted. Do you need to de-brief or would you rather just enjoy the food?" Matthew asked, with classic avuncular concern.

"Food first, no doubt about it. But I have updates, unless you're sick to death of the whole thing. Would you ever pass the bread over, Matthew? My stomach feels like my throat's been cut."

They ordered chorizo, quails' eggs, tortilla, Gernika peppers, kidneys in sherry, octopus, three kinds of ham, green beans and asparagus, with plenty of bread.

As the plates arrived, Beatrice saw Matthew's eyes widen and a sense of calm settled on her. Not every Beatrice-related experience meant disaster. Meanwhile, Ana ate and talked at a similar speed.

"All four of Aguirre's muscle men refuse to talk. Aguirre himself accepts all the wine fraud charges, but won't even discuss the murders. Still insists Luz killed herself. The whole guilt-over-pregnancy deal is blown, as the autopsy showed she wasn't."

"Do they know if the test belonged to her sister?" asked Beatrice.

"Haven't heard yet, but that's the premise I'm working. Salgado is subject to an internal police investigation. Word is that it's going to be a slap on the wrist and early retirement. Milandro's slated to take over. New broom and all that. God, this ham with the acorn oil – I could just roll in it. Now we're not talking just the police, but governmental organisations, media and major companies. Lots of dirty fingers in mucky pies. Everyone's likely to get splattered now the shit has hit the fan. Ah, sorry, we're eating."

Adrian bit into a tiny egg and followed it with a nibble of asparagus. "Don't worry. It would take more than that to put me off this food. You know, I'm almost looking forward to coming back for the trial. We simply must revisit this place. Every mouthful is a joy. Now what about Jaime?"

Beatrice stopped chewing.

Ana shook her head. "No sign. My guess is the Aguirre network set him up elsewhere, new identity, the whole shebang. Turns out Jaime Rodriguez wasn't even his real name. Dirty little scumbag slipped the net. If I could get my hands on that stinking heap of ..."

"You won't," said Beatrice, prodding a kidney. "Write him off and focus on the trial. The Aguirres will take care of their own."

She felt the weight of Matthew's gaze, but raised her glass as deflection.

"A toast. To a successful collaboration and justice served."

Glasses glinted and sparkled, as three voices repeated her words.

"Justice served!"

They drank, met each other's eyes and returned to the spread. In the contented appreciative silence, Beatrice made another decision. Her sabbatical was over. It was time to get back to work.

# Acknowledgements

With grateful thanks to the readers who helped wrestle this novel book into shape: Sheila Bugler, Jane Dixon-Smith, Gillian Hamer, Liza Perrat and Catriona Troth (Triskele Books); The Writing Asylum; Lorraine Mace, Julie Lewis and Alison Lopez. I'd also like to thank Aine, Zak and David Ambrose for their invaluable help and insights; Carl Knobel of weinpassion for sharing his expertise; Jane Dixon-Smith and James Lane for their visual talents, Darren Guest for forcing me to change the title and Julie Lewis for leading me to this one.

# Also by JJ Marsh

## Behind Closed Doors

"*Beatrice Stubbs is a fascinating character, and a welcome addition to crime literature, in a literary and thought-provoking novel. I heartily recommend this as an exciting and intelligent read for fans of crime fiction.*" – Sarah Richardson, of Judging Covers

"*Behind Closed Doors crackles with human interest, intrigue and atmosphere... author JJ Marsh does more than justice to the intelligent heroine who leads this exciting and absorbing chase.*" – Libris Reviews

"*Hooked from the start and couldn't put this down. Superb, accomplished and intelligent writing. Ingenious plotting paying as much attention to detail as the killer must. Beatrice and her team are well-drawn, all individuals, involving and credible.*" – Book Reviews Plus

## Raw Material

"*I loved JJ Marsh's debut novel Behind Closed Doors, but her second, Raw Material, is even better... the final chapters are heart-stoppingly moving and exciting.*" Chris Curran, Amazon reviewer.

"*Some rather realistic human exchanges reveal honest personal struggles concerning life's bigger questions; the abstruse clues resonate with the covert detective in me; and the suspense is enough to cause me to miss my stop.*" – Vince Rockston, author

# Cold Pressed

*Editor's Choice – The Bookseller*

*This is J J Marsh's fourth, snappily written crime mystery featuring the feisty but vulnerable Stubbs, a most appealing character. It's all highly diverting, and an ideal read for those who like their crime with a lighter, less gruesome touch.* – Caroline Sanderson, The Bookseller

# Human Rites

*"Enthralling! The menace of Du Maurier meets the darkness and intrigue of Nordic Noir. Keep the lights on and your wits about you."* – Anne Stormont, author of *Displacement*

*"Human Rites has got it all: organised crime, Beatrice Stubbs, nuns, Stollen, wine, Adrian and Expressionist art, with the added delights of a German Christmas, gay men's choirs and a farty Husky. She's back and she's brilliant!"* – The Crime Addict

# Thank you for reading
# a Triskele Book

If you loved this book and you'd like to help other readers find Triskele Books, please write a short review on the website where you bought the book. Your help in spreading the word is much appreciated and reviews make a huge difference to helping new readers find good books.

Why not try books by other Triskele authors?
Receive a complimentary ebook when you sign up
to our free newsletter at

**www.triskelebooks.co.uk/signup**

If you are a writer and would like more information on writing and publishing, visit http://www.triskelebooks.blogspot.com and http://www.wordswithjam.co.uk, which are packed with author and industry professional interviews, links to articles on writing, reading, libraries, the publishing industry and indie-publishing.

Connect with us:
**Email** admin@triskelebooks.co.uk
**Twitter** @triskelebooks
**Facebook** www.facebook.com/triskelebooks

Made in the USA
Lexington, KY
31 March 2019